SonicPING

sonicPING

by

Orlando Stephenson

Cover Design & Illustration ©2011 by Elizabeth Bromley

Copyright ©2011 by Orlando Stephenson
ISBN: 978-1-935897-43-9
MyGreenPublisher
P.O. Box 632 Richland, MI 49083
e-mail:publisher@pinkflamingo.com

Disclaimer:
All of the characters in this book are fictional. I did not set out to develop any personas that were related to anyone I know and as such any similarities are purely coincidental. The search engine company 'Sonic Ping' is also fictitious and the website sonicping.com is owned by me. In addition, the town of Pingree is also wholly a figment of my imagination as is most of this book except the real places and real events.

Printed in the USA

chapterONE

The woman chained to the post in the center of the stage looked lost. She was dressed in a flimsy harem costume that did nothing to conceal her body from the hundreds of prying eyes that devoured every exposed inch. The faint light of self awareness still visible in her heavily drugged eyes made it plain that she was terrified. That outpouring of fear along with her lack of clothing captured the attention and animal desire of every man in the room, slave buyers from all over the world. Their haze of cigar smoke, testosterone and just plain raw lust was so thick I would have needed fog lights to find my way to the bathroom. I waited for the auction to start and tried not to breathe the toxic atmosphere.

If she had been a complete stranger perhaps I could have turned my head and mind away from what was happening but if she had been a stranger I wouldn't have been sitting here. I was at this slave market in a city halfway around the world because that woman was my friend and the only way to insure that she didn't live out the rest of her life as a concubine in some sheik's harem was for me to finish as the highest bidder.

When the auctioneer stepped forward to start the bidding my heartbeat went up another thirty beats a minute. I glanced at my friend Rodger and then back at the petrified creature on the stage. Just for a second my mind flashed back to the path that brought us here. It had been less than a week ago when...

❧

The phone startled me. The clock read four am. I grabbed it before it could ring a second time and wake my wife. Caller ID showed it was Madeline.

"Hi," I whispered.

"Daryl, I need help," she said.

"Help?"

"Daryl, please…"

Her voice trailed off.

The words 'I need help' pushed my buttons. She was a damsel in distress and my heart and mind focused instantly on what I could do. The final plaintive 'please' was like waving a red cape in the face of a bull in a ring in Barcelona. I couldn't help charging to the rescue.

"What's the matter?" I asked.

Madeline and her husband, Brad, had been our best friends for ten years. We had done everything together. Our weekends revolved around each other: parties, dinners, movies, walks and hours and hours of just sitting around and talking. We could talk about anything and everything. Once in a while one of the four of us would get a little high on one horse or another but never for long. Our views, our beliefs, our life forces were incredibly the same. As much as human beings who are all molded by their experiences from birth to become the rainbow of colors that make up the human race could be, we were remarkably of the same mind.

Then he lost control on an icy road and a canyon swallowed him. It was as if someone had smashed a hammer into our cocoon and the whole thing fell apart. In one blinding instant Brad was gone, leaving a hole that could never be filled. I didn't know how much I loved him until he vanished from my life. It had been almost a month but the pain of his loss was still as raw as the night Madeline called so choked up with tears that it took an eternity to understand what she was saying. My mind still refused to believe he was gone. The simplest things like hearing a clever joke or reading an interesting news story or seeing a funny billboard would find me reaching for my phone to share.

"Daryl, I need you, please. Can you come?"

I heard her words, but the death or divorce of a member of a close knit foursome shatters the dynamic, and like poor humpty dumpty, it can never be put back together again. I hated what was happening. I hated the reserve that had crept into our relationship. It was as if someone had pulled an opaque shade between their side and ours. Madeline was on the other side of an intangible wall that seemed to grow cloudier every day. We could see her but not with the clear vision that we had when Brad's arm was holding her tightly.

"Daryl?"

"I'm here."

"Please…can you come over?"

"Five minutes," I said, scooping my keys from the dresser.

I quietly pulled on pants, a long sleeved t-shirt and was slipping into my shoes when my wife rolled over and lifted her head.

"Honey?" she said in a sleep drugged voice.

"Go back to sleep, sweetie."

"What's going on? Why are you up?"

"Maddy called," I said. "She needs my help."

"At this time of night?" she asked. "What's wrong?"

I didn't know what to say. Maddy hadn't told me what was wrong. I was running to her because I was drawn to helping damsels in distress and I was consumed with guilt about how we had lost touch since Brad's death.

"I don't really know, sweetheart, she didn't say," I said.

She sat up.

"Do you want me to go with you?"

She looked so beautiful and vulnerable all I really wanted was to climb back in bed next to her and take her into my arms. Bringing her along would probably be a great comfort to Maddy, but I knew how my wife operated, and if she didn't get enough sleep she was useless the next day. I also knew she had a major presentation at work in the morning. I crossed to the bed, sat down beside her, captured her face and kissed her. She responded. Thirteen years and the magic between us was still the same as the very first time.

"Go back to sleep, sweetheart," I said. "I'm certain it'll be fine."

"Are you sure?"

"Yes."

"Promise you'll call me if she needs me?"

"I promise," I said, "now go back to sleep."

I walked to the door and waited while she pulled the covers up and snuggled in. When I thought she had drifted back asleep my feelings overwhelmed me.

"I love you, Karen," I whispered.

She surprised me by raising her head, looking at me and saying, "I love you too, Mister Save-the-world."

CR

The streets were empty. In fact at this time of night the small town of Pingree, which straddled Massachusetts route 128 about an hour north of the hustle and bustle of Boston, was all but dead. The city figuratively rolled its sidewalks up at nine each night and things didn't get busy again until after eight in the morning.

Brad and Madeline's house was only two blocks away, but with the icy roads of early winter it seemed like an eternity until I pulled into their drive. She was waiting in the doorway with her arms wrapped around her chest against the cold. A petite woman who had lost her life's partner and now was losing her best friends. I ran to the doorway and hugged her.

"What's wrong," I asked, "nightmares?"

"All the time," she said, "but no, not tonight. Tonight I haven't slept."

I pulled her inside. Her face was red and streaked from crying which made her look lost and vulnerable. The thin robe she wore revealed more than it covered. The combination caused my body to respond and I hated myself for it. I had a wife I loved dearly and my reaction confused and upset me.

"What's going on?" I asked, holding her gently.

"Brad was…"

She stopped and a hint of fear and uncertainty flitted over her face. I waited for her to continue.

"Brad was mixed up in something really bad," she said.

"Bad? Like what?" I asked.

"Do you remember that dot com company he started about a year ago?" she asked.

"Boomslash," I said. "That was a great idea. I begged him to let me invest in it."

"You know how Brad was," she said. "There was no way he would have let a friend put money into something before he was sure."

"Yeah."

"Anyway, we had almost five hundred thousand dollars of our own money invested when he died," she said.

"Five hundred thousand! That's not possible," I said, "Brad told me that…"

"He lied to you because he was ashamed that it had taken that much, although it was finally starting to take off and we were beginning to make money and then…"

I looked at her eagerly waiting for her to continue.

"A few weeks before his accident he got sidetracked and began spending all of his time on something different," she said.

"What?" I asked.

"I'm not sure, but I know that he was excited about it," she said.

"It was something better?" I asked.

"I don't know. I'm not sure," she said. "He didn't tell me but…"

I waited.

"Daryl, I'm in trouble," she said.

"What do you mean trouble?" I asked.

"Someone's been calling and threatening me. It's something to do with whatever this new thing Brad was working on. They want the money they claim Brad borrowed and…some papers they say belong to them," she said.

"I don't understand," I said.

"They want me to make good on the additional two million they say Brad borrowed just before he died," she said.

"Two million dollars? Just before he died?" I repeated.

"Yes."

"Did you know about that?" I asked.

"No… well… Brad said something about having figured out a way to get a lot of money but not that he borrowed it," she said.

"Is this money in one of your accounts?" I asked.

"Daryl, I look for loose change in the sofa when I want to treat myself to a movie," she said. "What you see here in this house is all I have and the house is mortgaged."

I looked around the three bedroom ranch that they had shared and that she still lived in. Even located on the prosperous side of Pingree it was only worth a maximum of three hundred thousand dollars. I knew he also had a 401K, but it didn't have more than two hundred thousand in it. I snorted.

"Tell them to piss off," I said.

"I did," she said, "the first time they called."

"So what changed?" I asked.

"They took Jennifer."

"Jennifer's been kidnapped?" I asked.

Jennifer was her niece. She was twenty-seven years old, with inky black hair, clear intelligent smoky green eyes and a smile that could easily power a small third world country. I loved that girl as did almost anyone who met her. My heart threatened to beat its way out of my chest. The enabler part of me was on high alert and a mantra began beating a tattoo in my head. I needed to help, but the horror of it had me temporarily swamped.

"They called me just before I called you," Madeline said.

"And?"

"If they don't get what they want they are going to...sell her."

"Sell her?"

"Yes."

"You can't sell someone," I said.

"You can."

"This is the United States of..."

"Daryl," she interrupted, "they aren't kidding, they will."

"But..."

"I need your help, please."

I stopped protesting and looked at her.

"What can I do?" I asked.

"Hold me," she said.

I moved her into my arms without thinking. I captured her body and hugged her as if it were the last time. She moaned and snuggled her face into my neck. It felt like she should be there forever and it scared me. I was married and had no business even thinking about another woman. My physical reaction to her soft available body frightened me. I knew that men had roving eyes, but that had never been my way, and yet... I wanted her. It terrified me.

"Daryl?" she asked, interrupting my guilt.

"Mmm?" I hummed into her neck.

"Do you like me?"

"Uh oh," I thought.

"Of course I do," I said. "I've always..."

I stopped because that was a downhill slide that I had no intention of going down. I was happily married and here I was with an extremely desirable half naked woman in my arms. What was I thinking of? I brought myself back to the present by letting go of her, moving to the couch and sitting down. She sat down next to me, put her arm across my shoulders and snuggled into my chest.

"What can I do to help?" I asked, pushing her to arms length.

"I need two million dollars," she said.

"That's not going to happen."

"But, what about Jennifer…"

"We'll get her back, I promise," I said.

"How?"

"I don't know," I said truthfully. "When are they going to call again?"

"They said… they said a few days and… and I better have the money and…," she sobbed.

"Did they call this phone?" I asked, pointing to the phone next to her.

She nodded.

I reached across, picked the phone up and looked at the caller ID list. The last call had come in as 'unknown'. I didn't think they'd be that stupid but you never knew.

"Rodger might be able to trace that call back," I said.

"And we can find Jennifer?" she asked.

"Maybe, we'll see."

She snuggled back into my chest, put her face into my neck and kissed me. I could feel her nipples brushing my chest and her hand creeping places that were not safe for my restraint. I reached out and captured her wrist before she could inflame me further.

"Maddy, we are going to get her back," I said, trying to bring the subject back to the reason I was here.

She wiggled out of my lap and dropped to the floor in front of me. She wrapped her arms around me in a soft embrace and settled her head in my lap.

"You've been such a good friend," she said.

A wave of guilt washed over me. Since Brad's death I had been anything but a good friend. With each passing day an increasingly wider chasm had been growing between us while I stood dumbly by and let it happen. I was sickened by what a lousy friend I was.

I stroked her hair softly and vowed silently to be a better one. She rubbed her cheek on my thighs and my body started a slow burn. A building wave of desire threatened to engulf me. If I let this go on I would hate myself. She was beautiful, barely dressed and vulnerable. I pushed her off my lap and stood up, trying to hide the fact that my body was betraying me.

"I have to go," I said.

"Oh… yes, I guess you do. Thank you."

I helped her stand, turned and walked to the door. At the door I turned back to her and kissed her cheek.

"Goodnight, Madeline," I said, "I hope you can sleep."

"Daryl? Will you come again?"

"You mean when they call?" I asked.

"And…"

"What?"

"Please, if I need you. Will you come?"

"I…"

"I promise I will only call when it's like tonight," she said. "In addition to the phone call I really needed to see you tonight. I promise. Please."

"Ok, but…"

"I promise."

chapterTwo

When I got home I undressed in the hallway and tried to quietly slip into bed so as to not wake Karen. It was a waste of time. Either she had been lying awake or on the verge because as I lay down beside her she rolled over and gently kissed me. I chastely kissed her back and tried to leave it at that, but she had other ideas. She kept kissing me. It felt so good I responded by dragging her into a 'movie star kiss'. That caused her to writhe which kindled my desire for more. What I'm saying is that I'm no different than any other guy, intimate stimulation inflames me. Our first chaste kiss led to more kissing and then to intense kissing which eventually led to petting and when her hand found its way below my waist I went with the flow.

ॐ

"Wow, that was fantastic," she said after we both returned to the real world.

"It was, wasn't it?" I agreed.

We snuggled for about ten minutes before she asked, "So, what did Maddy say was wrong?"

"Jennifer's been kidnapped," I said.

She sat up.

"What? Why?"

"I'm not sure, but I think it's related to something Brad was working on just before his accident."

"Boomslash?" she asked.

"No, it seems he went off in another direction."

"Oh."

"Anyway they're asking for her to give back some money they claim he borrowed and some papers."

"What are you going to do?" she asked.

"I think Rodger might be able to trace them so I thought I'd go to his place in the morning and ask him to help."

"Is there anything I can do?" she asked.

"More than what you just did?" I said. "Well, it's been ten minutes. I'm feeling…revitalized. I suppose you could…"

"I'm talking about helping Maddy you goofball," she said.

"Oh."

I pushed her head gently down on the pillow and snuggled in beside her.

"I can't think of anything right now, sweetie," I said. "Let's try to get some sleep."

☙

She drifted off almost immediately but sleep eluded me. I lay there instead listening to her soft breathing and thinking about my desire for Madeline.

Karen and I had been having a little bit of a rough patch lately but we had been working it out. I had never been one to look at other women, even so I found myself constantly thinking about Maddy which upset me. My wife was beautiful and until recently she had been number one in my thoughts. Was this the beginning of one of those mid-life crises?

I shook my head to clear it and tried to think of how to stop the direction I was traveling and reconnect more with Karen, but my thoughts kept drifting back to Madeline. My attraction to her confused me. When it finally got late enough I slipped out of bed, showered and headed to the one place I thought I might get some answers on who had taken Jennifer.

CR

Rodger's Electronics was situated in a rundown strip mall located on the opposite, older, seedier side of Pingree where the town had originally started. The town had begun as a carriage stop on the old coach road from Boston to Gloucester in the late seventeen hundreds when Icabod Pingree established a post house for travelers. A blacksmith and a livery sprung up nearby and in 1770 those three merchants banded together, incorporated and the town of Pingree had been born.

Pingree's main claim to fame happened on December 16, 1773 when Icabod traveled to Boston and was one of the protesters who helped dump hundreds of bales of tea into the Boston harbor. Icabod might have gone on to become an important factor in the budding Continental Congress and formation of the Republic but Icabod was killed in a minor skirmish with the British termed the Battle of Gloucester in August of 1775. The town lapsed into obscurity for the next two hundred years.

The original center of town had been situated on the stretch of Massachusetts 133 that runs north between 128 and the town of Essex. It remained a sleepy backwater until the tech boom of the 70's when it exploded. Because of poor planning by the city fathers and cheaper land away from main downtown Pingree, old town was left behind. All of the new construction and high rises were built along both sides of 128 and around the two small ponds located on either side, leaving the center of old Pingree to become a virtual slum.

The entrance to Rodger's shop was so non-descript and unappetizing that even the most cavalier of clients thought twice before they entered. Rodger liked it like that. He didn't want walk-in business. He kept the storefront as a modicum of respectability, but he never took business from strangers.

Once in a while some unsuspecting and probably brain dead patron would brave the entrance and bring in a computer or other device for repair. What they got was an experience that they remembered for a lifetime. To describe Rodger as rude, boorish, impolite, unpleasant, overbearing and nasty to strangers would be like describing Hitler as a potential candidate for pope. Most of the foolish patrons who braved his door backed out like a cobra was striking at them.

I was one of Rodger's few friends as a result of a strange convergence of my nature and luck. One afternoon at the end of our eighth year a group of bullies had cornered him where the back schoolyard fence and the building met. It was a cul-de-sac trap, completely out of sight of any authority. I happened around the corner while eight ninth graders were pounding on him.

I didn't know who he was. I only knew him as 'that nerdy kid who never talked'. What I did know was that my temperament wouldn't stand for what was happening so I waded in like I was some avenging angel in a B-movie who couldn't be hurt or killed. In reality I didn't think of that. I was pissed and it showed. I fought as if I was invincible and the blows that hit me had no effect. The truth is that at the time they had no effect. Later I thought I was going to die I hurt in so many places. I drove them off and Rodger and I limped away. We have been friends since.

Something about that day changed Rodger forever. Oh, he was still nerdy, but he was no longer a weakling. He started lifting weights and developed an impressive set of muscles. He learned judo, karate, Tang so do, Tai Kwon Do and a host of other fighting disciplines. He also learned how to use weapons. In addition to knives and guns he was an expert using throwing stars, swords, clubs, sticks and a multitude of other more non-conventional weapons. By the time we finished high school he was one dangerous guy.

In June at the end of our senior year he joined the Navy. His original assignment had been in Information Technology where the nerdy side of him blossomed. He had always been good with computers, but his first assignment was at a counter-espionage school where the Navy had assembled some of the world's best computer brains to track and try to crack our enemy's efforts in cyberspace. He learned from the best.

Then someone discovered his expertise with weapons and he was sent to Navy Seal training. By the time he got out of the service and came back to our little Massachusetts town of Pingree he was a computer genius who also happened to be a well oiled killing machine.

He never flaunted it, but other men could sense the menace and raw power that emanated from him and left him alone. More than once I had observed three hundred pound bruisers step off of the curb into a puddle rather than disturb his path. For his part he never seemed to notice, although I had long since learned that those seemingly tranquil eyes rarely missed anything.

I tried to join the Navy with him but had been turned down, so I went off to college instead. I graduated with a degree in electrical engineering, married a Sarah Lawrence girl and went to work for a firm in nearby Boston designing circuit boards. I hated it. It was dull boring work. My way out of the corporate world came as a result of my love of cooking.

At age thirty I had my fill of the terrible excuse for vegetable slicers called mandolins that were available on the market. Hard to use and even harder to clean, I knew there had to be a better way. I spent six months designing and prototyping a clever design which I sold to a big kitchen appliance company for enough money that I would never have to work again. I then turned my hand to helping people in trouble, especially beautiful women, which didn't always sit well with my wife. When Rodger returned from the Navy he began helping me. We made a great team.

"Hey, Daryl," he said as I entered.

Now that might seem like a normal thing to say to a friend, but he was facing away from me and engrossed in a video game. I don't know if he had some hidden surveillance system or ESP or both. There was no way he could have known it was me, but he had. It always astonished me.

"Hey," I answered.

"What do you need this time?" he asked, not missing a beat on his video game.

"Why do you always assume that I need something?"

"Daryl," he said, "even you hate walking through that doorway. When you do it's because you really need something."

"Maddy's in trouble."

That got his attention. He had loved Brad and Madeline as much as I had. He had been the fifth wheel in our dynamic but not a passive or 'golly I wish we didn't have to put up with this guy' fifth wheel. He had been a part of our lives and a good part. Brad's death hit him almost as hard as it hit me. He dropped his game controller, spun around and speared me with eyes like laser beams.

"Trouble?" he asked.

"Maddy says that Brad borrowed a lot of money from some bad people and they want it back," I said.

"Tell them to piss off," he said dismissively, relaxing his shoulders.

"That's exactly what I said," I said.

"So, what's the problem?"

"They took Jennifer."

"Huh?"

"They took…"

"I heard you," he interrupted.

I could see the cloud of turmoil in his face and it surprised me. Rodger had never expressed interest in any particular woman and Jennifer had been no exception. Before Brad died we had regular Sunday dinner at Brad's house or mine at least once a month. Rodger had almost always been there and many times so had Jennifer. He had never indicated the slightest interest in her and yet his reaction to my news was as if the love of his life was gone.

"Rodger?" I asked, "What's wrong?"

He looked at me and the reflection of pain in his face was chilling.

"Rodger?"

"What?"

"Buddy, are you okay?" I asked.

He was staring at me but his mind was somewhere else. Then I watched the concern, panic and pain drain out of his face. The Rodger I knew came back and a frozen wintry look filled his eyes. I had seen that look once before when he and I had been involved in bringing down a child pornographer. I remember thinking that it was lucky for the sick bastard that two policemen were with us when we finally caught up to him because it had been clear to me that Rodger would have killed him like he would have stepped on a cockroach.

"What do you have?" he asked.

"What?"

"Look, you came here for my help. You didn't come empty handed so, what do you have?"

I looked at him uncomfortably, "Nothing."

"Nothing?" he said politely, but with a menacing undertone that sent a shiver of fear up my spine.

"Rodger, I'm one of the good guys," I said.

He blinked and some of the menace left his face.

"Just give me what you have from the beginning."

I laid it out for him. The late night phone calls, the demand for two million dollars and the papers, the kidnapping and that they were going to sell her if they didn't get paid. He listened as if in a trance, but I had seen that look before and I knew he was totally focused and processing every word as if his mind were a Cray supercomputer. Actually, I had seen that mind in action many times and it was better than a Cray. When I finished I sat back and waited.

"You're right," he finally said. "You've got almost nothing."

"I'm sorry, I…"

"Daryl," he said, holding up his hand to stop me, "the operative word is… almost."

I watched, fascinated as the wheels in his mind arranged themselves like a slot machine in Vegas lining up for the mega jackpot.

"So the phone call came in to Madeline's just before four in the morning," he mused, his fingers flying over his keyboard.

That sentence wasn't directed at me. He was talking to himself as his mind worked its way through the problem. I kept my mouth closed and continued to watch. I had seen him work his magic before and observing it in action was always mind-boggling. That he operated outside of the box was a tame description of what he did. He could take the tiniest, most insignificant component of a puzzle, something that a normal person might consider trivial, put it together with another seemingly unimportant piece and voila! he had a solution. It was awesome and terrifying at the same time. It was at times like this that I was grateful we were on the same side.

"Shit," he grunted finally pushing himself back from his computer and staring out the window.

Rodger only used profanity when he was surprised, scared or completely baffled. He was hardly ever baffled and plainly not scared so I had to assume that he had found something he didn't like. I waited while he processed what he had.

"It doesn't make sense," he finally said. "The call traces back to a cell phone owned by Sonic Ping and the call was routed through a cell tower close to their building."

That really didn't make sense. SonicPing.com was a relatively new, but super hot, dot com company that specialized in web searches. Their headquarters were located in the center of new Pingree. It was an up and coming Google competitor and, while not as big as Google yet, it had a whole new algorithm for internet searching that had made serious inroads into Google's web traffic and thus their pay-per-click revenue. The company had been founded by Mikahyl Dashkov, a second generation

Russian immigrant who had received his Ph. D. from MIT in computer science. Mikahyl was one of those boy geniuses that computer technology seemed to spawn. He was a Google copycat but a brilliant copycat as he parlayed his idea and expertise into big bucks.

On the surface Sonic Ping was a totally legitimate company with a revenue stream already in the billions of dollars. It didn't add up for them to kidnap Jennifer for any reason and certainly not for a paltry two million dollars.

"Sonic Ping?" I said dumbly, shaking my head.

"I didn't get it wrong," he said. "Something very strange is going on and it isn't about two million dollars."

"What can we do?" I asked.

"First, let's get Jennifer back," he said.

"How?" I asked.

"The phone that called her is on right now. I've put it on a permanent trace. Next I plan to set up a series of repeaters that will help me follow it and pinpoint exactly who is carrying it," he explained.

"But how will that get us to Jennifer?" I asked.

"I need you to talk to Maddy about the next time someone calls," he said. "When they do she needs to lie to them and say she's got what they want. But first she needs to hear Jennifer's voice."

"Okay."

"I'm assuming that since they haven't been too bright thus far, they will either let Jennifer talk on that phone or call on another one," he said. "Either way I'll be ready."

I thought about them not being too bright. They had caller ID blocked and it was a cell phone which was almost impossible to trace. Certainly law enforcement wouldn't have been able to tap into them. I was sure they were confident that they couldn't be found. They just hadn't reckoned on Rodger.

"And then what?" I asked.

He looked at me with those arctic eyes and my stomach shriveled up.

"You don't want to know," he said.

"Oh."

"Just be ready to help Maddy with Jennifer when I bring her, okay?" he asked.

I gulped and nodded.

chapterTHREE

The call came three days later. I was in a meeting with my banker when my caller ID lit up with Maddy's name. I didn't even excuse myself. I grabbed my bag and headed for the door, waiting until I cleared the room to speak.

"Did they call?" I asked.

"Yes, I just hung up with him and called you," she said.

"Did you talk to Jennifer," I asked, fearing the worst.

"He let her say hi for just a second," Maddy said. "She sounded scared."

"Did you let Rodger know?" I asked.

"I used the speed dial on my cell to call him while I was talking," she said, "but…"

"But?"

"He already knew they were talking to me," she said. "In fact he told me he was listening in. How does he do that?"

"I don't know," I said.

"What do we do now?" she asked.

"He said wait and he'd bring her," I said.

"Bring her?"

"Yes,"

"To my house?" she asked.

"Yes."

"Daryl, I promised I'd only ask you to come when I really needed you but… I… I do right now. I can't do this alone. I'm worried about Jenifer and… can you come?"

I was already getting in my car. My brain had somehow overlooked the fact that I had a wife and a happy home. I wanted to be close to her and nothing was going to stop me.

"Sure," I answered as if I didn't care one way or another, but it would have taken more willpower than I possessed to keep me from driving there as fast as I could.

∞

She was waiting in the doorway again except this time instead of a thin robe she was wearing a black mini skirt and a teal blouse. She looked incredible. I hugged her and didn't want to let go.

"Daryl, thank you for…"

I captured her face and kissed her to stop her from saying what I so wanted to hear, words that would have pushed me down another step on a path I knew was wrong. I didn't have a clue how my life had taken this twist. I was developing an interest with my best friend's wife and… it turned out it didn't make any difference that I had stopped her from talking because when I removed my lips she said the words anyway.

"I love you," she said.

"Oh, Mad, I-I love you too, but…"

"I know. I understand. I just want to thank you for helping me," she said.

"Have you heard from Rodger?" I asked.

"No."

"Well, don't worry," I soothed, "he said he'd be here."

"Do you think he'll… he'll have Jennifer?" she asked.

I thought about that for a moment. I remembered the look in Rodger's eyes as I left his shop three days ago and shuddered.

I wouldn't want to be the poor bastard that was holding Jennifer and I surely didn't want to think about what Rodger might do to the guy if he had harmed her in any way.

"Yes," I said with conviction, "he'll have her."

"Oh, Daryl, please hold me," she said, slipping into my arms as if she belonged there. "Just hold me close."

I wanted to push her away but my body had other ideas. We stumbled over to the couch, fell onto it and began necking like we were teenagers in the first blush of love. Things progressed over the next half hour from first base to second base and would have eventually gone past the point of no return when we were saved by the crunch of tires in the drive.

Maddy leaped up and hurriedly put her bra and blouse back on and dashed off to the bathroom. I ran my hand through my hair to arrange it so that it didn't look like I had just climbed out of bed, picked up a magazine from the end table, promptly put it back, then went to the front door and threw it open.

Rodger had Jennifer in his arms climbing the steps. I moved out of the way and let them pass.

"Rodger, you're being silly," Jennifer complained. "I'm okay."

Rodger didn't speak. He placed her on the couch gently, arranged some pillows under her head, stepped back and stood looking happier than I'd ever seen him. Maddy crossed to the couch, sat next to Jennifer and crushed her in her arms.

"I take it that it went well," I said, dryly.

"No problem," he laughed. "I think they got my message."

I heard Jennifer choke like she was suppressing something that was bursting out of her.

"If your message was that you are an alpha male and no one messes with your woman I think they did," Jennifer said.

"His woman?" Maddy and I echoed simultaneously.

"Well...I mean...uh, figuratively speaking," Jennifer stammered.

I looked at Rodger and he was blushing. That was a first. I glanced back at Jennifer and she was blushing also. Wow!

"So, are you going to tell us what happened?" I asked.

"Daryl, we might have a bit of a problem," Rodger said. "I had to break some eggs."

I knew what that meant. It meant that things had gotten rough and someone had gotten hurt or even killed. I looked at him and waited for him to explain.

"Daryl, you wouldn't believe it," Jennifer gushed, "he took the guy's arm and…"

"Jenn," Rodger interrupted, "it's better if they don't know the details."

"Oh… okay."

"The less they know the less they have to lie about when the cops come," he explained.

"The cops?" I asked.

"Yes," he said, "the police will probably be asking Maddy some questions."

"But how will they know to come here?" I asked.

"Cell phone records," he said. "It will take them a few days, but even they will find the calls to here and show up asking questions."

"So, what should she tell them?" I asked.

"The truth," he said. "She was asked about the two million dollars and she doesn't know anything about it."

"And the other stuff?"

"Forget about the other stuff," he said forcefully.

"Okay," I said carefully, "but why?"

"I'm not sure."

"You're not sure?"

"Daryl, something is seriously wrong. There is no way that these guys are worried about the money. It's just a cover to dig around for papers, documents, records… frankly I don't know what the hell they are looking for," he said.

"How bad can it be?" I asked.

"They fucking kidnapped Jennifer," he hissed.

I had never heard the word fuck from him before. Something had him frightened.

"So what do we know?" I asked.

"Almost nothing," he said. "Brad was mixed up in something that happened as a result of his dot com company. All we know at this point is that he was working on something else the three weeks prior to his accident but..."

He stopped talking and shook his head.

"I think it's better if you come by the shop tomorrow and I'll lay out what I've got," he said.

"Sure, buddy," I said. "So what do we do now?"

"Do?"

"Yeah."

"Well," he chuckled, scooping Jennifer off of the couch as if she weighed ten pounds. "I'm going to interrogate my suspect."

"Your suspect?"

"I suspect that she and I have a lot of things to say to each other," he said.

Jennifer struggled in his arms but not much, she plainly liked the attention.

"I'm going to take Jennifer to my place," he said, "I think she'll be safer there."

"Rodger, that's not really necessary," Jennifer protested. "I don't think that..."

"Jennifer," Rodger interrupted, "I'll feel better if you stayed in one of my spare rooms until Daryl and I sort this out."

She opened her mouth to protest but closed it again and snuggled into his arms.

"Okay," she said meekly.

"See you tomorrow, buddy," Rodger said walking to the door with Jennifer.

He turned at the door and looked at Maddy.

"I don't think that break-in you had last month was random," he said. "I think they were looking for something and I don't think they found it."

"Really?"

"I certainly, seriously, discouraged them for now, but I don't think it will stop them," he said.

"What do you mean?" she asked.

"Why don't you let Daryl look around a bit?" he suggested.

"At what?" she asked.

"Let him look through Brad's things."

"But the police already said that it was just a random break in and that nothing was missing," she said.

"I know, but Daryl might notice something the police missed."

That didn't sit well but she nodded and said, "Okay."

"And don't worry, Jennifer is safe with me," he said.

"Thank you for getting her back."

"No problem," he said, backing out the door with his bundle.

I looked at Maddy's stricken face and my heart melted again. I knew it was wrong but I couldn't help myself. I walked over and gathered her into my arms.

"What could they have been looking for?" she asked.

"I don't know," I said.

"I don't understand," she said. "Brad never kept anything from me."

"Mad…"

"Daryl, there has to be some mistake," she wailed. "I would have known."

"Mad, just let me poke around Brad's stuff a little to be sure… okay?" I asked.

"I suppose."

"Thanks."

CR

I spent the next five hours digging through Brad's things. I started in his closet and went through every pocket of every jacket and every pair of pants. I found seven credit card receipts. Four were for meals at various local restaurants, two were ATM withdrawals for two hundred dollars each from the same ATM only a few minutes apart and one was a charge to Boxes, Inc.

Then I went through his drawers one by one. The only thing I found out of the ordinary was a stash of porn magazines in the drawer under his bed. They were all pictures of big breasted women which seemed kind of strange because Maddy was a very petite woman with almost mannish breasts. In one of the magazines I found another credit card receipt from "Explicit Things" which was a local adult porn store.

The only other two items of interest were a piece of paper taped underneath his end table drawer that had a string of numbers written on it and a key that I found in his toolbox. The key caught my eye because it was new. It had B.I.656 engraved on it.

I put my meager haul into an envelope and put it in my pocket to show to Rodger in the morning. Maddy was napping on the couch when I came back into the living room. I wanted to lie down on top of her and resume our earlier interruption, but my smarter half kept me from stupidity. I coughed and she opened her eyes.

"Find anything?" she asked.

"Not really," I answered.

"Want to... hold me?" she asked.

Oh god I did but that would lead to...

"Maddy, I'm sorry, I really have to go."

"If the cops come can I call you?"

"Call me?"

"To be with me when I talk to them," she explained.

I walked to the window and looked at my car as if somehow that would give me the courage to back away or find some excuse as to why I couldn't come. I realized that I was being stupid.

"Sure."

chapterFOUR

Something was different about Rodger's shop when I dropped in the next morning. I couldn't put my finger on it, but the unfriendliness was missing. No, it was way more than that. I felt good about walking in. For the first time since I had been coming here I didn't have to overcome my dread and screw up my nerve to walk through his door.

I looked around. Everything looked the same. The only obvious difference was that Jennifer was sitting on the old ratty couch. She smiled warmly at me. Rodger was sitting with his back to me working on his laptop, but it didn't keep him from knowing it was me.

"Hey," he said. "Find anything?"

"I'm not sure," I said. "I found a few things that don't make sense, but certainly no smoking gun."

"Me either."

"Where do you want to start?" I asked.

"Sit next to me and let me show you what I've got."

I pulled up a folding chair and leaned over next to his shoulder so I could see the computer screen.

"From what I can see," Rodger began, "about three weeks before Brad died he stopped paying attention to his dot com company and went off in a different direction."

I looked at his computer and the home screen for boom-slash.com was showing. That had been Brad's internet site. It had been an awesome idea. The concept was simple. A totally integrated instant advertizing model using a combination of widgets and texting to simultaneously update your own website, Facebook, Myspace, Twitter, and any other web presence while sending the same update to thousands of cell phones. The potential customer base had been any business that could benefit by being able to bring customers through the door when they were having a slow day or entice customers to buy something on impulse. That was practically every retail business on the planet.

I had been so excited when he told me about it that I had wanted in. I begged him, but he refused to take my money. It was too risky, he claimed. If he went bust he didn't want to take me with him, though he promised that if it went big he would give me a piece. The thing about Brad was that he wasn't normal when it came to money. If it had gone big I never doubted for a minute that he would have insisted on sharing with me. Whether or not I would have accepted was a scene that was never going to play out. It ended when he died and I was never going to... I stopped drifting and turned back to Rodger.

"So what's the different direction?" I asked.

"It's not related to this at all," Rodger said. "I found it by searching the server where boomslash.com is hosted. I looked at every other web site on that server and there was one other site that is almost certainly Brad's."

I cocked an eyebrow and waited.

"It's under a 'Doing Business As' name that I suspected was his from the name," Rodger said. "A check of the county records verified it."

"What's it called?" I asked.

"Bigooh," he said.

I laughed. It was so like Brad to use a name like that. For years as kids when a hot chick walked by us our adolescent response was ooh. We fell into the childish habit of rating girls by the ooh criteria. It got to be a silly game and eventually evolved into gradients of 'ooh'. You can imagine the variations. Little oohs, ooh oohs, ooooohs, oh my oohs, well, the list was endless. The best and most desirable ones were always 'Big Oohs'.

"So the web site is bigooh.com?" I asked.

"You got it," he smiled.

"Sounds like Brad," I said. "So, what's the big deal?"

His fingers flew across the keyboard and the screen changed to bigooh.com. I looked at the display. It was a site that sold T-Shirts. To me it looked like thousands of e-commerce sites that I'd seen on the net, but I could tell from the grin on Rodger's face that I was missing something.

I put my right hand on the mouse and clicked my way around the site. It had some really stupid looking T-Shirt designs. None of them were shirts that I would ever order, but I supposed there were kids who thought they were cute enough to spend money on. The checkout icon showed that you could pay with either Master Card or Visa. It was pretty normal stuff.

"I don't get it," I said with exasperation. "So he had a site that sold T-Shirts, so what?"

"You didn't notice anything strange?" Rodger asked.

I looked again. In addition to the featured designs there was a home page with both Facebook and Twitter links, a search bar powered by Sonic Ping, a design page with lots more of the stupid looking patterns that they would print on a shirt for you and the normal 'about us' and 'contact us' links. It was a very simple site, but still nothing strange jumped out at me.

"No, I don't."

"How much are they?" he asked cryptically.

I looked and didn't see any pricing.

"The pricing is probably on the order page," I said.

"Order one then," he suggested.

"Rodger, those designs are for cretins or brain dead half-wits," I complained. "I don't want one of them."

"Try."

I put my hand back on the mouse and clicked on a design. A larger picture of it came up. I looked for the order button but there wasn't one. I clicked on it again and it went back to normal size. I clicked on the back button and looked for some link to get to the order page, but I couldn't see one. I moused over to the checkout icon but it wasn't a link. What the hell?

I tried everything I could think of including putting the word 'order' in the search bar. That led me to some Sonic Ping sponsored links that would allow me to order at other sites like Amazon or Barnes and Noble, but not here. I finally pushed myself away from the computer in frustration.

"You either can't order or my mind isn't working right this morning," I said.

"Your brain is fine," he said. "You can't order."

"That doesn't make sense," I complained. "Brad wasn't stupid. He knew how to write code. There is no way he would make a mistake like that."

"I agree," Rodger said.

"So what's going on?"

"I don't know."

"But…," I blustered, "no one would put a site up to sell something, even something as stupid as those shirts and not have a way to take orders."

"I agree," he said. "There has to be some other reason for the site, but for the life of me I can't see what it could be."

"What about the 'Sonic Ping' search bar?" I asked.

"You tried that and it didn't go to the order page either," he said.

"No, I mean the coincidence that SonicPing.com seems to be involved in the kidnapping of Jennifer," I said.

"Good point."

"What about the guy you found her with?" I asked.

"He was hired muscle," Rodger said. "From his accent I'd say the Ukraine."

"But you said he was using a phone registered to Sonic Ping…"

"He was, but he let me break both of his arms without telling me who he worked for," Rodger said.

"You broke both of his arms" I asked, incredulously.

Rodger swiveled his head so that he was looking at me. Two glacial pools reflected my face back to me. I gulped.

"He was lucky," he said. "I was…"

He stopped and looked over to Jennifer. She pushed herself up from the couch and walked over to us. She put one hand on my shoulder, the other around his neck, leaned down and kissed him.

"He was happy to see me," she giggled. "I think that made him merciful."

Rodger grabbed her around the waist and pulled her into his lap. I was treated to a mini demonstration of how to make love with your clothes on.

"Merciful?" I thought. *"He broke the guy's arms."*

"So, what did you find?" Rodger asked, pushing Jennifer away.

I pulled out my stash and laid it on the counter in front of him. He took a few minutes looking at each piece.

"Well," he said, "I'd say that the meal receipts are probably dead ends, but I'll go around to each place and talk to the help and see. What about this one from "Explicit Things?""

"He had a stash of magazines in the drawer under his bed," I said uncomfortably, "they were all… 'Big Breasted Babes' or…"

"You're kidding me," Rodger interrupted. "But, Maddy doesn't have…"

"I know."

"Well, I'll stop there as well and check," Rodger said. "It's probably also a dead end."

"Probably," I agreed.

"And the two slips from the ATM?" he asked.

"No idea," I said. "Why would he need four hundred dollars? And why is there only a few minutes between withdrawals?"

He turned to his computer and within seconds he grunted and sat back. Brad had surprised him again. I waited.

"It's located inside of Teasers," he said.

"But that's a very private gentleman's club," I protested. "Brad wouldn't have gone to a place like that. I mean, you have to be a member or know someone just to get in."

"Maybe they let him in to use the ATM machine," Rodger said.

That got a laugh from me as well, but my mind was occupied with why Brad had been there, and the obvious reason why one might need a lot of cash in a place with scantily clad women. It didn't make sense and it certainly didn't mesh with the Brad who had been my friend.

"Rodger, what's going on?" I asked.

"Don't really know, buddy," he said. "It sure doesn't fit with the Brad we knew, does it?"

"No."

He picked up the final credit card slip which was from Boxes, Inc, grabbed the key and flipped it over so he could see the inscription.

"What do you think?" he asked.

"The same thing you do," I said. "He rented a box at Boxes, Inc."

"Yeah. Why, I wonder?"

He shook his head in bewilderment, put his fingers back on the keyboard and within a minute he had Boxes, Inc on the screen.

"They only have two locations in Pingree," he said, "and one of them is way on the north side. It's probably the closer one in Center Street Mall. You should check it out."

"Sure," I said, taking the key.

"So, that leaves these numbers…"

I watched the Cray computer in his head crank up. His fingers were a blur on the keyboard. Screens came and went so fast that I couldn't see how he had time to read them. Abruptly he stopped and sat back.

"Oh, my god," he said, shaking his head.

Oh, my god from Rodger was like a normal person screaming and kicking his chair. It got my attention.

"Oh, my god?" I asked.

"It's an account in the Cayman Islands at First Caribbean Bank," he said.

"Brad had an offshore account?"

"Uh huh."

"Does it have money in it?" I asked.

"A little over ten million dollars," Rodger said.

"Ten million dollars?"

"Yes. It's been coming in at the rate of about one hundred thousand dollars a day since a week before he died."

"From where?" I asked.

"I can't tell," he said. "It bounces through quite a few IP addresses before it ends up in the account."

"Can you trace it?"

"Probably, but it will take time," he said. "It would be better if we had something more to go on."

"Like?"

"Don't know, bud, perhaps there will be something in the box he rented."

"I'll go over there right now and…"

I was interrupted by my cell phone. Caller ID showed that it was Madeline, which didn't make sense because it hadn't been long enough for her to feel a desperate need to see me. Even so I felt warm all over as I answered.

"Hi, Maddy."

"Daryl, can you come?"

"Maddy… I…"

"Detective Sampson just called," she explained. "He wants to come over to talk to me."

"What? Hold on, Maddy," I said, pulling the phone away from my ear. "Rodger, Dan Sampson just called Maddy."

"Wow!" Rodger exclaimed. "That was fast."

"You think it's about what happened with Jennifer?" I asked.

"Don't you?"

I did, but I was still surprised that they had traced everything so rapidly. I put the phone back to my ear.

"I'm coming right now," I said.

Detective Dan Sampson had grown up with Rodger and me. I had been friends with him since grade school and after I bonded with Rodger in the eighth grade he and Rodger had become allies if not true friends. During our senior year he had been the first string football quarterback, which had put him in a completely different social group, but even so, we'd remained friendly. That had continued as he went off to State on a football scholarship, blew out his knee and came back to join our police department.

Now he was sort of a friendly enemy. Some of the areas that Rodger and I got into while helping our helping of damsels in distress were grey ones in Dan's mind. It created conflict. Our bringing down the child pornography ring had been a case in point. He had been happy with the results but angry at some of the methods we had used. Even so we usually managed to get together and put the outside world aside once a month to have a few beers and watch a game.

Dan had been the detective who came when Brad had died, and again when Maddy had her break in. As small as his department was it still strained belief that he would have also been assigned this case. I looked at Rodger to see if he was bothered by the coincidence also.

"I'd say he knows I'm involved," Rodger said.

"How'd he put that together?" I asked.

"Let's go ask him."

"What about Jennifer?" I asked.

"She better come along."

chapterFIVE

Twenty minutes later we pulled into Maddy's driveway. Dan was waiting with another young detective that I didn't recognize. Rodger and I piled out leaving Jennifer in the car and walked up the driveway to where they were standing.

"Hi, Daryl, Rodger," Dan said.

"Hey, Dan," Rodger and I said in unison.

"Detective Kirkwood, this is Daryl Morgan and Rodger Truscott," Dan introduced us.

We both put out our hands, but Detective Kirkwood wasn't having any of it. He glared at us and kept his hand at his side.

"So you two are the hot shots who think they can take the law in their own hands," he said coldly.

"Bruce," Dan said with exasperation.

"I've heard about some of the shit you've pulled," he said. "If it had been me you boys would be locked away. And now this deal. What makes you think you have the right to break...?"

"Bruce," Dan interrupted, "wait in the car."

"Dan, we're supposed to do our interviews together," he sputtered.

"Wait in the car," Dan said firmly.

Bruce didn't like it, but he turned, walked over to the car, climbed in and slammed the door.

"He's young, fellows," Dan said, "cut him a break."

"With that open mind I'll bet he solves lots of cases, huh?" Rodger said.

"He doesn't know you two like I do," Dan said. "He's got a funny mindset that it isn't okay to go around breaking people's arms for no reason."

"Is that what you think?" Rodger asked.

"No, of course not," Dan said pleasantly. "I'm sure in your mind you had a very good reason."

"If I had broken any arms," Rodger said carefully, "I would have had a damn good reason."

"I'm sure you would. So what happened?"

"Dan, why don't we go inside and see Maddy and you can tell us why you're here," I suggested.

"Want to ask Jennifer to join us?" Dan asked, glancing at the car where Jennifer was sitting.

"Why?" Rodger asked.

"Just a hunch that she's involved," he said.

"A hunch?" Rodger said.

"Us detectives are big on hunches," he said.

Rodger walked back to the car, helped Jennifer out and we traipsed up to the porch and rang the bell. Maddy opened the door and ushered us into the living room. She squeezed next to me on the couch and held my arm like it was a lifesaver and she was the next poor soul being forced to leave the Titanic. I smiled at her and some of the tension left her face.

"So what happened?" Dan asked.

"Why don't we play let's pretend," Rodger suggested.

"Let's pretend?" Dan asked.

"Yes, let's pretend that you are a real Detective who is here to find out if we know anything about whatever it is you think we might be mixed up in," Rodger said.

"Okay, Rodger," Dan sighed. "Let me lay it out for you."

"Do that."

"Last night a guy was dropped off at the emergency room with two broken arms. He is a Ukrainian, in the country illegally and was using a cell phone that is being paid for by Sonic Ping."

"So?"

"So, you already knew that," he said.

"I did?" Rodger asked.

"Yes, and that he had made a phone call here three days ago and then again just an hour before he was dropped off at the hospital," Dan said.

I could see the faint tick in Rodger's right eye that was his tell. Dan had surprised him. I kept my face blank, but his words shocked me, too. We had been going under the assumption that the police hadn't a clue. Rodger recovered before my brain fully processed the implications.

"So, the department has some new equipment, huh?" Rodger asked.

"We do."

"So, what was he up to? Did you listen in on the calls?" Rodger asked.

"Our equipment isn't as good as yours, Rodger," Dan said, "so the answer to that is no."

"Mmm," Rodger said noncommittally.

"How about we share, Rodger?" Dan asked.

"Share?"

"Yeah. I'll tell you something that you don't know and you'll tell me something I don't know… it's called sharing."

"Dan…"

"Tell you what," Dan interrupted, "I'll tell you something I don't think you know and if I'm right you tell me why the guy was calling here."

"Sounds fair," Rodger said, winking at me.

Dan caught the wink, snorted and shook his head in exasperation.

"The Sonic Ping cell phone that called here was in Brad's cell phone speed dial," Dan said.

Rodger looked at him blankly as if he didn't care, but I could see the tick.

"Brad called it about an hour before his accident."

The tick got faster.

"We have reason to believe that Brad's accident wasn't really an accident."

Maddy gasped and tightened her grip on my arm. Rodger opened his mouth to speak and then closed it again and waited. It seemed like a wise move because it was clear that Dan wasn't quite finished.

"We've had a trace on that phone since we discovered the connection," Dan said. "It was pinged from the closest tower to this house the day that someone broke in here."

This time Rodger opened his mouth and said, "Okay, what they wanted was the two million dollars they claimed they lent Brad just before his death. They threatened Maddy if they didn't get it."

"And?"

"And what, Dan?"

"That's Sonic Ping for Christ's sake," Dan said. "There is no way they would be making threats over two million dollars. What else?"

"We don't know," Rodger admitted. "They think he had some records or something, but we haven't found them."

"Who looked?"

"I did," I piped up.

"And you didn't find anything?"

"No," I lied.

"They are not going to stop just because you broke some guy's arms," he said, looking at Rodger.

"I don't know what you're talking about," Rodger retorted.

"How is Jennifer involved?" Dan asked.

"Why do you think she's involved at all?" Rodger asked.

"She's here."

"We're dating," Rodger said.

Dan glanced from Rodger to Jennifer. He must have liked what he saw because a big grin cracked his face.

"Wow!" he exclaimed. "Congratulations!"

"I didn't say we were getting married," Rodger said testily. "I just said…"

"I heard what you said," Dan said, looking smug.

I was still processing an earlier part of the conversation. I thought Brad died in an accident and now…

"What did you mean when you said that Brad's death might not have been an accident?" I asked. "It was icy, he lost control."

"His brake lines were severed," Dan said.

Maddy started sobbing. I stroked her arm.

"How come that didn't come out?" I asked.

"We weren't sure if they had been cut before or as a result of the accident," Dan said.

"And now?" I asked pointedly.

"We're still not sure but it looks like…"

His voice trailed off as he realized how badly the conversation was affecting Maddy. Her face was buried in my chest and she was weeping.

"Maddy," Dan said gently. "I'm sorry."

She looked up. Even with tears running down her face she was one of the most beautiful women I had ever seen. She looked at him tenderly.

"I-I know, Dan," she hiccupped. "You've been a good friend."

A pang of jealousy hit that threatened to consume me. A good friend? When?

"I didn't mean to upset you," he said.

"I know," she said. "You've been very supportive."

I saw the way he looked at her and realized that my friend Dan had the same hang-up that I did regarding Maddy. The major difference was that Dan was single. My jealousy wasn't rational, but I couldn't help the burn in my stomach.

"What's the next step, Dan?" Rodger asked.

Dan reluctantly dragged his gaze away from Maddy.

"The guy whose arms you… well, someone, broke is a dead end. INS has him and he will be deported. The only other unexplained item is that there were two other numbers in Brad's cell phone that belong to Sonic Ping. One of them belongs to the Vice-President of their security department, but we don't know who the other one belongs to yet. We also don't have the faintest idea why Brad had those numbers, or why they might have killed him, or what they are looking for," Dan summarized.

"There were two other Sonic Ping numbers in Brad's phone?" I asked.

"Uh huh."

"And one is a Vice-President?"

"Yes."

"I don't get it," I said. "Why would Brad have anything to do with Sonic Ping?"

No one answered. I assumed they were as baffled as I was. Then the thought twisted around in my head and the real question hit me.

"Wait!" I exclaimed. "Why would Sonic Ping have anything to do with Brad? And at that level?"

"What do you mean?" Maddy asked.

"Do you have any idea how hard it is to get through to an executive at that level in any large company?" I asked. "It's about like trying to call the President of the United States. You don't."

"So?" Maddy asked.

I thought about it. His instant advertizing concept wasn't something that Sonic Ping wanted or needed and the whole model had, in fact, never gotten off the ground properly. His T-Shirt site, bigooh.com, used a Sonic Ping search bar, but so did tens of thousands of other sites. Why did he have access to high up company executives? I looked at Rodger and he shook his head.

"So," I said carefully, "each time we get another piece to the puzzle it makes less and less sense."

"Yes," Rodger said, "but one thing is clear and that is that everything seems to lead back to Sonic Ping."

"It does," Dan said, "but I'm afraid it's a dead end."

"Dead end?" Rodger said. "Why can't you pursue the two numbers and see where they lead you?"

"My boss doesn't think we have enough probable cause and has asked me to drop it," Dan said.

"That's crazy," I said. "You've got a possible homicide. What more do you need?"

"The powers that be think that Brad's death was an accident and the one possible lead just had both of his arms broken and is being deported," Dan explained.

"What about the threats to Maddy?" Rodger snapped.

"Rodger," Dan interrupted, holding up his hand. "As far as the police are concerned there was nothing but some phone calls and a possible break-in."

I thought about that. Dan didn't have as much information as we did and certainly didn't know about Jennifer being taken. I looked over at Rodger and I could see he had processed the same facts and had already twisted his focus.

"Could you share those cell numbers with us?" Rodger asked.

Dan shook his head in exasperation and responded, "You know I can't. Anything in an active file is off limits and anyway the department frowns on vigilante work."

"The department certainly didn't frown when we helped you break up that pornography ring two years ago or catch that child molester last year," Rodger said.

"Selective memory," Dan said. "They only remember the rules you broke not the results. Right now there is a faction that wants you and Daryl strung up. My new partner, Bruce, is one of the most vocal."

"I can get the numbers elsewhere," Rodger said.

"I know you can, Rog," Dan said, laying a folded up piece of paper on the coffee table. "I'm counting on it."

Rodger put the paper in his shirt pocket, stood up and pulled Jennifer to her feet.

"How do you want us to play this?" he asked.

"Look, I'm not going to expect you to actually let me know what you're doing," Dan said, "just…"

"Keep you in the loop?"

"When you feel like it. Yeah."

"Sure."

Dan got up with us, but instead of moving to the door he crossed to where Maddy was standing and took her hands.

"Mad…Madeline," he stammered, "I know you said you weren't ready but I really want to…"

"I'm not ready, Dan," Maddy said forcefully, interrupting him in mid sentence. "Truthfully I probably never will be ready. I loved Brad and never ever believed that I could have feelings for anyone else."

"I understand," Dan said, dropping her hands and turning away.

"But…"

He turned back and looked at her with eyes that radiated so much longing my breathing seized up like someone had slashed a karate chop to my throat. I couldn't speak. I stood in shock as their little drama played out.

"But?"

"I-I'd like to see you as a friend."

The wave of jealousy that washed over me was like being covered by a forty footer at the Banzai pipeline. I watched Dan step back to her and recapture her hands.

"Would you like to have dinner with me?" he asked.

She nodded.

"Tonight?"

She nodded again.

"Daryl," Rodger said, grasping my shoulder, "we need to go."

I broke my gaze from Dan and Maddy and looked at him. I could see the concern in his eyes and hated myself for putting it there. I shook myself as if that would make it all right again.

"Want to talk about it, buddy?" he asked softly.

I shook my head and walked to the door.

chapterSIX

It was late in the day before we finally made it to the mall. I parked close to the south entrance where Boxes, Inc. had an outside door that allowed patrons to access their boxes twenty-four hours a day. There was only one other person inside as we entered and he was just leaving.

Box 656 was a jumbo sized one located in the middle of the lower tier. I put the key in the lock and it opened. Inside was a laptop, a notebook and a key that looked like one of those security keys that pop machines use. Rodger tucked everything into the shopping bag we brought, handed it to Jennifer and we were out of the door within a minute of entering.

As we approached the car Rodger shocked me by holding out his hand and asking, "Mind if I drive?"

I was surprised because, while Rodger was a much better driver than I, he never drove when we were using my car. I looked at him questioningly, but he cocked his head, smiled and held out his hand. I fished the keys out of my pocket, gave them to him, helped Jennifer into the back and climbed into the front passenger seat.

Rodger started the car and then began fussing with the rear view mirror. When he turned it into an impossible position I started to swivel around to see what he was looking at.

"Don't turn around," he said.

I turned my head back to the front.

"What's going on?"

"We've been followed since we left my shop and I just want to give him time to get to his car so he doesn't lose us," he explained.

"Followed, we're being followed?" I asked.

"Yes."

"Why?"

"Golly, Daryl, I haven't a clue. Could it be the missing two million dollars and the stuff that we have in that shopping bag?" he said.

"That's not what I meant."

"What then?"

"What I mean is, how could someone have connected you to this?"

"He might have followed you to my shop this morning," Rodger said.

"Oh."

"Anyway, since he's on our tail and I want to find out more about him, I plan on losing him – hopefully without him realizing that it was intentional."

"And then what?" I asked.

"We'll follow him and see," Rodger said, backing the car out.

We started in the general direction of the strip mall where Rodger's shop was located. Now that I had been told we were being followed I couldn't resist looking in the passenger side mirror. I noticed a dark green Nissan that drifted about four car lengths behind us.

"The Nissan?" I asked.

"Yeah."

"Is he any good?" I asked.

"He is."

"How'd you spot him then?" I asked.

"I'm better," Rodger said.

"So, what's the plan?" I asked.

"I'm going to lose him at the next light," he said, "and then circle around and follow him."

"Isn't that Hollywood movie stuff?" I asked.

"It is when they do it," he said, flicking his eyes between the light and the rear view mirror.

The light went from green to yellow just as we approached and I felt the tug of the brakes. At the last instant he let off and we sailed through as it went red. I watched the car behind us come to a stop which trapped the Nissan behind him. We went over a slight rise and dropped out of his sight. There was a dumpster at the curb in the next block. Rodger pulled in front of it and backed up to it tightly so that we were shielded from view until any cars passing us were abreast. Even then our pursuer would have to swivel his head ninety degrees to see and recognize us in the half second that he was passing us.

"I don't think that he'll see us," Rodger said confidently, "but if he does I already have his plate so I can still run him down."

"Then why are we doing this?" I asked.

"On the off chance that when he realizes that he has lost us he will lead us to someone higher up."

"I can't believe he'll be that stupid," I said.

"I don't think so either," Rodger said, "but we don't have anything to lose."

At that moment the green Nissan went screaming by us. The driver was so intent on watching the road ahead that he missed us entirely. Rodger waited a few beats, letting two other cars zip by before we pulled out in traffic.

We spent the next hour following the Nissan as it frantically shuttled back and forth between the strip mall where Rodger's shop was located and my home. The driver was plainly upset that he had lost us. He finally gave up, drove into the main downtown area, parked in the Comerica Bank building garage and entered the attached elevator. We parked about twenty spaces away and watched him get in the elevator. It stopped on the eighth floor.

"I ran his plate," Rodger said, holding up his cell. "He's a private investigator named Maynard Baxter and keeps an office on the eighth floor."

"If he's any good he knows we came up with something at Boxes, Inc.," I said.

"I'm sure he does," Rodger said.

"You knew he was out there from the time we left your shop," I said. "Why didn't you lose him before we went there?"

"Because I wanted him to see that we found something," Rodger said.

"I don't get it," I said. "Isn't that just going to stir them up more?"

"They are already stirred up," Rodger said, "but we don't know who they are. What I'm counting on is that he has been instructed to let them know immediately and will be talking or emailing them as we speak."

"I see."

We climbed out of the car. Rodger helped Jennifer into the driver's seat and gave her the keys.

"Lock the doors and wait here," he said. "If anything suspicious happens, text my cell phone with any random string of three letters and drive out of here. If no one is tailing you, drive to the Comerica Bank main street entrance and wait five minutes in the loading zone. If we don't get there in five minutes, drive off and go to the safe house I showed you. If you have a tail, go to the 3rd precinct instead, park in the no parking zone in front, leave the car, find Dan and tell him everything."

"Rodger, you're scaring me," Jennifer said.

"Why, Jen?" he asked tenderly.

"You're making it sound like you could get killed or something," she said.

"I'm sure everything is fine," he said. "I'm just being careful."

I knew better than that. When Rodger put this much thought into what seemed like a simple meeting it meant he had a premonition. I kept my face blank when Jennifer glanced at me. It soothed her because all she did was pull Rodger down for a kiss.

ᘒ

"Are you carrying?" Rodger asked as the elevator door closed.

"No."

"Here," he said, handing me a nine millimeter Glock.

"What's this for?" I asked, ejecting the clip to check it and then reinserting it and chambering a round.

"Just a strange feeling I'm having," he said. "Maybe it's nothing."

"That's what you said just before that pipe bomb went off," I said, as the elevator stopped on eight.

The eighth floor was deserted. At the end of the corridor we found an office marked 'Maynard Baxter, P.I.' with the door open to a reception area that held a desk and three chairs. On the desk was an old fashioned call bell with a sign that said 'ring me'. There was no sign of Maynard, but there was another door at the back of the room and we could hear someone talking behind it.

"Sounds like he's on the phone," I said, nodding toward the door.

"Probably filling his client in," Rodger said. "Might be a good time to interrupt him."

"Do you have a plan?" I asked.

"No. I thought we'd just step in and see what happens," Rodger said.

He turned the knob, kicked the door open and we stepped inside with him going left and me to the right. Maynard was seated behind the desk with his feet up and a cell phone parked in his left ear.

"Speak of the devil," he said into the phone. "They just walked into my office."

He listened for a second and then said, "Sure, I'll hold them until you get here."

He swung his feet to the floor. His right hand pulled his desk drawer open and slipped inside. He didn't get it back out before Rodger had slammed it shut on his hand and deftly caught his cell phone as he dropped it from his left.

I had seen Rodger go from zero to a blur many times, but even so, it always amazed me how he could move. When he went into faster-than-light mode it looked like teleportation because one moment he would be standing next to you and the next he would be across the room.

"Hello?" Rodger said to the phone.

He listened for a second and then snapped it shut.

"I guess they didn't want to talk," he said, putting the phone in his pocket.

"My… my hand," Maynard whimpered. "You broke it."

"Did I? Let's make sure," he said, slamming the drawer shut on Maynard's hand again and then yanking the drawer open.

"What's this, Maynard?" Rodger asked, removing a .38 revolver from the drawer.

"You have no idea who you're dealing with, buddy," Maynard said.

"Tell us, Maynard," Rodger said.

"Fuck you."

"I think I know anyway," Rodger said, "and I'm sure your phone will confirm my suspicions."

"Fuck you."

"Really repetitive, Maynard," Rodger said, rummaging through his drawer and bringing out a set of handcuffs.

"Give me your hand, Maynard," Rodger said politely.

"Fuck you, man."

"You're starting to bore me," Rodger said, capturing his left thumb, swiveling it around and bending it back in a classic thumb hold.

Maynard came off of his chair. The beauty of that hold is that with only three to four pounds of pressure you can control someone who normally could pick you up and throw you across the room.

"Cuff him to the desk, will you, Daryl?" Rodger said.

I took the cuffs from Rodger, snapped one on Maynard's damaged right hand and the other through the handle on his desk.

"That's not going to hold if he wants to get loose," I said.

"I know, but that and his broken hand will slow him down a little," Rodger said, "and that's good enough."

Rodger crossed to Maynard's one file cabinet, pulled each drawer open and thumbed through the files.

"Wow," he exclaimed. "Almost everything in here is something he has done for Sonic Ping. He's a kept man."

In the third drawer he came out with a thin manila folder that he put on the desk and flipped through.

"This is a file on Brad that was started about three weeks before his accident," Rodger said. "Scumbag here was keeping tabs on him."

"Does he have any notes on the day Brad died?" I asked.

"Why?"

"Just thinking of what Dan said about the..."

"Oh, yeah, good point," Rodger said turning pages. "Nothing is jumping out at me, but we can take this along to go over in detail."

"Hey man, that's private," Maynard whined. "You can't..."

"I can't, Maynard?" Rodger interrupted.

Rodger's phone chimed with an incoming text. He looked at it and then at me.

"Message from Jen," he said, "Three guys, guns."

"Better than a random string of three letters," I said.

"Yes. Let's go," he said.

We walked back down the hall to the elevator and saw that it was on its way up.

"What do you think?" I asked.

"Probably all three of them in the elevator because they're stupid," he said.

"Want to surprise them?" I asked.

"Maybe next time," he said, heading for the stairs. "We don't know enough yet."

We started down the stairwell and were rounding the third floor landing when we heard someone bang the eighth floor door open and start down behind us. Rodger got Maynard's cell phone out of his pocket.

"Think that is all three of them?" I asked.

"They aren't that stupid," Rodger said. "At least one of them is on the elevator."

As we entered the ground floor corridor the elevator dinged preparatory to opening. Rodger hit redial on Maynard's cell phone, stepped to one side and pulled his pistol. I moved over behind him and pulled mine also. The doors opened. Rodger stuck his gun right in the face of the guy who was stepping out, reaching in his pocket for his ringing phone. He stopped and wisely put his hands up. Rodger snapped Maynard's phone shut and the ringing stopped.

"Are you the boss?" Rodger asked.

"You have no idea what you're dealing with, asshole," the guy said.

"So we keep being told," Rodger said.

"When my men get here I'm…"

"Back up," Rodger interrupted, forcing him to the back of the elevator, reaching in and punching a button at random and withdrawing his hand as the door shut.

chapterSEVEN

"What's next?" I asked.

"Run away, live to fight another day," Rodger said, heading for the front entrance.

As we went through the outer doors I could see the other two from the stairwell push open the hall door and spot us. They were three hundred feet behind. Jennifer was right where she was supposed to be in the no parking zone. She scooted over when she saw us coming. Rodger climbed into the driver's seat, I jumped in back and we were at the corner before the two chasing us made it to the street.

"Thanks for the heads up, Jen," Rodger said, squeezing her neck.

"Sure."

"Didn't you think they showed up awfully quickly?" I asked.

"Not really," he said, checking the rear view mirror for pursuit. "I think they came from the Sonic Ping building which is just across the street, and I'll bet our friend in the elevator is their head of security."

"Makes sense... so what do we do now?" I asked.

"I'm not really sure," Rodger said. "I was kind of surprised by their reaction to us doubling back on Maynard. I mean... sending three guys with guns?"

"Well, you had one of your *'I can't explain it but something's going to happen'* moments," I said.

He thought about that and looked at me.

"I guess I did, didn't I?"

"Let me think," I said. "You told Jen to text us if she saw anything, you handed me a pistol, you..."

"I got it, Daryl," he said.

"So, what now?" I asked.

"We need to go somewhere and look at what we got from the storage box and Maynard's file," he said. "But first we need to get rid of our tail."

I couldn't help myself. I spun around and looked in the rearview mirror. I fully expected to see a big SUV inches from our bumper. There was nothing. I turned back and looked at him smiling at me in the mirror.

"Not yet," he said, "but soon."

We pulled into a mega gas station that had pumps for cars and a huge area for eighteen wheelers. He parked in the trucker's area, pulled his laptop out and plugged Maynard's phone into it.

"This phone is a real liability, but the info in it could be important," he said, his fingers flashing over the keys. "So we keep the information and use the phone to distract."

Unplugging the phone he got out of the car and sauntered along between a couple of semis that had plates from Louisiana and California. He took his time, finally disappearing behind them. When he got back he no longer had the cell phone.

"Where'd it go?" I asked.

"I think it's on its way to Mexico," he said.

"Confusion?" I asked.

"Yes, they will trace it and follow where it is going instead of following us," he said.

"It might slow them down."

CR

Thirty minutes later Rodger pushed the laptop we had retrieved from Boxes away from him and ran his fingers through his hair.

"Wow," he said. "I didn't know that Brad was that good."

"That good?" I repeated.

"Well, I guess I knew," he said reflectively, "I'm just surprised that he felt the need to protect this so well."

"What did you find?" I asked.

"That I need help getting past all of his layers of protection," he said.

"You can't get in to his laptop?" I asked, incredulously.

"I figured out his user password, but the files we want are encrypted and I haven't a clue what the key to that is," he said.

"Surely if it was that difficult he would have had to leave himself a hint," I ventured.

"He did," Rodger said. "I think it's in that notebook, but I can't figure out how to use it."

I opened the notebook and paged through it. It looked like he had begun it when he had first conceived of Boomslash.com as a way of keeping his thoughts organized. Just reading his notes got me excited all over again. The idea of combining texting, widgets, websites and interfacing with all of the current social networking giants had been an awesome concept and now it was becoming clearer to me that it might not have failed as I'd thought.

The notebook showed a steady progression of how Boomslash was succeeding until the startup of Bigooh. Then he seemed to have gotten completely sidetracked. The final pages were nothing but doodling. SonicPing and Bigooh were prominently displayed with arrows flowing from SonicPing containing big dollar signs. The last page contained only one sentence followed by the number twelve which was circled. I read it three times before I looked up.

"What the hell does 'The five boxing wizards jump quickly' mean?" I asked.

"It's one of the shortest sentences you can make using every letter of the alphabet," Rodger said.

"Really?"

"It only contains thirty-one characters and it makes a sentence that makes sense, unlike some of the shorter ones," he said.

"I thought the shortest one was 'The quick brown fox jumps over a lazy dog'. That's what I learned in school."

"That has thirty-three letters," he said.

"So that's the hint?" I asked.

"I think so, but I don't see how to use it."

"I have an idea," I said.

"How to use it?"

"No, how to find out," I said.

"What?" he joked. "An ad on Craig's list?"

"Almost," I said, "I was thinking of Wikianswers."

"You're kidding me, right?"

"No."

"But…"

Rodger was one of the sharpest people I had ever met. I think part of his uncanny ability was that he didn't allow his mind to get muddled up with the why not's in the world. Instead of getting hung up with thinking about how stupid a question was or how stupid the person asking it was he listened and evaluated what he was hearing without considering the source. I watched his brain work on my suggestion for the three or four seconds that it took for really difficult things.

"What a great idea," he said, turning to his keyboard. "We'll let someone else work on this."

Within moments he sat back.

"Now we can concentrate on our other problems," he declared.

"Which are?"

"Your car, Jennifer being kidnapped, the stuff we found, especially the laptop, the information about Brad's death, the websites, ten million dollars, the keyword we don't know,

Maynard following us, the new three guys from Sonic Ping and ten million dollars," Rodger said.

"You said ten million dollars twice," I pointed out.

"That's because it's worth mentioning more than once," he said. "Besides it's probably closer to eleven million by now anyway."

"So where do we start?" I asked.

"Let's start by swinging by your house, parking your car and using one of my clean ones until we have this sorted out," he said.

"What's wrong with my car?" I asked.

"Maynard knows it for sure," he explained.

"Right."

"What I want you to do is drive it to your house and park it in your normal spot in the carport. Pack a bag for a couple of days and explain to Karen that you are working on a case with me," he said. "Then have her drive you to the 'Four Points Hotel' downtown. Enter the lobby and then go down the left corridor to the rear and out the back where Jen and I will be waiting."

"Should I look for a tail?" I asked.

"Sure."

"Think someone will be there?"

"I would imagine that either Maynard or one of the goons will pick you up as you leave your house, but they won't be prepared for the switch through the hotel," he said.

"What about Karen?" I asked. "Won't that get her involved?"

"I can't see why," he assured me. "They are going to be focused on you and Karen isn't even on their radar screen."

"Could I call a cab instead?"

He looked thoughtful for a moment and then nodded and said, "Maybe that would be better."

☙

When I got home I didn't see any obvious stakeout which in some ways was a relief. It gave me time to spend some quality time with my lovely wife. Time to hug her, time to tell her how much I loved her and plenty of time to fill her in on the latest developments and suggest that tomorrow might be a good time for her to visit her sister upstate. I helped her pack her bag, packed one for myself, gave her a kiss, grabbed my laptop and called a cab.

I watched carefully again when my cab pulled out of my drive, but either there wasn't anyone on my tail or they were very good. At the hotel I let the doorman take my bag inside as if I was checking in. When I got inside I gave him a five dollar tip and took my bag back, telling him that my friend had already registered and I'd find my own way. I walked to the rear of the hotel and out the back door where Rog and Jen were waiting outside.

"Any problems?" Rodger asked as I slid into the back seat.

"I didn't see anyone following me at all. Just in case I made it look like I was checking in," I said.

"All the better," he nodded.

"Where to now?" I asked.

"I need to swing by the shop and pick up a few things," he said.

"Aren't you worried that we might get tagged while we're there?" I asked.

"Not really. I've been watching the place remotely and no one has been back yet plus I have an alternate way in and out," he said.

ʘ

We drove into the mall lot fifteen minutes later and parked at the far end from Rodger's shop. He opened his laptop and watched his webcams for a bit before getting out of the car and going into the pizza carryout five doors down from his place. Thirty minutes later he reemerged from the pizza store dragging a roll aboard suitcase that he put in the trunk.

"I think I've got everything we need," he said, sliding back behind the wheel.

"Any trouble?" Jennifer asked, touching his sleeve lightly.

"One threatening message on the machine," he said, patting her hand reassuringly. "Not what I'd call trouble."

"Who was it?" I asked.

"He didn't identify himself but I think it was Victor Underwood," he said.

"Who's that?" I asked.

"He's the guy we met in the elevator," Rodger explained, "the Vice President of Security for Sonic Ping."

"What did he want?" Jennifer asked.

"He said that whatever we found at Boxes, Inc. is stolen property from Sonic Ping and they want it back," he smiled.

"Whatever we found?" I asked. "So they don't actually know what we have?"

"No."

"And if we don't give it back?" I asked.

"He didn't say, but the implication was that they will send someone to do their dirty work like they have before."

"Could we just give them something and claim that..."

I stopped because it was not only a stupid idea, but it made me realize that even if we turned over what we found they wouldn't believe it was everything and still come after us.

"Shit," I said. "We're fucked."

"Well, we are certainly going to have to make an effort to stay out of their path until we solve this puzzle," Rodger said.

"Have we gotten any hits from Wikianswers?" I asked.

Rodger turned and lifted an eyebrow at Jennifer. She shook her head.

"Jen is monitoring that board and I guess the answer is no," he said.

chapterEIGHT

An hour later Rodger called Dan and filled him in on our meeting with Maynard and the boys from Sonic Ping without giving him the really ugly details. Even so, he gave Dan enough of the particulars that he wanted us to come in and make formal statements. Rodger put him off with a promise that we would be in soon and then switched off his phone.

We spent the next two days in one of Rodger's safe houses. Except for when Rodger and Jennifer treated me to one of their quiet love-making sessions, where I had to turn the TV up to drown them out, it was boring.

We didn't get anywhere on finding out what Brad had been up to, but it wasn't from a lack of trying. Jennifer spent each day checking Wiki for an answer and posting the same question to as many other places she could find. Rodger used his time writing password solving programs, also to no avail, and I spent my time trying to find some logical reason why Brad had constructed an e -commerce website from which you couldn't actually order a single thing.

We did have a moment of levity the first day when we found out on the news that two employees from Sonic Ping had been arrested trying to stop a truck of video gaming machines bound for Guadalajara.

By the end of the second day, when Rodger retrieved messages, I was climbing the walls and thinking that perhaps we should put ourselves in harm's way if for no other reason than to provoke action.

"We got two messages on the machine," Rodger said, putting the phone down. "The first one is from Victor frothing at the mouth for what we did with Maynard's cell phone."

"I kind of thought it was clever," I said.

"The second one was from Dan saying he absolutely has to see me," Rodger said. "He sounded upset."

"It's probably something to do with Sonic Ping complaining about the phone and his superiors and especially his hotshot partner upset about us 'loose cannons,'" I said.

"Maybe," he nodded, "but he sounded really shook up."

"Want me to come along?" I asked.

"Perhaps we should all go," he said.

◌

Thirty minutes later we parked the car at the far end of one of Pingree's busiest shopping malls and staked out a table at the back of 'Dugan's Restaurant and Bar' which was located at the other end of the mall from where we left the car. Dugan's was never busy at this time of day. Rodger had spoken with Dan extremely briefly on our way and then had shut his cell back off. In fact we had all been keeping our cells phones off as it was one less path leading to us.

Rodger picked Dugan's because there was a back way out of the bar that led through service corridors along the length of the mall and then out to where our car was parked should things go wrong. The second reason for choosing this spot was evident when Dan entered with his hand covering his eyes. It was very dark inside and, for a moment until their eyes adjusted, we had an advantage on anyone coming in.

Dan made his way to the rear, spotted us and stopped dead. His face looked as if he had just seen a ghost.

"D-Daryl," he stammered. "What are you doing here?"

"You didn't tell Rodger to come alone," I said, getting out of the booth. "If there's a problem Jennifer and I can…"

"No, there's no problem. It's just…"

"What?"

"Daryl, we need to talk," Dan said.

"So talk," I said.

"Your car…"

He stopped talking, looking stricken. He opened his mouth to speak but nothing came out. I waited as long as I could and then asked, "My car?"

"Daryl," he responded, changing the subject, "when's the last time you talked to Karen?"

"Yesterday… no, day before when I was home," I said. "I was going into hiding with the rest of my gang and she was going to head out of town to visit her sister, why?"

"You haven't talked since…"

"My phone's been off," I said, "because the bad guys can find us. We did mention the bad guys, didn't we, Dan?"

"Call her."

"Huh?"

"Please, humor me and call her."

I turned my phone on and as soon as I had a signal I pushed and held down the number one key. My wife was the first number in my speed dial and, when my primal urges didn't overpower my better sense, she was number one in my thoughts also. Lately it seemed like my sexual desires were getting in the way of that. The call went right to voicemail and I listened for a moment because the sound of her perky voice caused a wave of soft loving memories to rush over me.

"Daryl?"

Dan's voice brought me back to the present. I tapped the disconnect icon and looked at him.

"Her phone's off," I said. "She's probably at a movie with her sister."

"What about voicemail?"

"I didn't want to leave a message," I said. "I'll call her back later."

"No," he said, shaking his head again, "I meant, did she leave you one?"

I tapped the phone call icon again and checked. The little symbol was in the upper left hand corner letting me know that I did have voicemail. I clicked it and waited while it connected. I had one new message and it was from her.

"Hi, honey," I heard her voice say, *"I know you told me that you were going to have your phone off, but I wanted to tell you that I love you."*

"I love you to," I whispered.

"And I hope it's alright if I use your car because my battery is dead again."

I disconnected again and looked at him.

"So?" he asked.

"Just a personal message."

"Where is she?" he asked.

"She didn't say, but I assume she's with her sister," I said.

"Because?"

"Look, Dan, I don't get it," I said, with a tone of real exasperation creeping into my voice. "What the fuck difference does it make where my wife is?"

"Because her car is still in your carport," he said.

"That makes sense," I said. "Part of her message was that she was going to use mine because her battery was dead."

"Daryl, your car was involved in an accident yesterday afternoon," Dan said.

"An accident?"

"Yes."

"But, what about my wife?"

"Daryl, sit down for a minute, will you?"

"What about my wife?"

"Daryl, will you sit down?"

I sat down angrily and looked up at him.

"What is this about my car and an accident?" I asked.

"On the expressway about fifty miles north of town a semi ran over the back of your car. It burst into flames and…"

"Dan," I interrupted, not wanting to hear or believe what was coming, "there is no way. My wife was a great driver and…"

My throat closed up and I couldn't speak. I knew what he was trying to tell me, but my mind didn't want to believe that what he was saying had really happened. I felt tears on my cheeks and I brushed them away, but there were more in their place. I wiped them away again and even more took their place. I stopped trying.

"How?"

"We don't know how," he said. "It looks like her brakes weren't working and she was trying to slow down to stop and the trucker behind her wasn't paying attention and…"

"Huh?"

"It looks like someone tampered with the brakes on your car and…"

I held up my hand and stopped him. My wife was dead, that was clear. A huge part of my life was over, that was also clear. I was wounded and some of the hurt that radiated from my core was never going to leave me, that was also clear, but some tipping point in me had also been passed. Some threshold had been crossed.

"Tampered with my brakes?" I asked coldly.

"Uh."

"Like Brad's?"

"Well…"

"Yes or no, Dan?"

"We can't tell, but it looks sort of similar," Dan said carefully.

"And your bosses?" I asked.

"My bosses?"

"Yes. What do they think?"

"Daryl, Sonic Ping is a huge force in this town and they…"

"Don't want to bite the hand that feeds them," I finished.

"Damn it," Dan said angrily. "I'm on your side, but they are saying that there isn't enough to go on."

"So, if it quacks like a duck and nips like a duck and waddles like a duck it can't be a duck?" I asked.

"They want more proof," he said.

"I see."

"Listen, I tried but…"

"Dan, I'm not blaming you," I said. "I understand how powerful Sonic Ping is, but even a four year old could see that there is something wrong."

He nodded.

"Someone tried very hard to bury this with Brad and now is trying even harder to keep us from putting the pieces we have together," I said.

"What do you have?" Dan asked.

"We really don't have much more than we told you," I said, "and none of it makes any sense."

"Look, Daryl, I know you and Rodger like to play things close to the chest, but we've had two suspicious deaths and…"

He stopped talking and looked at me.

"So, you're not going to play the 'you are interfering with an active police investigation' card, huh?" I asked.

"It wouldn't do me any good, would it?" he asked.

"No, and especially not now," I said.

"What can you give me?"

I glanced at Rodger. He nodded slightly.

"When you get back to your office look up Bigooh.com and tell me what you think," I said.

"That's it?"

"That is a lot, Dan," I said seriously.

"Oh."

"Dan," Rodger said urgently. "Who did you tell you were coming here?"

"No one," Dan replied. "Well…, my partner, of course."

"Jen, Daryl, we've got to go," Rodger said, pulling her from the booth and pushing her ahead of him toward the service door in the rear.

"What's going on?" Dan asked.

"Your partner is in bed with our Sonic Ping friends," Rodger said gesturing at the window.

Outside we could see Victor. He was heading for the door to the restaurant with two other guys. Four others were fanning out to each side.

"What the hell?" Dan sputtered.

"Do you need more proof that something is really wrong?" Rodger asked, shoving open the service door and pushing Jennifer and myself ahead of him.

"Hey, Rog, I'm sorry. He's a…"

"Good kid," Rodger completed.

"He is," Dan insisted.

"If you keep on believing that it is going to get you killed," Rodger said, letting the door close behind him.

We raced down the corridor past the rear door of 'Victoria's Secret's, Williams Sonoma, Fox Jewelry' and a host of other stores that were a blur. When we reached the exit door where our car was parked Rodger stopped and cracked it slightly. Two suits were camped close to the car looking toward the obvious direction from which we should have been coming.

"Time for plan B," Rodger said.

"I didn't even know we had a plan B," I said.

He looked at me and shook his head.

"Daryl, I always have a plan B."

He pulled out his iPhone and punched a few numbers. I watched through the crack in the door as one of the two suits reached in his suit pocket, fished out his phone and answered it.

"Get back here," Rodger said into his phone. "We've got them trapped in the bathroom."

I watched in disbelief as the guy snapped his phone shut, yelled at his friend and the two of them went trotting back toward the other end of the mall.

"How did you do that?" I asked, as we ran to the car and piled in.

"Magic?"

"Rodger, why would that guy believe his boss called him?" I asked.

"It said so on his caller ID," he said.

"How did you do that?"

"I used an iPhone app called SpoofApp that spoofs the caller ID. It showed him that the call was coming from Victor's cell phone," he explained, "it also disguised my voice."

"But…"

"He heard what he expected to hear," he said, checking the rear view for a tail.

"What now?" I asked.

"First we warn Dan again and then we get rid of this car," he said.

"We need to get rid of this car?"

"Did you notice that those guys were waiting near our car?" he asked.

"Yes."

"How do you suppose they knew about it?" he asked.

I thought about that and nothing occurred to me. I shrugged.

"Someone with really good access to DMV records who also knew we were coming here," he suggested.

"Dan's partner, Detective Kirkwood?" I said.

"Got to be," he said, punching a speed dial number on his cell.

He waited a second until the phone was picked up, said, "They knew about our car, Dan."

He listened for a few seconds and then shut his phone off.

"I think he might be starting to believe."

chapterNINE

Hiding in a safe house wasn't an option anymore. First, I had to go back home and take care of the hundreds of decisions that needed to be made because of my wife's death and second, and more importantly, I was angry and I wanted to lash out and I couldn't do it by hiding. I was furious that someone thought that it was okay to murder my best friend and then my wife just to cover something up. I was even angrier that the police seemed unwilling to find out why or even believe that two murders might have taken place.

That angry part of me was hoping that whoever was involved would try again and I'd get a chance to punish them. The stupid part was that I was in such a daze the first two days after she died that I wouldn't have noticed a rhino charging me. Luckily I didn't encounter any rhinos and no one tried to kill me either because I would have been a pushover.

The memorial service three days after the accident was horrible. I mean the service was beautiful and moving and special, but somehow her parents blamed me for her death and that spoiled the whole thing. They had never liked my dabbling in dangerous pursuits and even though this had nothing to do with anything that I had started it didn't make any difference. Guilt by association or *post hoc ergo proper hoc* thinking was their mindset. Somehow they had heard about Brad's similar accident and… well, grief and wanting someone to blame for the unthinkable can do terrible things to otherwise rational minds.

I didn't blame them but it was still hard.

What was harder than the service was coming back home with my wife's sister after the service and looking at her things. My wife had a shoe fetish that I had always classified as Imelda Marcos on steroids. I think that I read somewhere that Imelda had three thousand pair of shoes. It seemed to me that my wife had at least that many in boxes in the garage which didn't count the ones she was really using that were in her closet. I suppose that was just me being a typical guy and exaggerating, but it did seem that she had more than she could ever wear. None of that mattered now as all I wanted at this point was to move my gaze upward from every pair I looked at and see her standing in them.

Then there were the jeans and the dresses and the makeup and the perfume and the jewelry and… I couldn't do it. Everywhere I turned something reminded me. I went through an entire box of tissues trying to control the weeping. All I really wanted was to lie down and wake up from the nightmare with her holding me.

Her sister took pity on me and spent three hours dragging all of her things out and down to the storage shed so there wouldn't be so many horrible reminders every time I opened the closet door. It didn't really work because the scent of her in the shower and in the empty closet and even in the pillow, when I lay down to try and rest, did me in.

Madeline stopped by and offered to help my sister but I could see that her mind was elsewhere. She had Dan along and it was clear that they had plans of getting to know each other better. I could have asked her to stay but it would have been jealousy driving me. I could tell that Maddy was getting closer to Dan and keeping her to help me would have been senseless torture, so I declined.

How my wife's sister did it was beyond me. I couldn't get further than halfway through filling one box of clothes before I'd remember the red dress that she wore to last year's Art Museum party or the jeans she wore traipsing around Toronto, and the feeling of loss would so overwhelm me that I had to stop.

Going through her jewelry was the hardest because most of it we had purchased together. The diamond necklace that we bought in that cute little boutique in Amsterdam or the Ruby bracelet we bought in Bangkok or the really unusual Sapphire pendant and earrings that we found in the factory mine shop in Ilakaka, Madagascar. Memories of things we'd done and places we'd been that would have been fun with her next to me. Now they left a taste of ashes and pain.

We finally finished up around eight that evening. I sent her sister home and lay down to get some sleep, fully intending to call the Salvation Army in the morning to take away the things that she didn't want. The phone rang at four am and just for a moment I thought it had all been a bad dream, that it was my wife calling me to come get her. The caller ID said 'unknown' and the voice on the other end was disguised.

"We want the stuff you took from Boxes, Inc.," the voice said.

"Fuck you," I said, coming fully awake. "We are going to track you down and when we do…"

"Look, asshole," the voice interrupted, "this is way bigger than a couple of cowboys like you and your friend."

"You killed my wife," I said.

"We want the stuff," he said, ignoring me.

"Fuck you," I said again.

"Put it in a box and take it to…"

"At the risk of sounding repetitive," I hissed, "fuck you. It's not going to happen. We are going to find you and bring you down."

"The next message we send you is going to be worse," he said, angrily, "much worse."

"Worse than killing my best friend and my wife?" I asked.

I was talking to a dead line. I dialed Rodger.

"Rodger, I just got a call asking for the stuff back," I said.

"What'd you tell them?" he asked.

"I was kind of repetitive with my verbiage," I said.

"And?"

"He was angry and claimed the next message they sent would be much worse."

"Well, I've got Jennifer safe and we can get Dan to get some police protection for Maddy, so perhaps we can catch one of these guys red handed," he said.

"I hope so," I agreed. "Any progress on the hard drive?"

"Jen has been a trouper about getting it out there, but no, nothing so far."

"I'll call Dan in the morning and fill him in," I said.

"Watch your back, buddy," he said.

I hung up and went back to bed.

ʘ

The next morning I called the station. They put me through to the squad room.

"Third precinct, Detective Kirkwood speaking."

"I'm looking for Detective Sampson," I said.

"He's not here right now," Dan's partner said. "May I help you, sir?"

"Can you tell me when I might reach him?" I asked.

"I'm not at liberty to give out that information, sir," he said. "Would you like to leave a message?"

I so did not want to leave a message with Kirkwood, especially since both Rodger and I suspected that he was working with Sonic Ping, but I couldn't see an alternative.

"Ask him to call Daryl when he gets a chance, will you? Tell him it's very important."

"Your number, sir?" he asked.

"He has it," I said.

"I'll see that he gets the message," he said and hung up.

At the time I thought that if I didn't hear from him by the end of the day I'd try again and, if necessary, go over to Maddy's and keep her company or watch her house myself until he could arrange something. Then I got involved with calling the Salvation Army and helping them load my wife's things and one thing led to another. I started drinking at three in the afternoon and the rest of the afternoon and evening was and still is lost to me.

❦

I woke up under the dining room table with a splitting headache. The phone was ringing. I crawled to it and held it gingerly to my ear.

"Daryl," Rodger said. "Are you okay?"

"No," I croaked.

"What?"

"I drank too much," I said.

"Daryl, they took Maddy," he said.

My hangover vanished. I was on full alert.

"How?" I asked.

"She had a date with Dan last night," he said. "They were jumped in the parking lot when they came out of the restaurant."

"Date?" I said, focusing on the pang of jealousy that hit me.

"Daryl, are you listening?"

"Sorry."

"Have you heard from them?" he asked. "Have they tried to call?"

I thought about the fact that after about five o'clock yesterday afternoon a cruise ship could have blown its horn next to my ear and I wouldn't have heard it. I looked down and my message light was flashing.

"They might have," I admitted. "My message light is on."

"You drank that much?" he asked.

"Rodger, the Salvation Army came and…"

"I'm sorry, buddy," he said. "Check, will you, and call me back?"

"Sure."

I hung up and pushed the play button. There were three messages. All three were from the thug with the disguised voice and by the third he was very angry.

"Okay, asshole, you think you're so fucking smart and won't pick up?" the voice said. "Your friend's wife is history."

I dialed Rodger back.

"I fucked up, Rog," I said. "They called me three times and he was really angry the last time."

"What'd he say?"

"That Maddy is history. Oh shit, Rodger, I really fucked up and…"

"Daryl, stop it," he interrupted. "We'll get her back."

"But, what if they…"

"Daryl, focus," he said. "We'll get her back, I promise."

"Okay."

"Give me a few hours to do some traces on the calls to your house and Maddy's and…"

He stopped talking. Something else was bothering him.

"What?"

"Dan's in the hospital," he said.

"Huh?"

"They jumped him as he was opening the car door," he explained. "He didn't have a chance."

"Is he okay?"

"He's going to live, but he won't be working for at least a month," Rodger said.

"Well, the good part is that the police will be busting ass to find out who did it," I said.

"That's what doesn't make sense," Rodger said. "They've swept it under the rug."

"You're kidding."

"No, I think that little snake partner of his managed to quell any possible investigation."

"Oh shit!" I exclaimed.

"What?"

"I called yesterday morning and left a message for Dan to call me," I said. "I left it with his partner. I thought at the time that he didn't recognize who I was but…"

"Yeah."

"I'll go visit Dan and see what I can find out," I said. "Where is he?"

"Valley Central."

"Okay. I'll check in with you in a couple of hours."

"Daryl," Rodger said forcefully, stopping me from hanging up.

"What?"

"Be careful. These guys almost killed a cop."

I thought about that. Sonic Ping was a huge economic force in our town, but to almost kill a police officer and sweep it under the rug? I needed to pay attention.

᎒Ꮹ

Two hours later I was standing in Dan's room. His face looked like someone had pushed it into a belt sander. His left arm was in traction, and in addition to the vitals monitor, he had an IV drip and a morphine pump. I stood over him for forty-five minutes before he finally opened his eyes.

"Daryl," he croaked.

"Dan."

"Ask Rodger to send Tiny," he said.

I leaned in thinking I hadn't heard him correctly.

"I want Tiny," he repeated.

Tiny was a three hundred and fifty pound mass of muscle, bone and brains that Rodger and I used when we needed a bulldog with a mind to protect someone. Tiny was the best there was at what he did, which was protecting a client no matter what. If Dan was asking for Tiny he knew his partner was bent and he was scared. I couldn't resist digging at him.

"Dan, you're with the police. Why would you need protection?" I asked.

"Daryl, do I have to fucking beg?"

That made me blush.

"Sorry," I said in earnest, "I'll get him here right away."

"Tell Rodger to brief Tiny that he is not to trust anyone except yourself and him."

"Wow, what the hell is going on?" I asked.

"I'm slow but I'm not stupid," he said. "Too fucking many coincidences and the last one was that the only one that knew where we were going last night was my partner."

"I see."

"What do you know about Maddy?" he asked.

"Only that they took her," I said.

"They told me to tell you that they were going to sell her," he said.

"That's what they said about Jennifer," I said.

"They mean it, Daryl," he said. "They plan to move her out of the country right away."

"Unless what?" I asked.

"There is no unless. They're going to do it to send you a message that when they call again you better give them what they asked for," he said.

"Fuck."

"Daryl, what do you guys have?"

"That's the problem, Dan, we don't have anything that makes any sense," I said. "Just bits and pieces of nothing and they wouldn't believe us anyway.'

"So what are we going to do?" he asked.

"You aren't going to do anything," I said. "You can't even walk."

"Daryl, I love her. Please, you have to help."

I don't know why that hurt so much, but it did.

chapterTEN

Dan pushed the feed button on his morphine pump and five minutes later he was asleep. I called Rodger.

"Dan wants Tiny," I said without preamble when he answered.

"Wow, he must really feel threatened," Rodger said.

"He says that only his partner knew where he was going last night," I explained.

"Can you stay until he gets there?" Rodger asked.

"Yes."

"Stay put. I'll get back to you," he said and hung up.

I sat down in the chair next to Dan's bed where I could see the door. I turned off the TV and stared at the wall.

❧

I was still staring at the wall two hours later when the door opened and Tiny walked in.

"Hey, Daryl," he said.

I came out of my trance and looked up. Tiny looked around the room. I had forgotten how big he was. Rodger and I had originally met Tiny eight years previously when he had been part of the local security detail for a very famous rock star and I had been working for a single mom who's daughter had run away from home and become a groupie. It had helped that we were pursuing similar goals, but even without that we would have become friends. That kind of attraction can't be explained, but sometimes when you meet someone you just know that they are someone who will be a friend for life. Tiny was one of those.

He was fearless in the face of danger and had earned a Silver Star in Iraq for rescuing one of the men in his squad who had been shot and was unconscious. He had run twenty yards from cover to scoop his buddy up and carry him through fierce enemy fire to safety. It had also earned him a Purple Heart for the leg wound that he ignored during the rescue. With Tiny on the job they would have to kill him to get to Dan. I stood up.

"Tiny," I said warmly, attempting to wrap my arms around his more than gigantic frame.

"What happened to Dan?" he asked, looking at the bed.

"Some guys jumped him and took Madeline and…"

"Wait," he interrupted, "he's a cop. Why isn't this place swarming with cops?"

"Dan's boss thinks it was just a random mugging," I explained.

"But you and Rodger don't?" Tiny said.

"No, we don't but Dan asked for you himself," I said.

"Oh. So, who do I trust?" he asked.

"Myself and Rodger," I said.

"Not his partner?" he asked.

"Especially not his partner," I said. "We're all pretty certain Kirkwood set the whole thing up."

"Daryl," Tiny said, shaking his head, "perhaps you should start from the beginning."

I sat down and started to talk. By the time Dan roused from his morphine induced stupor I had given Tiny a complete grounding in the events of the past two weeks. Summarized like that it seemed even more unbelievable than it had as it happened. Dan opened his eyes and reached for the trigger on the pump, stopping when he caught sight of Tiny.

"Tiny," he croaked. "You came."

"You're looking kind of rough, buddy," Tiny said dryly.

"Did Daryl fill you in?"

"Uh huh."

"I need you to stay close, okay?"

"I can do that," Tiny said.

"Thanks," Dan said, again reaching for the trigger to the pump.

I saw a cloud pass over Tiny's face. He glanced at Dan and then at the morphine pump. He took two steps to the bed, ripped the morphine IV out of Dan's arm, bundled the tubing and pushed the apparatus across the room and out into the hall.

"I'm going to do my part but you need to stay alert, okay?" Tiny said.

"What?" Dan said raggedly.

"No more drugs, Dan," he said gently.

Dan looked at his arm where Tiny had pulled out the IV. It was seeping blood. He looked up at Tiny's determined face and nodded.

"Okay."

Tiny moved his gaze to me and winked.

"I think I've got it handled, Daryl," he said.

I stood up to leave, and Dan's partner burst through the door before I could get to it.

"What the fuck are you doing here?" he asked me angrily then glanced at Tiny. "And who the hell is that?"

Tiny moved around me and planted his formidable body in Detective Kirkwood's chest, pushing him back toward the door.

"I'm Dan's bodyguard," Tiny said with his face inches away from Bruce's, "who are you?"

"Bodyguard?" Bruce asked. "Why would he need a bodyguard?"

Tiny didn't answer. He just kept pushing on Bruce's chest, moving him closer to the door. Bruce craned his neck around him so that he could catch Dan's eye.

"Dan, what is going on? A bodyguard? This is a joke, right?"

I was thankful that Tiny had pulled the morphine drip out of Dan's arm, because if he was still zoned out I was sure that Bruce would have found some reason to remove us from the room. Dan was still clearly under the influence, but he didn't leave any doubt about his intentions.

"I want him here," he said.

"Dan, we can protect you," Bruce said.

"Who's we?"

"The police, Dan, we're the police. We can do a way better job than some amateur like this bozo," Bruce blustered.

"Really?" Dan said. "Like the job you've been doing so far? Like the one that got me here?"

"That was just some random mugging," Bruce said. "You can't blame us for that."

"You guys can stick with the random mugging idea all you want," Dan said, "but there have been too many random acts in the past few days for my cop radar to adsorb. I want a body-guard and I intend to have Tiny here until I can fend for myself, got it?"

"Uh…sure, Dan, whatever you want," Bruce agreed.

"Any progress on Maddy's whereabouts?" Dan asked.

"No," Bruce said shaking his head, "but I'm sure she'll turn up. I think maybe she's hiding because she's scared or…"

"So you guys don't intend on paying any attention to my report about what really happened," Dan interrupted.

"Look, nobody gets kidnapped and sold into slavery in another country," Bruce said. "I don't know what happened between you two or how much you had to drink but…"

"Get out!"

"Huh?"

"I said get the fuck out of here, Bruce," Dan said, "before I turn Tiny loose on you."

That got Bruce's attention. A tinge of fear crept into his eyes, but after all, he was a cop with the complete force of the law on his side. His back stiffened.

"Turn Tiny loose on me?" he scoffed. "Are you nuts? I'm a cop. You can't do that. I could shoot him and claim…"

"Bruce," Dan stopped him, "I'm not sure what's going on or how you are mixed up in this. Maybe you are as naïve as you act, but I'm telling you that you are on the wrong side of this and for your own well being you'd best leave it alone."

"Dan…"

"One last time, Bruce," Dan said coldly, "leave or I am going to have Tiny remove you bodily."

"Fuck you," Bruce said, turning and walking out.

We watched him try to slam the door, which was quite a trick as hospital doors are not designed to be able to slam. We looked at each other. Silence reigned. It was Dan who spoke first.

"I still can't believe that he is really mixed up in this," he said. "I still think that he is a clueless kid who has no concept of the bad out there, but I want you both to play it as if he is a part of why Maddy has gone missing."

We both nodded and the silence stretched out again. I think we were all thinking of the same thing, but it was Dan again who finally interrupted our reverie.

"Daryl," Dan said, his voice catching, "is she going to be okay?"

I didn't know what to tell him. I knew what Rodger had said about her being sold into slavery and the prospects of recovering her didn't seem good. I knew he didn't want to hear that so I lied.

"We are going to get her back," I promised.

"I love her," he said.

That twisted something in my heart, but I put it aside. My friend was lying in a hospital bed all banged up and incapable of going after the woman he loved. My enabler half was going to try and make it right.

"We'll find her, buddy," I said. "Just get better."

He nodded and closed his eyes. With a final thumbs up to Tiny I walked out looking for dragons to slay.

chapterELEVEN

It took me more than an hour to get back to the safe house where Rodger and Jennifer were waiting, using some of the tricks that Rodger had taught me over the years. I doubled back on myself, ran red lights, changed lanes for no reason along with other tricks designed to throw off a tail. The most important was leaving my car in a parking lot to make it look as if I was running an errand, then walking through a busy store to the other side and grabbing a cab, then changing cabs again.

The direct route was only twenty minutes, but I didn't dare take it. I wasn't sure who was involved, but at this point I didn't need to find out. Some part of me wanted to so that I could throttle the information out of them, but with Maddy's life at stake I wasn't willing to take the chance.

When I finally got there both Rodger and Jennifer seemed engrossed in their computers.

"Anything new?" I asked.

"I tracked all of the phones that we know are involved in this and two of them pinged towers close to the restaurant where Maddy was abducted. One was Victor's," Rodger said.

"From there they went across town and then split up. Victor's appears to have gone home and now his phone is pinging the tower closest to Sonic Ping so I assume that he is at work."

"What about the other one?" I asked.

"It stayed put for most of the night and then was turned off. Maddy's was pinging the same location until it was turned off also."

"Where?" I asked.

"From the tower location I'd say that they took her to Teasers," Rodger said.

"Teasers? That club that Brad went to?" I asked.

"Yep."

"Do you think she might still be there?" I asked.

"It's a long shot, but you should check it out," he said.

"What about you?"

"I have a bite on the internet from some guy who says he has the answer to the password problem and I don't dare break contact with him," Rodger explained. "Holler if you need cavalry."

chapterTWELVE

Teasers was located in a seedier part of old downtown Pingree, not far from Rodger's shop. The entrance was a small non-descript metal door off of a parking lot in the middle of a cinderblock wall with a tiny sign. Unless you knew that the club was there you would have never stumbled on it. In fact, I had asked the parking attendants when I drove in where Teasers was located and both had expressed ignorance. Clearly, if you didn't know where it was then you had no business trying to go there.

Luckily the parking lot and surroundings were well lighted and with enough traffic for people going to nearby shops that I didn't stand out. I hung around next to my car until a large group of partygoers began making their way toward the door and then I attached myself to them. Several of the girls were quite drunk so it was easy for me to drape my arms around one of them and join in the giggling and laughing as if I were with the group. My plan almost fell apart at the door when the bouncer stuck out his hand and stopped me.

"He with you, Selma?" the bouncer asked the girl on my right arm.

She looked at me with clear, interested, intelligent eyes. There wasn't a trace of the copious amounts of alcohol that her bearing indicated she had consumed. She plainly knew I wasn't part of her group. I looked at her with a sick horrified look. She smirked and nodded.

"Yes, Jared, this is Two Shoes Buckypaper, my new boy toy."

Jared laughed and removed his arm. I stumbled into the club. Inside, Selma kept her hand firmly clutching my bicep. It was clear that I had been wrong about her being drunk, but I still assumed that she would forget about me as soon as something interesting happened to distract her. I was wrong. She steered me to a quiet corner in the entrance hall and leaned in like she was going to kiss me.

"What's your story, Two Shoes?" she whispered with her lips just inches from mine.

"Just having a good time," I said.

"Do this a lot, do you?" she asked.

"Sometimes," I said cautiously.

"Bullshit, Bucky," she said. "I come here every weekend and I've never seen you before. What's your angle?"

"I uh…"

"Looking for someone I bet."

This wasn't going the way I expected or needed. Too much curiosity from this one was going to get me noticed. Plus, I could probably use her help. I grabbed her by her shoulders and pulled her into a passionate kiss. She responded.

"Wow," she said, "very nice, Buck."

"The name's Daryl," I said, "and you are… Selma?"

"Yes."

"Well, Selma, would you like to help me?"

"Depends," she said. "What do I get out of it?"

"What do you want?" I asked.

"You," she said, "but I'm betting that's not going to happen, is it?"

"I…"

"Lucky girl," she said.

"What?"

"The one you're looking for, she's a lucky girl."

I glanced away and thought about my feelings for Maddy and how I'd had to deny them because of my wife and now because of Dan. I looked back and tried to keep my face from showing the storm raging in me.

"I'm helping a friend," I said.

"Oh. It's like that, huh?" she said.

"Will you help?"

"You think she's here?" Selma asked.

"Yes."

"Why?"

"Because… well, that's what I was told," I said vaguely.

"Let's look around then," she said, dragging me out of the hallway alcove and toward the main room.

"Wait."

She stopped and looked at me.

"Wait?"

"Yes, what do you want from…," I let my sentence trail off as I realized that the end of my thought might be offensive.

"Want from you?" she asked.

I didn't know how to put delicately what I was thinking. I nodded.

"Like, do I expect money?" she said bluntly.

"Well…"

"What I want is for you to escort me for the evening," she said.

"That's it?" I asked.

"Do you see that creep over there who followed us in?" she asked, nodding down the entrance hall where a really buff looking guy was pretending to look at a wall poster.

"Creep?"

"Trust me, his looks are deceiving," she said.

"Is he stalking you?" I asked, my protective radar finally engaging.

"Down boy," she said, hitting my arm. "Just stay close, okay?"

"Why is he following you?" I asked.

"I don't know," she said. "He's been around for about three weeks and it's starting to scare me."

Just then two really nice looking young women passed us. The blond on the left put her right hand around my neck, moved her lips close to mine and whispered, "Come see me later, won't ya?"

I flushed with embarrassment which made Selma laugh.

"You don't come to places like this ever, do you, Daryl?"

I shook my head like a naughty schoolboy and she laughed again.

"Come on, let's look."

The main room of the club was huge but didn't overpower you. The lighting was subdued, the chairs were large and leather and big enough to seat two people and the tone was restrained elegance. Except for the almost naked girl spotlighted on the stage it might have been a posh old boys club or an exceptionally tasteful library specializing in obscure and very rare manuscripts.

The other thing that would have stopped me in my tracks, except that Selma had a grip on my arm and kept me moving was the number of good looking women. Actually, good looking was simply too average of a description. The place was filled with great looking women, most of them dressed in leather or costumes.

Maddy wasn't in sight, but I hadn't really expected her to be. In the corner close to me was an ATM machine that I assumed was the one Brad used. Beyond it was a curtained doorway that was guarded by a brute of a guy.

"What's behind that door?" I asked.

"That's where the semi-private rooms are," she explained.

"What goes on back there?"

She sidled up very close to me, put her lips an inch from my left ear and whispered, "Want me to show you, Bucky?"

My mind said no but my body was getting other ideas. I shook my head in exasperation and put my hands on her waist to keep her from getting closer.

"Selma, can we look?"

"What's her name?" she asked.

"Madeline."

"Okay, follow me," she said, pulling me across the room.

As we passed the ATM machine I stopped her.

"Wait, this place takes credit cards, doesn't it?" I asked.

"Of course they do," she said.

"So why would someone need a bunch of cash?" I asked.

"Is that a joke?"

"No. My friend was here a few weeks ago and he withdrew... uh... a lot of money from this machine and I just wondered why," I said.

"What's a lot of money?" she asked.

"Four hundred dollars," I said.

"Oh."

"So?" I asked.

"What did he look like?"

"Huh?"

"Your friend, what did he look like?" she asked.

"About six feet tall, short curly black hair, granny glasses and ..."

"Brad?" she said interrupting me.

"Uh...yeah, his name was Brad," I admitted.

"Nice guy," she said. "He came here a lot about a month ago."

That was news to me.

"Really?"

"Uh-huh."

"Why?" I asked.

"I'm not sure," she said. "He seemed to be looking for something."

"Like?"

"I don't really know," she said. "He spread a lot of money around among the girls. I think he was looking for a girl who he says came through here and disappeared."

"Disappeared?"

"The girls come and go," she said. "There are lots of clubs all over the states, all over the world for that matter."

"Oh."

"So, do you see your friend?"

"No."

"She probably didn't come here," Selma said.

"We traced her here with her cell phone," I lied. "I know she's here."

"Uh oh," Selma said shaking her head.

"What?"

"That means she's in the…uh…special members only section."

"So?"

"So, only a person who has been a member for at least a year is ever allowed down there."

My heart did a back flip off the high board and ended up in my feet. There was no possible way I could wait a year to get downstairs. There had to be another way.

"What about guests?" I asked.

"What about them?" Selma said.

"Can a special member bring a guest?"

"Yes."

"And?"

"And what?"

"Are you a special member?" I asked.

"I happen to be, yes."

"Well?"

"Well what, Daryl?"

"God damn it, Selma. Stop being so fucking dense," I said. "Will you take me down there or not?"

"That depends on you."

I got it. Actually I didn't get it, but I got the fact that she was going to blackmail me into something for escorting me downstairs.

"What do you want?"

"I want the same thing I wanted the first time you asked, Daryl," she said. "You."

"No."

"Ok," she said.

She turned and started walking away from me.

"Wait, god damn it."

She turned back and looked at me, "What?"

"What do you mean me?" I asked.

"Do you know why guys come here?" she asked.

"Looking for love?" I replied.

"Sort of," she said. "Do you know why most of the women come here?"

"Uh, to make money?" I said.

"Some maybe, but for most money's secondary," she said.

"Secondary?"

"Daryl, do you know what this place is?"

"It's a gentlemen's club, isn't it?"

"Not really."

"Huh?"

"Most people who know about this place think it's a gentlemen's club that is very hard to get into. In fact it's a 'lifestyle' club and is almost impossible to get into unless you are recommended by an existing member," she explained.

"A lifestyle club? What's a lifestyle club?"

"It's a place where lifestyle people can come to play and act out their special needs," she said.

I was totally lost and my face must have showed it because she snorted and shook her head.

"Tell you what," she said. "Spend thirty minutes in a private room with me and I'll take you downstairs."

"Doing what?" I asked suspiciously.

"I'll leave that to you," she said, turning away and expecting me to follow her. "Use your imagination."

She whisked me through the main room of the club with its bar and leather couches crowded with normal looking people drinking and talking to the rear of the club where a three hundred pound guy stood guarding a velvet curtain.

"Two for a private, vanilla, thirty minutes," she said.

He looked at me and smirked, "Vanilla, Miss Selma?"

"Jerome," she said, "Bucky Two-Shoes is new."

"Pardon me, Miss Selma, I just can't remember the last time you used a vanilla room," he said. "He must be special."

"Don't know yet, Jerome," she said, taking a key from him and pulling me after her down the hall. "I hope so."

We entered a private room where she flipped the sign outside to 'occupied' and locked the door behind us. Before I could glance around the room she had me lip-locked and tumbling toward the couch. We ended up prone with me on top and somehow my hands found their way to first base. My hands liked what they were holding. The rational part of my mind wanted me to push myself away, but some other part was telling me to go for it. It was Selma who broke the kiss.

"So Bucky, what do you think?" she asked.

"What is it with this Bucky stuff?" I asked. "My name is Daryl."

"Oh," she purred, dragging me in again.

"And what the fuck is vanilla?" I asked when we resurfaced.

"Most people," she answered.

"Most people? God damn it, Selma, I…"

"Hold that thought," she said plucking a ping pong paddle from the end table and putting it in my hand. "What does that make you think of, Bucky boy?"

"Paddling your ass," I said without thinking.

"Now you've got it," she said happily, spinning around and planting herself across my lap.

I don't know what possessed me, but I began using the paddle on her rear and the more I did the more I liked it. So did she. I didn't hit her hard and I stopped after every blow and ran my hands over her globes. I loved that they were so firm and warm.

"So, Selma," I asked, "is this shaping up to what you were thinking of?"

"Don't know yet, Buckyboy, but it seems like it."

I kept spanking her and found that the little whimpers she made were turning me on. It seemed that what I was doing was wrong. After all, I was still in mourning, but my body wanted her. I looked around the rest of the room and saw it also had a

King sized bed with handcuffs on the four corners. I put the paddle down, scooped Selma up and threw her on the bed.

"If this gets to be more than you are looking for just tell me to stop," I said, using the handcuffs on the headboard to capture her wrists.

"Stop isn't a safe word, Bucky."

"Huh?"

"Just keep doing what you're doing," she purred.

I secured her ankles with the cuffs on the footboard and stepped back to admire. My god she was exquisite. Her streaked blond hair swirled around soft creamy white skin set off by blue-green eyes and red kiss-me lips. Her eyes had clouded over in lust and she was plainly ready for me to make love to her.

For my part the changes and frustrations of the past few days had combined to drive me over an edge I didn't even know existed. I thought about continuing to spank her with the paddle, but in her present position other thoughts intruded. I stretched out on top of her, captured her mouth with mine and forgot about everything for a while.

೦೩

"Downstairs?" I asked softly after reality returned.

"I guess you've earned it," she said, giving me a look that made me want to crush her in my arms and do the whole scene over. I smiled instead.

We went back out into the hall and turned away from the curtained entrance where Jerome stood. At the other end of the hall was an elevator in front of which stood a guy who could have been Jerome's twin.

"Miss Selma," the brute said politely, "you planning on going downstairs?"

"Please, Tyrone, if you'd be so kind," Selma answered.

Tyrone pushed the button next to the door and it opened. He stood out of the way as we entered, then reached in and pressed the B button, withdrawing his arm as the doors closed.

"You come here that much?" I asked.

"Why do you say that?"

"Because everyone knows you and treats you like a fixture," I said.

"It's probably because I tip really well," she said by way of brushing off my inquiry.

The elevator dinged and the doors opened to a third mega sized guy in a suit. He stood out of our way. We were in a short hall with another door at the end. As we approached it Selma grabbed my shirt and swiveled me to face her.

"Etiquette is: Look all you want, but don't interrupt a scene and don't talk to anyone who has a collar on," she said. "If you are unsure ask me, clear, Bucky?"

"Collar?" I asked stupidly.

"Just stay close to me and look for your friend," she said, pushing the door open.

We walked into a room that had some leather couches with several people sitting and talking. There was a large dressing room to the right and I could see a nice looking thirty some year old sitting at a vanity putting on makeup. A paunchy grey haired guy was just coming out of a dressing booth attired in a corset, wig, stockings and high heels. I must have stopped walking because I felt a tug on my arm and I was propelled into the next room.

We entered a large room that even though I'd never seen one before could only be described as a dungeon. It was a chic dungeon, not dark, dank, damp or gloomy. There was carpet on the floor, chairs to sit on and only a few flickering fake electric torches, but it was a dungeon none-the-less.

Scattered around the room were groups of people. A closer look revealed that they were in various stages of dress or undress. Some were in outlandish outfits and some were naked. There were cages, crosses, benches and tables with all kinds of strange goings-on.

Selma led me around the room so that I had a good look at each group and then we stopped at each of the doorways leading off of the main room. These doorways had windows that allowed you to peer into semi-private rooms. Most were unoccupied, however several had similar scenes taking place inside, similar to ones going on in the main room. I didn't see Maddy in any of them.

"Well?" Selma asked when I had done the circuit twice without finding her.

"She's not here," I said.

"How sure are you that she was here?" she asked.

I ignored her question because I was focused on a windowless door on the far wall.

"What's back there?" I asked.

She glanced in the direction of my gaze and shrugged, "Just the offices."

"Can we look?" I asked.

"Daryl, she wouldn't have been allowed back there," Selma said. "Only staff and owners can go back there."

"So we can't?" I said.

She looked at me, shook her head in exasperation and walked away from me toward the door. I followed. As we reached it she opened her purse, extracted a small key ring with only one key, put it in the lock and turned it. We walked through and she closed it behind her.

"Look around, Bucky," she said.

I grabbed her hand, the one still holding the key, and pulled her around to face me.

"Who are you, Selma?" I asked.

"Someone who's doing stupid things because of you," she said, putting her lips inches from mine.

It got the desired reaction. My mind stumbled over the outrage I'd had just seconds ago and all I could think of was how much I had enjoyed our time in the 'vanilla' room and repeating the performance. I put my lips on hers and closed my eyes. My hands moved up her back, under her top and around to her breasts. I slipped my hands under her bra and found her nipples. She moaned and I moved one hand down to pull up her skirt. I could feel her hand on my zipper when we were interrupted by a cough.

I gently pushed her back and turned. A nice looking guy about my age with grey streaks in his hair, loosened tie and a tired look on his face stood in the doorway of an office.

"Hi, Selma. New toy?" he asked.

"Oh. Hi, Jerry," she said without any trace of embarrassment, "just showing Daryl around."

"Around?" he said.

"I'm looking for someone," I said.

I saw a frightened look flit through his eyes, but it was gone almost before I could swear I'd seen it.

"Did you find him?" he asked.

"Her," I said pointedly.

I saw that flicker of fear again.

"Oh," he said, pretending disinterest.

I glanced around the corridor we were in. Besides the office he came out of there was one more door. It looked solid. It was bolted.

"What's back there?" I asked, nodding at the locked door.

"Just storage," he said.

"Can I see?" I asked.

He looked startled at my request. He opened and closed his mouth twice but nothing came out. Finally he looked at Selma.

"It's just a big storage area with an elevator to the service entrance in the alley," Selma said, "We actually never use it, but I'll open it and you can take a look."

She threw the bolt and pushed on the door but it wouldn't open.

"That's funny," she said, "we usually never lock this one."

She put her key in the lock, but it wouldn't turn. She pulled it out and put it back in and tried again, but it still wouldn't budge. She looked at Jerry.

"Why isn't my key working?" she asked.

"Well... uh... I rented that space out and they changed the locks," he said.

"You rented it out and didn't tell me?"

"Selma, I..."

"Aren't we partners, Jerry?" she asked.

Partners? I looked at her. Her being an owner here explained a lot. I turned to Jerry for his answer.

"Selma, you... I mean we were having some financial difficulties and I... we needed the money and..."

"And what?" she asked.

"They kind of implied that it would be bad for business if I didn't," he whispered.

"They threatened you?"

He looked down at the floor in shame, "What harm was there? We didn't use the space anyway."

"How long ago?" she asked.

"About two months," he said.

"Two months, and you didn't tell me?"

"Well you hardly ever ask about the business end and I..."

"To?"

"Huh?"

"That's a simple question, Jerry," she said coldly. "To whom did you rent it?"

"I'm not exactly sure. The guy who pays has a Russian accent and something I overheard made me think they might be associated with Sonic Ping."

"Do you have a key?" she asked.

Jerry hung his head, "No."

"Look, Jerry," she said, "I've been stringing my new friend Daryl along because I was pretty sure that we didn't have any place where someone could be hidden. Now you're making me look really stupid. I want this fucking door open and I want it now, got it?"

I looked at Selma with new respect. The sweet, easy going, pushover demeanor that she had exhibited so far was masking a structure of kryptonite. She was one tough woman.

"Selma, how do you expect me to do that?" Jerry whined. "It's a steel door and..."

"Get some of the boys in here and have them break it down."

"But, the guys who rented it are going to be..."

"Now, god damn it!"

"Selma, if I do that they'll kill me."

She could see the fear in his face. Even I could see that he was more frightened of breaking open that door than he was of Selma, and that was saying a lot. In her new incarnation she was formidable. He turned and scampered into his office leaving her fuming. Before she could react he was back, holding something in his hand.

"Here," he said, handing her a security key on a rabbit's foot key-chain. "This is a master key to the elevator entrance in the alley. I had the locksmith make me one when the locks were changed. They don't know I have it. If they catch you please tell them it's yours."

From the way she looked at him I didn't think that their partnership was going to make it, but she didn't say a word. Grabbing me by the arm she marched me back through the dungeon to the elevator and stood ignoring me until it came.

"Want to talk about it?" I asked as the door shut behind us.

She whirled on me, "You know, Bucky, if I had known how much trouble you were going to be I would have dumped you at the door before we came in."

"I think I'm kind of attracted to you too, Selma," I said, wrapping my arms around her and drawing her in.

Our lips melded and she melted into my body. The ride was way too short.

chapterTHIRTEEN

Ten minutes later we had worked our way out of the club, around the side of the building and into the alley. About halfway down the back side of the building was a door with a metal plate next to it, the plate at waist height with a key slot. She put the key in and turned it.

"What are we going to do if someone's here?" I asked.

"Tell them the truth," she said. "I rent the building and I'm showing you a potential sublease space."

"That's the truth?" I asked.

"Close enough."

The elevator came empty, we piled in and thirty seconds later it opened into the basement room that we hadn't been able to reach from the inside of Teasers. It was also empty.

Next to the entrance was a desk littered with papers, a computer and a printer. Beside it was a small refrigerator. In one corner on a charging stand was a compact electric forklift. There was a short hall in the back that probably led to the door we had been unable to use. Scattered around the room were good sized packing crates. The place was deserted.

"It doesn't look like your friend is here," Selma said, obviously ready to turn around and leave.

"Just give me a minute, okay?" I asked.

I moved to one of the crates. My attraction was that they were way too nicely constructed for shipping anything normal and I was curious as to what they might be sending from such a strange location. The crate I picked had the top cracked and when I put my fingers under the edge it swung up on hydraulic shocks to reveal the interior. For a few seconds my brain couldn't figure out what I was seeing.

The interior was padded with soft foam, molded into the shape of a person in a reclined position. At strategic points were restraint straps. In addition there was an IV that contained saline solution and a catheter.

"This looks right up your alley, Selma," I said.

"Daryl, that isn't something to joke about," she said. "They look like crates to…"

"Yes?" I asked.

"God damn it," she said, "they are shipping people in those crates."

"Is that a surprise?" I asked.

"Yes."

I looked at her and decided her surprise was genuine.

"We need to call the police," she said, reaching for her phone.

"Wait."

She stopped trying to dial and looked at me.

"Let me look at the computer and the paperwork first, please," I asked.

"Okay, but hurry," she said. "I wouldn't want to get caught down here."

She had a point. If what we were looking at was what I thought, getting caught down here was bound to get us both a trip in a crate, and to someplace where I'm sure we didn't want to travel.

I crossed to the computer, booted it up and waited while it came on line. It was password protected so I wasn't going to find out what might be on it until Rodger could take a look. I shuffled through the papers on the desk, but they were just copies of bills-of-lading. The shipping addresses were all the same bonded warehouse in Casablanca, Morocco. I unplugged the computer, gathered it up with the papers under one arm and stepped to the elevator.

"Let's call on our way out of here," I suggested, pushing the up button and fretting until the elevator arrived.

Thirty seconds later when the door opened on the alley Selma was looking down at her phone and dialing so she didn't see the guy blocking our exit. I did. I also saw the semi-automatic pistol leveled at us. I put out my free hand and stopped her. She looked up.

"What?" she asked.

"Back up, both of you," the guy said.

"Look, buddy," she blustered, "Perhaps you don't know who I am but I own this place and…"

"I know who you are, Selma," he said. "I've been following you for three weeks. Now, back up."

I looked more carefully and sure enough it was the hunky guy that Selma had labeled a creep who had followed us into the club. We backed up into the elevator until our backs were touching the other set of doors. He pushed the button for the basement and then stood with his back against the door on his side while we rode down in silence. When the doors opened behind us we stumbled backward and he followed. I turned, walked over and put the computer and papers down on the desk. I wanted my hands free in case he had a moment of inattention.

"That's far enough," he said.

I sat down on the desk and watched him, while Selma came over beside me and grabbed my bicep as if I was going to be able to save her. I patted her arm and waited. He pulled out his phone and speed dialed a number.

"I caught Selma coming out of the shipping room with some John," he said without preamble. "They had the computer and a bunch of papers."

He listened for a minute and then wiggled the gun at me.

"Toss me your ID," he said.

I reached for my back pocket and he came on full alert. His gun, which had been wavering loosely in his hand, got rock steady.

"Carefully."

I turned my right hip slightly toward him so that he could see my pocket as I fished my wallet out with two fingers. I gently tossed it on the floor in front of him. I was hoping that he would divert his attention, but his eyes remained riveted on mine as it landed in front of him. He reached down without lowering his gaze, scooped it up and thumbed it open to my driver's license.

"Daryl Morgan. 2212 North Lane. Date of birth is…" he stopped speaking as whoever was on the other end interrupted him.

He listened. His eyes became stony. He nodded twice and closed his phone.

"Step over to that crate," he said to Selma, then looked at me. "And you too."

We both walked over to the open crate that I had inspected earlier.

"Lie down in it, Selma," he said.

I didn't like where this was going, but the alternative was to have him shoot us. I nodded at her and she stretched out in the crate.

"Fasten all of the restraints," he said.

I buckled the straps around her ankles, her wrists and her waist. I left the one around her right wrist loose enough that she could pull her hand through it hoping that he wouldn't notice. He stuck the gun in my neck and pushed hard enough that it had to have left a bruise.

"Tighter, asshole," he hissed.

I tightened the strap and sat back on my heels. She wasn't getting out of that shipping container until someone helped her out.

"Now you," he said, motioning to the case next to hers.

I pulled the cover back, lay down in the cushy foam and fastened the ankle straps. My mind was finally catching up to the seriousness of what was happening and my body was rebelling. If I didn't find some way in the next few minutes of reversing our situation we were going to be on our way to the Middle East, or worse.

"Waist," he said calmly and I buckled the strap across my middle.

"Now your left wrist."

I glanced at the gun and sighed. This was not the way I thought my life was going to end, but who ever knows how that is going to happen? I pulled the left wrist strap tight and connected it. He leaned over and before I could react he slammed the gun against my forehead. By the time my vision cleared he had secured my right wrist. Both Selma and I were helpless. He put the barrel of the gun in the middle of my brow.

"Say goodnight, Daryl," he said.

I watched his trigger finger as he started to squeeze.

chapterFOURTEEN

The neat little round red-tinged hole that opened up in the middle of his forehead looked out of place. It was as if someone had used a single hole paper punch dipped in red paint on his brow. His eyes went lifeless, the gun clattered to the floor and my would-be killer slipped out of sight. I twisted my head around as far as I could and found Rodger's face smiling down on me.

"Cut that kind of close, didn't you, buddy?" I said.

"So, you knew I was here?" he said as he loosened the straps at my wrists.

"No, it's just the fear talking," I said. "I thought I was taking the long sleep. How did you get here anyway?"

"About an hour ago I had a premonition," he said.

"Lucky me," I said.

"Yes… anyway I came here and was in the parking lot when you went around the back. I saw our friend here follow you to the alley and wait. Then, when he walked you back into the elevator at gunpoint I went around front, got downstairs into the basement…"

"Wait," I interrupted, "you got downstairs? I thought that…"

"You needed to be a special member to get down here?" he finished.

"Yeah."

"I did Jerry a big favor when his daughter fell in with a bad crowd a few years ago," he explained.

"Oh."

"Anyway, I picked the lock on the steel door that leads in here and came in just in time to keep him from making permanent corpses of you both."

"Permanent corpses? Is there another kind?" I asked.

"You know what I mean, Daryl."

"Yes," I said sitting up to reach my ankles.

"Are you guys going to gab all night or is someone going to let me loose?" Selma crabbed from her crate.

"Who's that?" Rodger asked.

"Just a tart I picked up on the way into the club," I said. "Maybe we should just leave her here."

"Daryl," Selma sputtered, "when I get out of here I'm going to…"

"I thought you liked that kind of treatment," I said.

"Timing is everything, Daryl," she said. "Right now I'm feeling lucky to be alive and doing something kinky with you isn't even on my radar."

I walked over to her crate, undid her restraints, then lifted her out and held her tightly. She melted into me again. I liked the way we fit together. She broke our embrace, turned to Rodger and stuck out her hand.

"Hi," she said. "I'm Selma, Jerry's partner in the club. I just met Bucky on my way in tonight."

Rodger shook her hand, "Hi, Selma, I'm Bucky's friend, Rodger. How come Jerry didn't have a key to the door?"

"He says that he just rented the space out about two months ago and they changed the locks," she said.

"Slowed me down enough that I about didn't get here before…" he gestured at the body.

"Who was that guy?" she asked.

"I don't know, but he knew who you were and whoever was at the other end of his phone call sure knew my name," I said.

She walked over and looked down at the body like he was some new species of bug and she were an entomologist. I was surprised because most women would have been completely freaked out by what just happened not to mention the dead body.

"He tried to kill us," she said, nudging him with her toe. "Why?"

Rodger reached down, pulled the guy's cell phone out of his pocket and looked at the last number dialed.

"He called Victor," he grunted.

"Rodger," I said in exasperation, "this whole thing is starting to get ridiculous. We've got indications that people from Sonic Ping might have killed Brad and my wife and yet the police are ignoring it. Now it looks like Victor from Sonic Ping just ordered Selma and I to join the unliving and what do you think our chances of convincing the police are?"

"They won't want to hear it," he said.

"To top it off we have this dead guy who wouldn't be that hard to explain if we could trust the police, but somehow I think we'd end up in front of a jury for murder one if we called them," I said.

"I agree," he said.

"So what's our next move?" I asked.

"Put him in one of these crates and ship him," Rodger said.

"What?" both Selma and I said at the same time.

"Look," he said. "If we leave the body here we are losing control of the situation. If the police find him they might tie us here via Jerry, if the Sonic Ping guys find him they might stage things in their favor... anyway, the possibilities of a bad outcome for us are... well, I'm saying that we should use their shipping connections to ship him out of here."

"Where?" I asked.

"How about Victor's house?" he said.

I thought about that for a few seconds. It made sense. The dead guy could be traced back to working for Sonic Ping and Victor couldn't be sure what we might have gotten from him before he died. He wouldn't dare call the police when the crate came and it would use up some of his resources to get rid of the body. I stepped to the desk, reconnected the computer and booted it.

"You have your work cut out for you, Rodger," I said, "because this had password protection on it and who knows what else."

Rodger smiled at me and sat down in front of the computer.

☙

The main screen showed only one user, labeled 'Ship'. It was password protected. That didn't present any problem for Rodger as he used some trick he had to reset the Administrator password and then change the 'Ship' password so that we could get into that user. There were two files of interest on the desktop that he took a moment to copy to a thumb drive before opening. The first one was an Xcel file that contained eighteen lines. Each line appeared to be basic information about individual shipments to the bonded warehouse in Casablanca which looked as though it had been generated automatically by the shipping program. The last entry sent a dagger into my heart. I tapped the screen.

"What do you think?" I asked Rodger.

"Those are Maddy's initials and the ship date is correct for the time that she disappeared. I'd say that represents the crate they shipped her out of here in," Rodger said.

"Why would they do that?" I asked. "Why wouldn't they use her for blackmail?"

"They said they were going to send you a message," he said.

The second file was a detailed breakdown of each shipment. Again the last shipment was plainly Maddy, although it was missing entries in the last three columns.

"This is a list of each shipment, date shipped, tracking number, initials, date of birth, height, weight, color of hair, date received, amount paid, date of payment and the account number to which the money was transferred," he said. "The only open shipment is Maddy."

"Which column is the amount paid?" I asked.

Rodger pointed and I scanned down the list. The average seemed to be about 400,000 dollars.

"These aren't insignificant by any means," I said. "But why would Sonic Ping be risking what they have for these relatively small amounts?"

"Maybe it's a side venture of Victor's and he is using Sonic Ping as cover to keep the cops away," Rodger said. "Perhaps Mikahyl doesn't know it's going on."

"Do you mean Mikahyl Dashkov, that Russian guy who started Sonic Ping?" Selma asked.

"Yes," Rodger said. "But we haven't linked him to any of this yet."

"Do you think this operation is what Brad uncovered that got him killed?" I asked.

"It would make a nice neat package," Rodger admitted, "except it doesn't explain the money that keeps pouring into his Cayman account."

"Have you had any luck with the password?" I asked.

"Not really," Rodger said. "I did have one guy I told you about come out of the shadows who claims he'll send me a hint."

"Shadows?"

"Jennifer found a group of hackers who play around with things like that for fun," he explained. "They aren't breaking any laws, but they are on the fringe so they won't come out in the open to us. The hint should be there when we get back."

⚂

An hour later we were out of there. We found that the shipping service they had been using to pick up the crates would come at any hour of the day or night and arrange for overnight air to anywhere in the world. In this case we were just shipping across town. We printed out a bill of lading, the truck came and we watched the crate drive off to Victor's house. He was going to have a long and fascinating night.

My stomach was in knots because up until now I had not believed that they would actually sell Maddy into slavery. I had been convinced they were using the threat to get me to give them what we had. Plainly I had underestimated them.

Jennifer met us at the door. She looked at Selma with interest.

"Jen, this is Selma," I said. "It's a long story, but she's with us."

Jennifer welcomed Selma warmly, then kissed Rodger to get his attention.

"We got a hint from 'Venom'," she said excitedly.

""Who's 'Venom'?" I asked.

"That's the hacker I told you about," Rodger said. "What was the hint?"

"He said to tell you that there are thirty-one days in the longest month," Jennifer said.

Rodger stood still for all of thirty seconds. That hint didn't mean anything to me, but I didn't want to speak for fear of interrupting his thought process. Like me, the two girls remained frozen for the entire time. Finally I saw his face relax and then he grinned.

"Clever," was all he said and headed straight for his computer.

CR

I didn't see how that hint was helpful at all, but Rodger booted up Brad's computer, brought up the random password generator, typed in 'izardsjumpqu' and hit return. The program ran for about a minute before Brad's encrypted drive opened. I still didn't understand.

"I saw you do it but I don't get it," I said. "How did you know to type that?"

"Remember the clue?" Rodger asked.

"Yeah. Some months have thirty-one days."

"Right and we were dealing with the sentence 'The five boxing wizards jump quickly'," he reminded me.

I nodded.

"Today is the fifteenth of the month so I start with the letter 'i' and use the next eleven characters," he said.

"Why the letter 'i'?" I asked.

"It's the fifteenth letter in the sentence," he said.

"Oh, and a total of twelve letters because that was the number circled at the end of the sentence," I said finally getting it.

"Right," he said. "It was very clever of Brad and virtually impossible to break without the key because the password changes every day."

We both stopped for a moment and thought of our friend Brad. The hurt of losing him was still fresh and more than ever I wanted to catch the bastards. I shook myself and looked at the screen.

"What have you got?" I asked.

"To tell you the truth, Daryl, with everything we've been through today I'm wiped out," Rodger said. "Why don't you and Selma use the bedroom in the back that has the other adjoining bath and we'll start fresh in the morning."

I looked at the computer. A part of me was chomping at the bit to get started. Brad was dead, my wife was dead, Maddy was on her way to Morocco and the bad guys from Sonic Ping were out looking to kill us, but my better sense prevailed. Notwithstanding that Selma had just sidled up next to me and the smell of her perfume was interfering with my judgment. I looked down at her and my resolve to continue tonight went out the window.

"Probably a wise move," I said propelling her toward the bedroom.

chapterFIFTEEN

"I thought you were going to sleep and work on this in the morning," I said to Rodger's back.

"It is morning," he replied.

I glanced at the clock. It was four am. I had gotten out of bed after only three hours. My body kept telling me that I wanted to sleep but my mind wouldn't leave the problem alone. When I got up, Selma had been stretched out beside me in almost the same position she'd been after our marathon love-making session. That my relationship with her had progressed that far had really turned the guilt screws. My wife was gone less than a week and I already had deep feelings for another woman.

I had kissed her softly so as to not wake her and then padded out to the kitchen to build a cup of coffee, which is where I discovered Rodger sitting in front of Brad's computer. He pushed it away and turned to me.

"I found a possible reason why Brad and Karen were killed," he said. "If what I discovered is the reason, it's serious, and they aren't going to stop until they've eliminated anyone that might be a threat to their scheme."

"Their scheme?" I asked.

"Their scheme?" Selma asked from the door of our bedroom. "What are you talking about?"

"You found something that is bad enough that they have to kill to protect it?" Jennifer asked from the other doorway.

"Perhaps I should start at the beginning," Rodger said. "Jen, could you please make us all some coffee while I fill everyone in."

I looked in the fridge while Jen went about making coffee. I didn't see anything that looked like breakfast except a package of English Muffins and a jar of peanut butter. I got the toaster out and began making muffins for everyone while the coffee perked.

"To get the entire picture we have to go back to Brad's first company," Rodger said.

"Boomslash.com," I piped up. "That was a great concept. It should have gone viral."

"What was so great about it?" Selma asked.

"The idea was like one stop shopping for on-line, instant advertizing," I said. "The client could go to one web page and type in their changes and instantaneously it would update their web site, their Facebook page, their My Space page, their Twitter account and at the same time send out a text message to all of their customers."

"What does that have to do with Sonic Ping and selling slaves?" Selma asked.

"That is kind of convoluted," Rodger said, "but bear with me a minute and I'll explain."

The first set of muffins popped up. I put the second set in, spread peanut butter on the warm ones and handed them out.

"Boomslash was getting some customers and quite a bit of traffic," Rodger continued. "Things were taking off, but Brad wanted to build it faster so he turned to Sonic Ping to help him."

"How?" Jennifer asked.

"Pay-per-click," Rodger said. "He paid Sonic Ping to put a sponsored link up on their search page. Anytime that someone searched on Sonic Ping for key words specific to what Brad was offering, a link to Brad's site would appear."

"I see that all the time and it really makes sense," I said. "You just pay for the real customers who click on the link. Just the customers who are searching for exactly what you are selling."

"That's the theory," Rodger agreed, "but Brad seems to have discovered a dark side to the whole pay-per-click deal."

The three of us looked at him in anticipation. I put peanut butter on the next set of muffins and Jen poured us each a cup of coffee. Rodger stretched the moment out as long as he could.

"When he set up the pay-per-click with Sonic Ping he also set up a tracking system. His tracking followed the IP address of everyone who clicked and more importantly exactly which pages on his site they visited," Rodger said.

"I can't see how that would actually be that useful," I said. "I mean what do you care where they came from or where they went as long as they looked at the site and seemed really interested and signed up or ordered or…"

"It isn't useful," Rodger agreed, interrupting my sentence.

"It isn't?"

"No, that was just one of those happy mistakes that led him to the real problem," Rodger said.

"So?" I asked.

"It wasn't the information that was there, it was the information that wasn't," Rodger said cryptically.

I sat back. Rodger was on a mission to educate us and I was clearly the devil's advocate.

"What he found was that at least eighty per cent of the people who used his key words in their search and clicked on the sponsored link didn't check anything else out," he said.

I thought about that. It didn't make sense. Eighty per cent? I sat back for the finale.

"Think about that," Rodger said. "Someone goes to Sonic Ping to search for… fish oil, for instance."

Selma smiled at him and nodded for him to continue.

"Let's say that a fish oil supplement manufacturer decides to use Sonic Ping to build their traffic," he said to Selma. "So

'Natural Fish Oil' agrees to pay Sonic Ping to put up sponsored links whenever one of the key words they've selected comes up in the search string. Are you with me so far?"

"What key words?" Selma asked.

"For this example let's say, 'fish oil', 'free sample', and 'healthy'. Every time one of these is in a search string the 'Natural Fish Oil' web site link comes up at the top of the page so people can click and go to that site and see what they have," Rodger said.

"Okay."

"And every time that someone clicks on that sponsored link they have to pay Sonic Ping fifty cents," he said.

"Sounds cheap," Selma said.

"It does sound cheap, but what would you think if eighty per cent of the people who searched for those exact words and then clicked on that link and got to their web site didn't bother to click on the 'free sample' button or check out anything else at all on the site?"

"That doesn't make any sense," Selma interrupted. "Why would someone search for something and then find exactly what they wanted and then not look further?"

"That's what Brad wondered," Rodger said. "He thought about it and came up with a theory that he tested."

I had an advantage over the two women because I had seen more of the picture than they had. I could see what was coming.

"Is that why he started Bigooh.com?" I asked.

Rodger nodded. The two women looked at Rodger to continue. I did also because even though I'd made the connection I didn't really understand how it was related.

"Brad wondered why someone would search for a specific thing and then not investigate when they got to a site that had the exact thing they were searching for. The only theory that made any sense to him was that someone was making money by clicking on the sponsored link."

"You mean Sonic Ping was clicking on their own customer's links and pocketing the money?" Jennifer asked.

"No," Rodger said, shaking his head. "That would have been way too easy for a customer to catch on to. If Sonic Ping had been stealing from their own customers they would have gone out of business by now. Brad felt there had to be another answer."

"Anyone want any more English muffins?" I asked as Rodger paused. I got three head shakes.

"So?" Selma asked.

"He found that Sonic Ping has a plan called 'Ping Peers,'" Rodger said. "If you have a bona fide e-commerce site you can become a 'Peer' which allows you to put a Sonic Ping search bar on your site."

"Wait a minute," I said. "Anyone can put a Sonic Ping search bar on their site."

"Correct," he said.

"So what's the big deal with being a 'Peer'?" I asked.

"The big deal is that if you are a 'Peer' then whenever someone uses the search bar on your site Sonic Ping can track it and if a sponsored link comes up and the searcher clicks to look at it you get part of the revenue," he said.

"How much?"

"It depends on a bunch of factors," he said, "but roughly half."

"Half?" I said. "Like in our example of searching for a site for fish oil and coming up with 'Natural Fish Oil' and clicking on it the 'Peer' would get twenty-five cents?"

"Yes."

"I can see how that might be a nice source of supplemental income for a popular site, but it seems like small change to me," I said.

"How about a situation where you used an automated program that put search strings on your own site that clicked through to generate click revenue as fast as the program could click?" he asked. "Tens of thousands of clicks a day."

"The same search strings over and over?" I asked.

"Yes."

"Wouldn't that be repetitive enough that Sonic Ping would figure it out and...?"

"How about using a random sample of every key word that customers are paying for so it takes a long time to repeat?"

I thought about that. That would be thousands of different businesses. Probably tens of thousands of words, but still... I shook my head in exasperation. Surely Sonic Ping would red flag too many hits on the same key words or too many from the same IP address or...

"Top it off by using a program like *Change IP 2.5* or *IPRental* or an IP proxy router program that changes or spoofs your IP address every few seconds. Or any other of dozens of methods that makes it appear to Sonic Ping as if the hits that are coming through your 'Ping Peer' search bar are coming from all over the world. Of course you could also employ some other masking devices like varying the spelling of the key words and..."

"Holy shit," I interrupted as the magnitude of the fraud that could be perpetrated hit me. "If you could do that you could totally spoof Sonic Ping's system and make as much click revenue as... well, as much as you had sites that wanted to pay for clicks. That could be billions of dollars."

I thought about Bigooh.com which, on the surface, was a legitimate e-commerce site except you couldn't order anything and had a Sonic Ping search bar. It fit.

"Is that really why Brad started Bigooh?" I asked.

"I think so," Rodger said. "It looks like it was his test site to prove whether or not you could trick Sonic Ping's fraud check-ing software. I found the spoofing program he set up. He has it running on a server in Antigua. The money it generates bounces around several places and eventually ends up in that Cayman account."

"And how much does that account have now?" I asked.

Rodger's fingers danced around the keyboard for a minute, "Just over twelve million dollars."

"Damn it, Rodger," I said, "I know that's a lot of money and no doubt it proves that there is scamming going on, but really, it's not enough to explain why they killed Brad and tried to kill me."

"It doesn't, does it?" Rodger said.

I shook my head.

"I mean, even if he was threatening to expose the scam all they would have had to do was turn the whole thing around. They could burn him for even checking to see if it worked. Expose him to the authorities and get the government to file charges against him for click fraud. Then claim that his was a special case of getting around their safeguards, which they dutifully caught and reported," I said.

"You are right. With their money and legal power they would have buried him and no one would have ever caught on to the bigger message that eighty per cent of their five billion dollar revenue stream is suspect," Rodger said.

"So, if it's wasn't Brad threatening to expose the pay per click scheme or the slave trafficking then what the hell is it?" I asked.

"I don't know … there is only one other thing that pops up that might have some relation, but I can't see how it fits," Rodger said. "He didn't get anywhere with it. He was still checking when he died."

"What?" I asked.

"He was looking for a girl who disappeared about three weeks before his accident, the same time he started bigooh.com," Rodger said. "She seems to be tied to the pay-per-click deal some way and he traced her to Teasers, which is why he kept going there."

"I saw Brad there a few times," Selma said, "and some of the girls told me he was looking for someone, but it really isn't unusual for a patron to be looking for a girl so I never thought much of it. Do you have a name?"

"Misty," Rodger said.

Selma started giggling.

"What's so funny?" I asked.

"There are three Mistys working there right now. It's a stage name," Selma said. "What's her real name?"

"Brad didn't know and she seems to have disappeared just about the time he started looking for her," Rodger said.

"There was one 'Misty' who was a regular who vanished about that time, but girls come and go all the time," Selma said. "Her real name was Judy Green. She was a nice looking, high class girl who always arrived in a sedan limo with a driver."

"Wait," Rodger said, putting the thumb drive with the Xcel files from the shipping computer into one of his USB ports. "Those initials are… yes!"

We all looked over his shoulder at the computer. He had the file with the details of each shipment on the screen. The thirteenth shipment line had the initials J. G. in the name field. That shipment had occurred about four weeks ago and showed that they had received three hundred fifty thousand dollars about two weeks later by wire transfer.

"I'd say that is a pretty good indication of what happened to 'Misty'," Rodger said.

Selma leaned in and looked at the list. She shuddered and drew back. A big hiss escaped her lips. I pulled her to me and wrapped my arms around her.

"What?" I asked.

"Some of those other initials," she said, "they… they… might be…"

She stopped talking and started sobbing. I didn't know what else to do so I held her tighter.

"I told you that girls come and go," she said, controlling her breathing, "but the truth is that in the past few months more girls have left without notice than is normal and I…"

She stopped talking again, shaking her head.

"That fucking Jerry," she said.

I was pretty sure where she was going, but I waited for her to speak again.

"They were taking girls from my club and selling them. Jerry had to have known," she said angrily.

She whirled, grabbed both of my shoulders so that I was facing her and looked up at me.

"What are we going to do about this, Daryl?" she demanded.

"I thought I was just your boy toy and my name was Bucky," I said.

"Daryl, this isn't the time to be cute," she said. "These people are killers and kidnappers. What are we going to do?"

"The police?" I said, facetiously.

"Daryl, all that will do is tie us up explaining ourselves while the bad guys cover their tracks," she said. "We need to crack this open so that we can't be ignored."

"Crack this open? All we've got so far is a bunch of stuff that doesn't make sense," I said. "We've got a money trail that keeps getting bigger but not a real reason why someone would kill Brad."

"So what's our next step?" she asked, insistently.

Rodger coughed.

"I think Daryl and I are going to start in Morocco and try to get Madeline back. Then we can see where that leads," Rodger said.

"I'm going with you," Selma said.

"Me too," Jennifer chimed in.

"No," both Rodger and I said at the same time.

"You think that you're going to leave us here?" Jennifer asked.

"Alone?" Selma added.

"Look," Rodger said. "We are going to be dealing with some very dangerous guys who…"

"Is that some 'Me Tarzan, you Jane' thinking where the women need to guard the nest?" Jennifer asked.

Selma laughed and added, "Yeah. Like you'll have to be worrying about us if we're along and it will distract you from the real dangers?"

"I have to agree with Rodger," I said. "This could be very risky and if we have to worry about the two of you it could…"

"Give it a rest, Bucky," Selma interrupted, "we're going with you."

"So I'm Bucky again?"

"You are when you act stupid like you are right now," she said.

"Rodger?" I asked, looking for help.

"I'll book four seats to Casablanca," he said, turning back to the computer.

chapterSIXTEEN

Rodger managed to get us on the afternoon flight to Detroit that connected with an overnight Delta flight to CMN, the main international airport in Casablanca, Morocco, arriving the next morning at ten thirty. Luckily we all had up-to-date passports so it was only a matter of throwing stuff in bags, heading to the airport and then sitting in seats made for people half our sizes for a total of twelve hours until we landed in Morocco. We deplaned, passed through customs and made our way to the Le Meridian Mansour Hotel.

We picked that hotel for three reasons. One, it was a luxury hotel and thus would have more staff with knowledge of the area; second, it was close to the port where the bonded warehouse was located; and third, it was very close to *Rick's Café* which had been made famous by the movie *Casablanca*. Rodger had taken some time after booking our flights to contact the network of operatives that we used around the world. The head of the North African group we had used in the past arranged to meet us at 'Ricks' at six pm.

By the time we checked into the two bedroom suite it was noon. None of us had been able to sleep well on the plane so we unanimously decided to nap until four pm. It turned out to be a bit of a mistake as I actually felt more dragged out when I got up.

At four we drove our rental car to the port area and snooped around looking for the bonded warehouse. We eventually located it inside the port fence but in a spot where we could see both of its shipping docks. There was no activity for the two hours that we watched. At six pm an older woman came out and got into the only car in front of the office area and drove away. We decided to move on to *Rick's*.

Rick's Café was a mythical saloon in the 1942 movie *Casablanca*. The cafe had been created as a real place in 2004 by an American woman who had been living in Casablanca and working at the American embassy. It had since become a must stop, not only for the myriads of tourists who came to Morocco each year, but also many highly placed officials of governments around the world and the rich and famous. We entered the bar and the greeter, a middle aged Moroccan in a 'fez', welcomed us and seated us in the bar. I looked around the room but didn't see anyone who looked as if they could be our contact. A waiter came and we ordered drinks.

"Who are we meeting here?" I asked.

"Poison," Rodger said.

"What kind of name is that?" Selma asked.

"Anonymous," Rodger said. "We've worked with Poison on two cases but have never met, nor have we any idea of Poison's age or sex."

"What kind of cases would require someone halfway around the world?" Jennifer asked.

"One was a runaway twenty-two year old girl that we traced to Tangiers," Rodger said. "Her parents wanted to find her and get a message to her. The other was a fourteen year old boy who was kidnapped by his Algerian father when the custody battle didn't go his way."

"Algerian?" Selma asked.

"Poison has some great contacts from Morocco to Tunisia," Rodger explained.

Seven o'clock came and still no contact. We ordered another round and listened to the piano player, Issam, play *As Time Goes By* for the third time since we'd come in. I tried to sip my second drink slowly because jet lag and the first one were doing me in.

At seven thirty I excused myself to go to the bathroom. As I came out of the toilet a striking young woman in her thirties, dressed in form fitting jeans and an expensive blouse bumped into me. I excused myself and stepped around her in the narrow hall. As I passed she put her lips next to my ear and whispered, "Service entrance, five minutes, just you and your friend."

I went back to our table, sat down, took a large swig of my drink, looked at Rodger and said, "You and I have a date."

He raised his eyebrows and smiled.

"Poison?" he asked.

"Don't know for sure but I think so," I said. "She wants to meet at the service entrance."

"She?"

"Yeah."

"When?"

"We should go now," I said, standing up.

Rodger got up. I patted Selma's arm and we walked toward the back.

Rick's Café was a traditional Moroccan grand mansion originally built in 1930 in the old Medina section of Casablanca. It had fallen into disrepair until its rebirth as Rick's. The service entrance at one time had been the main entrance hall to the house but now was a narrow dead end. As we pushed through the 'staff only' doors the spectacular woman who had bumped into me stood in plain view smoking a cigarette and leaning against the wall. She flicked her smoke away and pushed herself off the wall.

"The boy's name?" she asked.

"Kevin Baroukel," Rodger said.

"The amount you wired to my account for that job?" she asked.

"In dollars or dinars?" Rodger asked.

"Dollars."

"Two thousand."

"I'm Poison," she said sticking out her hand, "and you guys are Seeker?"

"Yes," Rodger said shaking her hand, "but call me Rodger and this is Daryl."

I stuck out my hand and found a surprisingly firm grip.

"Wow," she said, "real names?"

"Yes," Rodger said. "You probably already have them anyway."

She laughed and visibly relaxed.

"I brought what you asked for," she said, nudging a small duffel bag with her foot. "I also checked out the bonded warehouse, so I know where the shipments go when they leave there and how you can get access to the... markets, at least here in Casablanca."

"Markets?" I asked.

"Uh..." she said and looked around nervously.

"He's just being dense," Rodger said. "He knows what markets you are talking about."

"Okay. The one here in Casablanca is on Wednesday nights and is at the old arena, although it looks like most of the crates that come through here go directly to Marrakesh."

"What about the two shipments that I asked about?" Rodger asked.

"The shipment three weeks ago definitely went there. The other one just arrived yesterday and left this morning. I'm pretty sure that it's also on its way to Marrakesh, but I'll be sure tomorrow."

"Thanks, Poison," Rodger said. "I might have some other stuff if you're available."

"You know how to reach me, Rodger."

"Can you help if I need some muscle power for an extraction?" he asked.

"Yes."

"So how do we access the Marrakesh market?" Rodger asked.

"It's at an address in the old medina, called Maafa. I put the directions in the bag," she said nodding at the duffel bag, "but frankly they never let anyone in that hasn't been before or who isn't vouched for."

"Don't you have someone who can vouch for us?"

"I'm sorry I don't," she said.

"Don't worry, we'll figure something out," Rodger said, picking up the bag.

"Wait," I said, "are you saying that we've managed to trace Maddy this far, but now she's been shipped to Marrakesh and we have no way of getting into the auction where she's going to be sold?"

"Maddy?" Poison asked.

"That last shipment happens to be a very good friend of ours," Rodger explained.

"So this isn't just a job?" Poison asked.

"No."

"Well, I'll put some extra effort into trying to find a way in, but…"

"Rodger," I said, "do you realize how terrified she must be?"

"Daryl, we'll get her back."

"How lost, lonely, scared, petrified and abandoned she must feel?"

"Daryl," Rodger said, spinning me around so I had to look him in the eyes. "We are going to get her back."

I twisted out of his arms and looked at Poison.

"When is the next auction in Marrakesh?" I asked.

"Day after tomorrow," she answered.

I felt helpless.

chapterSEVENTEEN

The drive from Casablanca to Marrakesh took us four hours. We checked out of the Meridian at eight in the morning. I took the wheel while Rodger sat in the passenger seat and inventoried the contents of the duffle bag. Poison had provided us some untraceable credit cards, a passport in Maddy's name with her picture so we could get her through passport control in the United States if we managed to get her back, instructions as to where and what time the market tomorrow night was being held and some simple weapons for Rodger.

The roadway from Casablanca to Marrakesh was a limited access expressway that took us past wide open green fields of crops that looked like grains such as wheat and barley. Except for a few subtle differences from time to time, like road signs in Arabic, we could have been on an expressway in the Midwest.

Then the flat plains gave way to rougher terrain as we climbed over the beginning foothills of the Atlas Mountains. The countryside became even more striking as the green fields gave way to more arid crops such as olive and date palm and we passed small quaint Kasbahs, Arabic walled fortresses that in an earlier age had served as places for local leaders to live and protect their tribes.

Our entrance into Marrakesh was spectacular. It is a vibrant city teeming with people. Known as the 'red city' because of the preponderance of red clay buildings, it has the largest traditional market, or souk, in all of Morocco. Adjoining the souk is one of the largest open squares in the world called Djeemaa El Fna. Poison had recommended that we stay at a traditional riad hotel called the Riad Les Hibiscis because she had a contact there in the event that we needed to communicate, and also because it was located within walking distance of both the souk and the main square. Furthermore, the address of tomorrow night's slave auction was inside the old medina which was also nearby both of those. We checked into the hotel and the four of us wandered down the street to the square.

The Djemaa El Fna has to be experienced to be believed and even then the experience comes across as surreal. It is worth a visit to Marrakesh just to visit that square.

It was only three in the afternoon so the real action had yet to get started. Even so we immediately encountered dancers and snake charmers and old men selling real teeth that have been pulled from living (and dead) people, brightly dressed Arabic traders selling sips of water (an item that used to be in very short supply, which now represents merely a tourist photo-op), spices, shoes, clothes, acrobats, storytellers, rugs, mussels, snails and argan oil.

Argan oil is one of those products that make you wonder how anyone ever put together the steps to come up with it and more importantly why. It is produced by pressing the oil out of the fruits of the Argan tree after goats have eaten them and eliminated them in their waste. It sounds foul but the oil has a distinct, toasted nutty, goaty and very rich flavor.

At sunset vendors set up dozens of kitchens that cook and sell hundreds of different kinds of things to eat, some of which is served in open air sit down restaurant fashion, but much of which is presented fast food style. Most of what is available are concoctions that the majority of westerners have never heard of and many are not and are never going to be on your radar as a dish that you might care for. Still, it is interesting to look and sample if you are brave or drunk enough. We found that looking too long was the same as if we had ordered and the vendors expected us to pay for the privilege. It spoiled some of the enjoyment because I found myself looking away from something interesting sooner than I might have in normal circumstances in order to keep from being accosted by a street vendor who expected me to pay.

Nevertheless, we did look and enjoy ourselves, but the necessity of finding some way into the auction swirled around in the background of each of our minds, managing to put a damper on our afternoon and evening.

At eight pm we stopped at a small restaurant for a bite to eat, after which Rodger and I dropped Jennifer and Selma back at the hotel. With the girls safely tucked away for the night Rog and I wandered one last time around the streets that bordered the building that held Maafa. We were looking for that elusive point of access we hoped that we had merely overlooked. We didn't find it. It was close to midnight when we agreed to give it up for the night and began walking back to the hotel.

Passing a cul-de-sac, the sounds of a scuffle caught our attention. We were alone, in a strange country, at night, in a potentially dangerous part of town and had the loss of Madeline to worry about. It didn't matter, something made us look. We peered into the darkened ally and didn't like what we saw.

A good looking young man in a crisp white linen suit was being pounded on by four big guys in turbans. It was the eighth grade bullies all over again. I looked at Rodger, he nodded and we waded in. We had no business interfering and if we'd given it a moment's thought we probably wouldn't have. As we stepped further into the blind alley, I picked up a short piece of scrap wood and applied it to the back of the head of one of the turbans. He dropped like a stone and, as his friend turned to find out what happened, Rodger let loose some of the moves that he has tried forever to teach me. Guy number two was down. Rodger shifted his stance to the other brutes and within seconds all four were groaning on the ground.

I dropped my piece of wood, grabbed the left arm of the dazed young man in the linen suit and dragged him from the alley. We pulled him down the narrow passageways that were the main streets of the old town until we exited into a real thoroughfare with traffic. I hailed a passing cab, shoved him inside, Rodger and I tumbled in behind him and we collapsed in the back seat. I used the only phrase of Arabic I knew to get the driver started toward our hotel. The adrenaline rush that had gotten me this far was gone and my body was shaking. I put my head down and waited for my breathing to return to normal.

The young man said something in Arabic to the driver and we abruptly swerved. I looked up to see that we had changed direction away from our hotel and shot a questioning glance to Rodger. He shook his head and smiled. I looked at the young man beside me and opened my mouth to object.

"Don't worry, my friend," the young man said in slightly accented English. "We are going to my home. You will be safe, Inshallah."

I could have asked for us to be let out of the cab, but the aftermath of the adrenaline rush had completely drained me. I put my head back on the seat and closed my eyes.

❧

I woke up when the cab stopped. We were at the gate of a huge estate where the guard clearly knew the young man beside me. He opened the gate, bowed deeply and waved us in.

We entered a lush oasis. In our short day of poking around Marrakesh and its environs we had never encountered anything remotely like this compound. During the hours of walking around to get a feel of what might lie in store for getting Madeline back we had been by a few homes of wealthy Moroccans, but they paled in comparison to this place. This was a palace surrounded by a forest of palm trees and running fountains.

As we reached the front entrance the cab door was opened immediately by a different servant who also bowed deeply. The young man stepped from the cab and turned to me.

"Please, come in, sirs, and let me thank you properly," he said.

Rodger and I climbed out of the cab to follow him. Yet another servant opened the richly ornate ten foot high front doors into a huge cavern of a rich marble entrance foyer with a blue tiled hallway running to the rear. Two more bowing servants greeted us inside.

The young man strode purposefully toward the back, leaving us to follow in his wake. At the end of the hall he glanced back just for a moment to insure we were still following and then threw open a massive oaken door.

The opening revealed an elegant dark mahogany high-ceilinged library with thousands of books. Seated at a handsome ornate teak desk on the left side of the room was a distinguished gentleman dressed in a jalaba with an embroidered ghutra on his head. He stood up as we entered. Our young friend crossed to him, embraced him and then launched into a long soliloquy in Arabic with gestures towards us. We waited patiently until the young man ran out of steam. The older man stepped around his son and looked at each of us carefully.

"Your names, sirs?" he asked.

"I'm Daryl," I said. "Daryl Morgan."

"And I'm Rodger Truscott," Rodger said.

"I am in your debt, Mr. Morgan," he said grabbing my hand and pumping it, "and yours, Mr. Truscott."

"Please, call me Daryl," I said, "and I'm sorry but I don't understand.

"I am Wazir Achmed Bakam al Saadin and this is my son Prince Hakeem," he said. "You saved his life tonight and for that I am forever in your debt."

"It was really nothing, Wazir, sir," I protested. "We just happened to be there."

"First, Daryl, you must call me Achmed," he said. "And secondly it was not 'nothing' as you say. He is my only son and my heir. They would have taken his life tonight if you had not saved him. For this I will always be in your debt."

That embarrassed me. I didn't want someone to feel indebted to me and I doubt that Rodger did either. We acted without thinking and I felt uncomfortable with the thought that if I had taken the time to evaluate the situation I probably would have run for my life and Prince Hakeem would be dead.

"I'll settle for a cup of tea," I quipped.

"No," Achmed said fiercely, "I will not settle my debt to you with a cup of tea, but we shall have one together."

He clapped his hands and a servant appeared as if by magic bearing a tray with cups and a pot. The perverse thought of what might have happened if I had asked for coffee flitted through my head, but I figured he would have been able to make that happen somehow. There was probably a different clap for coffee.

We sat on cushions at a low table and drank our tea. Over the course of the next two hours we talked and I learned that he was the Wazir of the city and province of Marrakesh, answerable only to the king. He had four wives. The first three had given him girls, which while he professed to love them, were not the necessary male heir that he needed to insure that his enemies didn't take over his sultanate. His fourth wife had given him Hakeem, the young man we had saved tonight.

Subtly, but with perseverance during those two hours, he tried his best to draw us out. When he asked us how we had come to his country we gave him vague answers. Rodger made up a story about sightseeing and wanting to see the mosques and the souk and the old medina. I chimed in about perhaps wanting to buy a Riad as a vacation getaway, and then, as if I had an afterthought, I asked if he had ever heard of a place called Maafa.

"Maafa?" he asked tipping his head. "I can't say as I have. Is it a club?"

"I think so," I said, realizing that he wasn't going to be able to help us.

"Do you know where it is located?" he asked.

"Um, somewhere in the old medina but it's not important," I said trying to deflect his interest.

He looked at me sharply, turned to one of his servants, said something in Arabic and then turned back to me smiling.

"More tea, Daryl?" he asked, already pouring me a fresh cup.

The last thing I wanted was more tea, but I didn't want to be rude so I sat back with my fresh cup in my hand so that it couldn't be filled again. I saw Rodger get my implied message as he carefully kept his cup in his hand also. The conversation drifted into the current weather problems and the unrest brewing in southern Africa as we patiently waited for a polite pause in which to take our leave.

ര

Ten minutes later we were interrupted by a servant who entered the room and urgently approached Achmed. I thought the interruption was a perfect time for us to excuse ourselves and get back to our hotel. I drained my cup and stood up so that we could say our goodbyes. Rodger followed suit. Achmed stood up also, took a step to my side, reached out, grabbed my arm and waited until he was sure he had my attention.

"So, Daryl," he said, "you and your friend are here on a mission to save a young woman, who was shipped into my country in a container and is now going to be sold off to the highest bidder as a slave, is that correct?"

I was stunned. How he had managed to put that together from our conversation about Mosques and the souk and Riads was beyond me. I looked at Rodger. He shrugged.

"Achmed, I'm sorry, but I don't have a clue what you are…"

"Daryl, I'm the Wazir," he said, "did you seriously think I had no idea about Maafa and what may be happening there?"

"Well, I…"

"I've been informed that the next auction is tomorrow," he said. "Is that the one you are attending?"

I looked at Rodger. My eyes pleaded for help. He turned to the Wazir.

"Achmed," Rodger said, "our problem is that we don't have a way in."

"No?" he said. "Do you have a plan?"

"Actually we do," Rodger said. "We hired four thugs to beat up Prince Hakeem so that you would feel so indebted to us that you would insist on helping us."

That startled him for a second and then he laughed and slapped Rodger on the back.

"You Americans have such a strange sense of humor," he said. "But of course I can get you in. It is the least I can do."

"You mean you've been there before?" I asked.

"No, I only have heard of the place," he said, "and I've heard the rumors of what goes on there. It is a very new venture, only about eight weeks old and if what I hear is true, it is very illegal. I have been meaning to personally investigate because if the hearsay is true this is very serious. We do not condone slavery in this country."

"So you know someone to vouch for us?" I said.

"I'm the Wazir, Daryl," he said. "I don't need someone to vouch for me. They would have to let me in. In this case, however, I will get someone to vouch for you because I would be recognized."

"Oh."

"Isn't it the same in your country?" he asked.

"Pardon me?"

"Your Obama person," he said, "couldn't he get into even the most private of places if he wanted?"

"Not necessarily," I said. "Just being President doesn't automatically mean that he would be granted entrance, private means private."

"The only place I can't go in this country without an invitation is the King's palace," Achmed said.

I felt as if a weight had been lifted from my shoulders. We were going to be able to get in to the auction. Our next obstacle was being the successful bidder and paying for our purchase, but

Rodger had assured me that he could access Brad's account with thirteen million and counting so I wasn't too concerned about that part of the problem. I stuck out my hand.

"Thank you, sir, I can't tell you how grateful I am that you are willing to help us," I said.

"Daryl," Achmed said, "I owe you and Rodger a debt that can never be repaid. It is a small thing you allow me to do."

By now it was well past two am and I was anxious that Selma and Jennifer would be getting worried about where we were. I tilted my head toward the door.

"We must be going," I said. "It's late and we want to be well rested for tomorrow."

"Nonsense, you and Rodger are my guests now," he said. "I have arranged for you to stay with me."

"But…"

"Don't worry, all of your things have been brought from your hotel, including your two lovely young women," he said. "The two ladies were frightened at first, but I think my wives have reassured them that all is well."

"You knew where we were staying?" I said.

"Daryl," he said, smiling. "You keep forgetting who I am."

He clapped his hands and two very pretty women came through the door escorting Selma and Jennifer. I could see the relief in both of their faces as they spotted us. Selma crossed to where I was standing and slipped into my arms.

"What's going on?" she asked. "What is this place?"

"That's a very long story, Selma," I said, "but the good news is that we have a way into Maafa. I will fill you in later, but for now I'd like to introduce you to Wazir Achmed Bakam al Saadin, our new friend and host. Achmed, this is my friend, Selma."

"Wazir?" Selma asked. "Like the Arabian knights?"

That brought a hearty laugh from Achmed.

"Do you remember the duty of the Wazir in the Arabian Nights?" Achmed asked her.

She shook her head.

"He provided virgin brides for the King to marry each day and then had them killed the next morning because the King believed all women were unfaithful," Achmed explained.

Selma shuddered but looked at him eagerly to continue.

"Eventually, the Wazir couldn't find any more virgins and was in danger of the wrath of the King. He didn't know what to do. Scheherazade, who was his own daughter, offered herself. The Wazir knew that it meant certain death the following morning for his daughter, but he reluctantly agreed. She became the King's next bride," he said looking at her with satisfaction. "My relationship with the King is somewhat different."

"And?"

"And what, Selma?" he asked, his eyes twinkling.

"Did she die also?" Selma asked.

"No, the very first night she told the King a story that she couldn't finish because it got too late. She promised to finish it the next night," he said. "He let her live to hear it. The following night she finished that story and started another that she didn't have time to finish. Each night she did the same. He always let her live to hear the end the following night. She would then start a new story that she couldn't finish. Our folk lore says she kept him enthralled for a thousand and one nights."

"Sort of like 'a cliff hanger a day keeps the executioner away?'" Selma said.

That brought another big belly laugh from Achmed.

"You Americans," he said, shaking his head. "I think we are going to be very good friends."

Selma smiled and said, "I think so also, Mister Wazir."

"Please call me Achmed," he insisted. "Your friend will explain why I owe him and Rodger a debt that can never be repaid."

"Nice to meet you then, Achmed," she said.

"And you, Selma."

"So, in your folklore how does the story end?" she asked.

"Do your stories always have happy endings?" he asked.

"Not always," she said ruefully. "Certainly not as often as I would like."

"Ours either," he admitted, "but this one does."

"Yes?"

"By the end of one thousand and one nights Scheherazade had born the King three sons," he said. "She finished her last story and didn't start another. Instead she threw herself on his mercy and begged him not to kill her and leave his three sons without their mother. By then he realized what a gem he had in her as a wife and partner so he pardoned her and they lived happily together from then on."

"Nice ending."

"Let us hope that the ending to your quest tomorrow is also a happy one," he said.

"Yes."

chapterEIGHTEEN

The breakfast spread the Wazir's staff laid out the next morning was an eclectic variety of foods of the region and the country, coupled with familiar American style fare. It looked great and I was hungry. Being hungry is a bad state to be in when faced with such a plethora of choices. There were so many selections I wanted to sample I ended up with two plates. Two heaping plates with some of almost everything they were serving.

I sat down next to Selma and glanced at what she had chosen. She only had one plate and it was empty. Well, not really empty, but compared to mine it was. Her single plate had a small portion of hummus, two strips of red pepper, four black olives, one fig and two dates.

In contrast my first plate was loaded down with three different kinds of olives and a bunch of pits from the ones I'd already eaten while waiting for Rodger to move along the line, a saucer of olive oil for dipping, two slices of Moroccan bread called Msamen, five strips of bacon, two poached eggs and two sugared squares of dough called Ahouifi M'semmen. My second plate had a bowl of some kind of soup called harira made from lentils and a heaping portion of laasida which seemed to be nothing more than couscous cooked with butter and water. I cleaned both plates.

Breakfast and the residual effects of jet lag did me in. My eyes were glazing over and I had designs on slipping away to get another hour or two of sleep when Rodger clamped his hand on my shoulder and brought me back to the real world.

"Daryl, you need to wake up. The six of us should go over all of the possible scenarios that might happen tonight and develop contingency plans," he said. "We can't let Maddy down."

That did it. My need to make everything right kicked in, remembering that the sole reason we were here was to rescue Madeline from her horrible situation. My body responded with a rush that wiped away my desire to close my eyes.

Rodger, Achmed, Selma, Jennifer, Prince Hakeem and I sat down in the same room where we had first been introduced to Achmed and tried to cover all of the contingences. We game planned the coming evening at Maafa for the remainder of the morning, stopped for a groaning lunch and then used most of the afternoon to do the same.

It shouldn't have taken us anywhere as long as it did to feel comfortable with our plan because early into our strategizing we all agreed that there was nothing that could really go wrong. Nevertheless we went through each possibility, carefully, for as many times as it took for all of us to feel comfortable.

If Maddy was offered for sale, as we expected, we believed we had more than enough money to outbid any other bidder by a factor of thirty times. We agreed that money wasn't going to be an issue. The serious scenarios we worked on were those where Maddy wasn't offered for sale or we were turned away from the entrance.

Poison sent us final confirmation that Maddy's crate had indeed been shipped to Maafa so, at this point we were fairly certain that Madeline was one of the two women who would be on the block tonight. If she wasn't there was nothing we could do about it now. Achmed assured us that he would track down where she had gone if she didn't appear for sale.

The possibility of us not gaining entrance was the serious one. Achmed could simply walk up to the door and would have to be let in, but the problem was, he was positive that the girls would disappear and all traces of illegal activity would also vanish. We, on the other hand, could get in without raising suspicion if we were vouched for, but that also carried the risk that something could go wrong and we would be turned away. We explored what might hold us up at the door or have us turned away and how we could react to change the outcome. While Achmed was certain that the person he had in mind to vouch for us was powerful enough to overcome any objections we decided that to be certain we should split into two teams. Thus, if one team was refused entrance we had a second shot.

I would be going in with two of the Wazir's most trusted bodyguards as one team and Rodger, Prince Hakeem, in disguise as a bodyguard, and another of the Wazir's bodyguards would enter separately as the second team. The Wazir found another trusted person to vouch for the second team.

Achmed wasn't going with us for fear of being recognized and neither were the women because women, except for the ones who worked there or were being sold, were not allowed in.

By five in the afternoon our strategy was fixed and we could relax. We all retired to bedrooms to catch a few winks before show time. I was ready for a nap, but Selma had other ideas and it didn't take much urging on her part to change my mind.

ଓଃ

Maafa opened at eight even though the first auction wasn't until midnight. Our fear of not being able to gain entrance was unfounded. We showed up at nine and both teams were easily admitted. We joined back up once we were inside. The three of us got a nice table near the stage, with the three bodyguards finding places in the rear.

The reason for opening the club at eight was obvious. With dozens of scantily clad women everywhere for company, and similarly dressed waitresses who would bring you whatever you desired to drink, it was clear that the people who ran Maafa wanted you relaxed and in a good mood prior to the start of the auction. Being a bit drunk when the bidding started probably didn't hurt either. For the next three hours we nursed drinks and watched the crowd. My stomach was wrapped around itself worrying about Madeline and our chances of success. The printed program on the table where we were sitting showed that there would be two offerings tonight. Neither of the descriptions matched Maddy, but I convinced myself that the second girl could be her and that they were just exaggerating her breast size.

ଔ

At midnight almost all of the laughter and wild behavior calmed down as if a switch had been thrown. The crowd sensed it was time for the first girl of the evening. We waited with anticipation. Then, the lights dimmed, the music that I hadn't even realized was in the background went into cinema 'something's coming' mode and a spotlight focused our attention on the stage. Whoever was running the show milked the moment, but eventually a big brute of a guy dressed like he had been cast in some Hollywood movie as a harem eunuch came into the light.

Stumbling along behind him at the end of a long sturdy chain that terminated on a three inch steel collar around her neck was an exceptionally pretty young blonde woman also dressed in a harem costume that left very little to the imagination. Her pantaloons were sheer as were the panties beneath them and her top was similar to what passes for a bikini top in Rio.

It wasn't Madeline, but as I had expected her to come second I wasn't concerned. She staggered behind her captor with a look of terror on her face. A stir went through the crowd and I have to confess that something ugly and sinister sparked inside of me. As barbaric as what was happening was in reality, in some dark recess of my psyche it resonated. I felt ashamed.

The brute paraded her around the stage several times allowing the audience a three hundred sixty degree view before looping the end of her chain on a post in the center of the stage effectively securing her in place. He exited and a handsome man in his forties dressed in an Armani suit stepped to the lectern on the left side of the stage and cleared his throat.

"Gentlemen," he said in English with just the barest trace of an accent, "as usual we will conduct tonight's proceedings in English. For those of you who don't speak any English please inform the young lady who has been assigned to see to your comfort for the evening and a translator will be provided. Further, all bids will be in US Dollars."

There was a flurry of activity at only one table. Prince Hakeem took the interruption to lean into the center of our table.

"That gentleman on stage is Mustafa, one of the two owners of Maafa," he said. "They are both from one of the Gulf Emirates and both have diplomatic immunity."

"Diplomatic immunity? What does that mean?" I asked.

"It means that after we get your friend back we can shut down their operation, but they will be allowed to leave our country," he said.

"But what they are doing is illegal," I said.

"It doesn't matter," the Prince said. "They could commit murder and we can only expel them. We cannot hold them responsible for their actions."

"What are you trying to say?" I asked.

"I'm saying that we will put a serious dent in their operation, especially if you and your friend put an end to their major source of procurement, but they will set up shop somewhere else and start over."

I looked at Rodger and saw the gleam in his eye. I'd seen it before. He hadn't liked Prince Hakeem's outcome and was already thinking about how to rectify what he saw as an unjust situation. It was the same look he always got before he, well, **we** ended up doing something that I always agreed with, even though we'd earned our reputation as vigilantes. Mustafa cleared his throat and the room quieted.

"Shall we begin the bidding?" he asked, glancing around the room. "Do I hear two hundred thousand?"

Someone raised their hand and someone else immediately followed suit. We were off and running with a fever pitch. I bid one time at the four hundred thousand mark to keep from seeming out of place but dropped out for fear of actually being the highest bidder and using up money I was saving for Madeline.

The bidding rapidly progressed to six hundred thousand and then slowed. At that price she would sell for well above the average that we had seen in the computer files we'd stolen. To my surprise two new bidders chimed in and the price jumped to over a million. She eventually went for two million three hundred thousand dollars. I looked at Rodger and he shrugged.

"There must be some new dynamic that we aren't aware of," Rodger said.

"Actually we only looked at what the operation in the United States was being paid," I said.

"True," he mused. "It could be as little as only twenty percent of the actual selling price."

"We're going to have to spend more than we expected," I said.

"What do we care?" he said. "It's not our money and there seems to be an endless supply."

"As long as we have enough," I said.

"We have thirteen million," he said.

"I know but…"

I was interrupted by the entrance of the brute for the second time. He was dragging another hapless woman who was stumbling reluctantly behind him. She was dressed as scantily as the first one and if anything was even lovelier. The problem was that it wasn't Maddy. I looked around as if someone had made a mistake and I could fix it by catching their eye and getting them to bring her out instead. I finally swiveled to Rodger.

"It's not Maddy," I said, stating the obvious. "What are we going to do?"

"I don't know, buddy," he said. "We are going to have to pretend to be interested in this girl and when we get out of here we can try to figure out our next move."

The bidding started at four hundred thousand and rapidly went to three million dollars before it slowed. The girl sold for just short of five million. Rodger and I looked at each other in amazement. We got up to leave. Mustafa walked back on the stage and tapped the mike to get everyone's attention. We were at the door when he spoke.

"I see some of you are leaving because we did advertize that we only had two offerings tonight and you think we are finished," he said. "I also see that quite a few of you are still seated and ready to continue to bid, which makes me believe that it's hard to keep a secret."

That stopped us and several others who were making their way to the door. We waited for him to continue.

"The rumors are true," he said. "We have one more girl tonight and this will be our last auction. We've decided to move on."

I turned that over in my mind and realized that one possible reason that the bidding had been more aggressive tonight is that the rumors had fueled a fire. Buying a slave such as these couldn't be an easy matter and now they were going to fold up shop, at least here and for now. This last girl would go for a fortune. Even so I prayed that it was Maddy.

Mustafa retired from the stage. We returned to our seats as did everyone else who had been preparing to leave, except for the Ayatollah looking guy who had just purchased the last lovely lady and was engaged in a heated discussion with a suave, well dressed, middle aged guy sitting behind a desk in an alcove near the door.

"Who is that?" I asked Prince Hakeem, nodding at the well dressed guy.

He glanced in the direction I was looking and smiled.

"That is Jabbar," he said, "the other partner. He is the money guy. I'd guess he is making sure that the funds are secure before he turns loose of the girl."

I would have continued to watch the drama at the door, but the music went into cinema mode again and the brute entered from the left side of the stage. My eyes watched each link of chain until the girl he was dragging onstage came into view. A tsunami of relief washed over me as I realized that Maddy was the final girl being offered and it was only a matter of time until we had her on a plane out of here. She walked docilely behind the brute as he led her around the stage two times and then tethered her to the post. Her movements and the hazy film covering her eyes made me realize that she was sedated.

"Gentlemen, do I have an opening bid of... how about five hundred thousand dollars?" Mustafa asked, looking around the room.

"One million," said a man seated at the table next to us.

I don't know what his intention was in doubling the asking bid, but what happened was that the room went into a feeding frenzy. Almost every table bid at least once. By the time bidding slowed down the price was up to eleven million dollars. We hadn't bid yet and there were still three active bidders. I was really worried.

"Rodger, what are we going to do?" I asked.

"Bluff?"

"Bluff?" I repeated. "What do you mean, bluff?"

"Pretend that we have the money and then figure something out later," he said.

"But what happens when that Jabbar guy finds out that we don't have the money?" I asked.

"I don't know, Daryl," he said, "but we really don't have a choice if we want her back."

I looked at her. She was standing there, tethered to the post and even in her drugged state, looking completely lost, lonely and vulnerable, she was delectable. I raised my hand and bid. My bid was immediately topped by someone, but I stuck my hand up again.

When the bidding reached sixteen million everyone but one other bidder had dropped out. The other table that was still in the contest had five men seated at it. Three of them were obvious bodyguards. The other two looked like a father and son, with the father doing the bidding. Gauging the interest from the son, I was sure that he was the intended owner.

The father was a very dark skinned Arab in a traditional white Dishdashah which his son was also wearing. That indicated that they probably came from one of the states on the Arabian Peninsula. As I stuck my hand up to bid sixteen million one hundred thousand the father glared at me and snapped out a bid of seventeen million. I raised my hand again to bid seventeen million one hundred thousand and before I could finish he had raised his hand again to eighteen million. It was clear that he had more money than sense. I looked at Rodger.

"What are we going to do?" I asked. "We aren't going to outbid this guy and if we manage to we are going to be in deep trouble with Jabbar when it comes time to pay up."

Rodger seemed lost in thought and didn't speak. The auctioneer got impatient.

"Gentlemen?" he asked. "Do you have a bid?"

"Can we have a minute?" I asked. "We need to confer."

"I'll give you thirty seconds to bid," he answered.

I looked back helplessly at Rodger.

"What's the trouble?" Prince Hakeem interjected.

"Money," Rodger said.

"Money?" the Prince repeated.

"We only have thirteen million," Rodger explained.

"But you've already bid more than that," the Prince said.

"We thought we could work it out," Rodger said.

"Why didn't you ask my father to help you?" Hakeem asked.

"We honestly had no idea that the bidding would get this high," Rodger said.

"A bid, gentlemen?" Mustafa interrupted.

I looked at Maddy and my heart crumbled. To be so close to freeing her and then to lose her like this was beyond unbearable. I glanced over at Rodger to see if he had a suggestion. He wiggled his head from side to side one time and defeat washed over me. I raised my eyes to Mustafa and shook my head.

"Sold to the bidder at table seven for eighteen million dollars," he said.

chapterNINETEEN

A wave of despair hit me. I had failed. My best friend's wife was going off in chains to live out her life as a slave and I had done nothing to prevent it. Well, I had tried to do something, but I had been horribly unsuccessful. I could feel my vision closing in along with a fierce hurt growing in my chest that felt like someone was pushing a fire iron into it along with a chunk of something clogging my throat that I couldn't swallow away. Before I could completely slip into self pity Rodger put his hand on my shoulder and squeezed.

"Plan B, buddy," he said.

"Plan B?" I asked stupidly. "I thought we already used plan B."

"Technically you're right," he admitted. "I guess this is plan C."

"What?" I asked. "I didn't know we had a plan C."

He smiled, turned to Hakeem and said, "Tell your father we're ready."

Hakeem opened his phone, thumbed a message and pushed send.

"It's done," Hakeem said.

I watched as the man who had just paid eighteen million dollars for Madeline walked over to Jabbar's table to settle up. His son was drooling at her as if she were some exquisite one-of -a-kind treasure that he had been searching the desert sands for all of his life and had finally unearthed. I hated him.

"When is plan C going to happen?" I asked, watching Jabbar and the father shake hands, clearly having concluded the transaction.

"Soon," Rodger said serenely.

About half of the bidders had already left the auction house as had both of the first two successful ones with their prizes in tow. Maddy had been delivered to the father and son table and was standing next to it like a lost soul. I hated the despair I could sense in her posture. The bodyguards were up and ready to leave and the duo were gathering their things.

"They're leaving," I said, hopelessness creeping back into my voice.

"Well, let's slow them up a little, shall we?" he said.

He stood up and moved toward their table. Hakeem and I stood and followed. Glancing around I saw our three body-guards detach themselves from the back bar and move to join us. We reached their table just as they had finally gotten organized and were turning for the door.

"Excuse me," Rodger said deferentially. "I wonder if we could have a word."

The father swiveled his head and stared at Rodger with an icy look.

"About what?" he asked.

"We'd like to talk about the young lady you just purchased," I said.

"She's not for sale," he snapped.

"We were thinking more like a gift," Rodger said.

"A gift?"

"Yes," Rodger said. "You could give her to us and save yourself some trouble."

That brought an involuntary laugh from the father who then turned and said a few words in Arabic to his three bodyguards. They stepped closer. The son clutched the chain leading to Maddy's collar and pulled her close behind him.

"Is that one of your American jokes?" the father asked coldly.

"No," Rodger said, "just a suggestion to try and save you from some problems that will inconvenience you seriously."

"Problems with you?" the father scoffed.

"Well, ourselves and Achmed Bakam al Saadin," Rodger said.

That brought another snort from him.

"Do you seriously think that because you happen to know the name of the Wazir of this region of Morocco that I'm going to become like a woman for you?" he asked.

"Like a woman?" Rodger asked.

"Become a pussy like you Americans are so fond of saying," he said.

"Is that a no?" Rodger asked.

"I promised my son a woman and I bought her," he said. "If you wanted this one so badly why didn't you outbid me?"

"We didn't have enough money," I said.

"Find another one then," he said.

"We want this one," Rodger said.

"Why?" the father asked.

Maddy had been staring at the floor, resigned to her fate, but finally the conversation had penetrated her fog of drugs. She raised her head and looked at Rodger and then at me.

"Rodger? Daryl?" she squeaked. "Why are you here? To save me?"

"Oh, so it's like that," the father said. "You Americans are always trying to save the world, aren't you?"

"It's a bad habit we have," Rodger said.

"I'm going to enjoy knowing that we have your woman as my son trains her," he snarled. "We will teach her to scream your names."

I blanched in horror, thinking of Maddy living her life like that. Rodger didn't even flinch.

"This is your last chance to do what's right," Rodger said mildly.

A dark cloud of anger mottled the father's face. He rattled off another sentence in Arabic and his three bodyguards stepped in front of him and began pushing Rodger backwards with their chests as they moved toward the door.

"We are leaving now," he said.

Rodger backed up and stepped sideways as if he were intimidated and was getting out of their way. The guards relaxed. As they moved past him Rodger's left foot swung up in a sweeping arc from the ground. It caught the center guard in the bridge of his nose, driving it at an angle upwards into his frontal lobe. He fell like a stone. At almost the same time his right hand chopped in a horizontal slashing motion to the bodyguard on the right, catching him in his Adams apple. He clutched at his throat and forgot about anything but trying to breathe. The third guy went for the gun he was wearing under his robe, but Rodger captured his arm, spun him around and used his momentum and a hand to the back of his head to drive his face into the table that they had just vacated. He slumped to the floor.

The whole process hadn't taken more than a few seconds and had created minimal fuss. Many of the men leaving hadn't even noticed. The son looked frightened and was passive as Rodger plucked the end of the chain from his hand and handed it to me. The father, on the other hand, was not in the least frightened and was plainly furious.

"So, you think you can steal what you are not able to buy?" he said coldly. "My friends who are still here or the owners of this place will have you killed."

In fact, now that some of the guests were becoming aware of what had happened they were edging toward us and motioning their bodyguards to follow. Jabbar and Mustafa signaled their security staff and five big guys started moving toward us with murder in their eyes. Rodger looked at the father.

"One last chance, my friend," Rodger said sweetly, "tell all of them to back off and I'll let you and your son walk away."

Dad ignored what Rodger had to say. He was on a mission and didn't think a young, naïve, punk American could possibly bring anything to the table that could have any effect on his life or his single-minded plan to own the woman he had just paid eighteen million dollars for. He was positive that the men in the room were on his side and that Rodger and myself were doomed.

"I'm going to enjoy watching them destroy you," the father said. "I'm going to ask them to let you live so that you can experience the rest of your life as a shadow of the man you should have been."

"Suit yourself," Rodger said serenely.

Just before the hordes reached us all hell broke loose as men in uniform poured in from the main exit and from behind the stage brandishing semi-automatic weapons, using police whistles and shouting something that must have been the Arabic equivalent of 'police, freeze'. The father figured it out right away and glared at Rodger. He smiled and shook his head sadly.

"I warned you," Rodger said.

It only took seconds for the police to secure the room. An officer came over to Prince Hakeem immediately and bowed deferentially. The Prince said something in Arabic and the guns that were pointed at Rodger and me were lowered.

In a few moments Achmed entered through the main door carrying a red velvet robe and crossed to where we were standing. He looked at Maddy and smiled.

"So, my friends," he said, "is this the woman?"

"Yes."

He placed the robe around her shoulders, belted it, turned to the bodyguards that were with us and said something in Arabic. Two of them stepped to either side of her. The one closest to me held out his hand for the chain. I gave it to him.

"You are safe now, my dear," Achmed said. "My men will take you to my palace where your friends are waiting."

"Safe? Friends?" Maddy said.

"Jennifer is here with us," I explained, "along with a friend of mine."

"Jennifer is here?"

"Yes," I said. "If you go with these men they will deliver you to the Wazir's palace where we are staying. Jennifer will be waiting for you."

"Wazir? Palace?" Maddy parroted, the drugs in her system still clearly ruling her comprehension.

"Just go with them please, Maddy," I said. "We will be right behind you."

"Okay."

She let herself be led out by the two bodyguards. I watched her until she disappeared out the door. One important part of our mission was finished but so many questions remained. I turned back to Rodger with a grin.

"Well, Rog," I said, "it didn't go down exactly as we planned but we got her back."

"That we did," he agreed. "Now we have to try to discover where Judy Green went, why Brad was searching for her, how she relates to the pay-per-click scam and Sonic Ping, and why they killed Brad and Karen."

A commotion at the side of the room drew our attention. Mustafa and Jabbar were in a heated argument with the two policemen who had AK47's trained on them. They were gesturing toward us and trying to walk in our direction but were being restrained. Achmed said something loudly in Arabic and the two guards moved out of Mustafa and Jabbar's way and followed them over to us.

I couldn't understand the next five minutes because it was all in Arabic. I did hear the word Wazir from time to time, which made me realize that both Mustafa and Jabbar knew who he was. Eventually the argument wore down and the two slave marketers stomped out the door with four officers in tow.

"You are probably wondering what that was all about," Achmed said, after they had departed.

"You let them go," I said in amazement. "They were selling innocent women into slavery and you let them go."

"I told you," Prince Hakeem said.

"I know but…"

"They have diplomatic passports," Achmed said. "I had no choice but to allow them to go."

"But…"

"No buts, Daryl, it is the way of the world," Achmed said.

"What was all of the arguing about then?" I asked.

"They wanted me to leave their establishment," he said, "because of all of the information and access to their funds that are on the computers and papers here."

"I thought they had diplomatic immunity," I said.

"They do, but it only extends to their persons, not their possessions, so I refused," he explained.

"What happens to them now?" I asked.

"They will be declared 'persona non grata' and expelled from Morocco," he said.

"So they are free to start their business again somewhere else?" I asked.

The Wazir looked embarrassed but kept his eyes on mine and answered, "Yes."

I looked around and my gaze fell on the father and son duo who had been with us as the raid went down and had been privy to all of the past few minutes of conversation. I turned to Rodger.

"What do you want done with them?" I asked.

Rodger turned and addressed the Wazir.

"Achmed, this is the man who outbid us for Madeline," Rodger said. "I gave him several opportunities to do the right thing and relinquish his hold on her, but he wouldn't. In fact he seemed gleeful that his son would be abusing her knowing that she was a friend of ours."

"Do you have a special way you want him punished?" Achmed asked.

Rodger looked at the father appraisingly. He glared back. Rodger shook his head in exasperation.

"I do, but it's cruel and inhumane and probably wouldn't do any good," Rodger said. "Achmed, here is a man who thinks it's okay to enslave a woman just because he wants to and can afford it. He gave Mustafa and Jabbar eighteen million dollars for Maddy just because he could. Clearly he would have bid a significant amount more, and would have done it without batting an eye."

"Nevertheless what these men have been doing is a serious crime and all of them will be brought up on charges," Achmed said.

He spoke briefly in Arabic, gesturing at the father and son and the rest of the bidders. In a few minutes the room was cleared, leaving the four of us and four officers.

"Achmed," Rodger said, "I know that your people are going to confiscate all of the files and computers here, but I wonder if we might have a peek at them first."

"I thought the woman was what you came here for," Achmed said.

"She is, but she is the tip of an iceberg. There were at least seventeen other women involved just from the club in the United States where our friend was abducted," Rodger explained. "Our good friend was killed about a month ago and we believe that in part it was because he was searching for one of the missing women."

"By all means, my good friends," Achmed said. "Take your time."

ॐ

We spent two hours in the office going through the files and computer system. It was very rewarding. We found names and addresses of the buyers of every single girl that had passed through the operation. In all they had sold a total of thirty-three women. In addition to the eighteen from the United States there had been women from the Ukraine, Russia and Latvia.

We also found all of the codes and passwords to the various bank accounts that Mustafa and Jabbar had been using to deposit their proceeds. Rodger took a moment to move the money into the same stream that Brad had used for bigooh.com, which meant that at least another thirty million dollars would end up in the Cayman Islands account.

ભ

We got back to the Wazir's palace at six am. The three girls were wide awake and waiting. Maddy looked shell-shocked, but most of the drugs had worn off so she was much more alert. I crossed the room to where she was seated, lifted her up and gathered her into my arms. She felt happy, soft and very desirable. In spite of my resolve a lump of heat formed in my stomach.

"Thank you, Daryl," she whispered.

"Sure," I mumbled into her hair.

"Is Dan okay?" she asked.

A pang of jealousy hit me. I looked over to Selma, she smiled and the fist around my heart eased. I relaxed my grip and let her drift away from me just enough.

"They beat him up pretty badly but he's going to be all right," I answered.

"I feel so bad about what happened. If only…"

"Maddy," I interrupted, "none of what happened is your fault."

"But Brad…"

"Brad found something out and they killed him for it," I said. "You didn't have anything to do with it. Dan got hurt because his partner is in bed with some bad element that seems to be tied to Sonic Ping."

"When can I see Dan?" she asked.

"As soon as we can book flights home," I said stroking her hair.

"Don't be silly, Daryl," Achmed piped up. "You are my guests and I owe you a debt that can never be repaid. I will arrange for my private jet to ferry you back to the U.S."

Maddy looked up at me, "What does he mean a debt that can never be repaid."

"Just something that happened, Maddy," I said. "I'll explain later."

I turned to Achmed. His offer was way too generous, but I knew that he'd be insulted if we didn't agree and we wouldn't be able to talk him out of it anyway.

"When can we leave?" I asked.

"I can have the plane ready in an hour," he said.

"Wow," I thought, *"an hour from now we can be on a plane home?"*

"I'd like to go with them, father," Hakeem said.

"By all means, son."

"I'll call our chief pilot," Hakeem said, leaving the room.

"After you get back home what is your next step?" Achmed asked.

I knew what I thought we should do, but I turned to Rodger to let him answer.

"I know that your people plan to turn over the lists we got from Maafa to Interpol for them to follow up on recovering the abducted women," Rodger said. "I would ask that you withhold one name on the list as a favor to us."

"Which one?"

"Judy Green," Rodger answered. "She was purchased by a Libyan industrialist who lives in Tripoli."

"Why do you want me to withhold that name?" he asked.

"We are fairly certain that Judy is the key to the puzzle as to why our friend Brad and Daryl's wife were killed," Rodger said. "We plan to mount an operation to snatch her away from him."

"I thought as much," Achmed said. "And I'm sorry but I can't do that."

"He can't do that?" I thought. Rodger was stunned as was I. *"What happened to 'I owe you a debt that can never be repaid'? What happened to...?"* My thoughts were cut short.

"Unless you are willing to let me help," he said.

We stared at him in disbelief.

"I was making one of your American jokes."

"So...you will help us?" I asked.

"Of course, Daryl," he said. "I owe you a debt that..."

Both Rodger and I burst out laughing.

ଔ

One hour later we pulled up to the Wazir's hangar at the Marrakesh-Menara International airport. RAK is a small gateway airport only about five miles from the center of Marrakesh. It took three SUVs to get us there. Two of them were for the six of us that were actually going on the flight plus one bodyguard and driver in each. The third SUV contained another four armed men as backup bodyguards. Clearly the Wazir had enemies and after the high powered men he carted off to jail last night the count had gone up significantly.

The entrance foyer to his hangar had a short access hall with a small office to the right with a receptionist. Straight ahead was a good sized lounge. The receptionist plainly knew we were expected and buzzed us through. The lounge was carpeted in a dark grey Berber with lighter grey oversized leather chase lounges, a big screen TV that was tuned to CNN, comfortable window bench seats looking out on the runway and a serve yourself snack bar. No check-in, no security, no baggage restrictions and no hassle. We waited in the plush seats while the ground crew finished fueling the plane and the flight crew did their final checks.

The Wazir actually had three planes. He used his Cessna Citation I short range jet for hopping around Morocco into the smaller airports when his duties took him to other provinces. His medium range Gulfstream II was used for trips to Europe and when he brought all four of his wives and their entourages and needed more space. Then there was the one that he rolled out for us.

His Gulfstream G550 sitting just outside the lounge was sleek, spacious, fast, and comfortable. It also had a range of over seven thousand miles, which was more than enough to reach the U.S. without refueling. Outfitted for sixteen passengers, it held the six of us plus two bodyguards with tons of room to spare. The crew consisted of two pilots plus a relief pilot and two lovely flight attendants. The plane also had a fully stocked bar and galley, but after the events of the past few days and the related lack of sleep, it was wasted on us. We all went to sleep while the jet was still taxiing out for takeoff. I woke up on the descent into our U.S. gateway airport and I was the first one to rouse.

chapterTWENTY

When Detective Sampson's front door imploded and sailed across the foyer, narrowly missing Selma, my brain watched it twist by her head in slow motion. A dozen scenarios as to why that door had come off of its hinges so dramatically flickered through my mind. The sheet of flame that accompanied it first made me consider that the gas main in front of the house had exploded. Then my brain moved on to the possibility that a drunk driver had missed the sharp right angle turn in front of Dan's house and had impacted the front porch at eighty miles per hour, propelling the door on its life-threatening journey. Those first speculations were replaced by additional fleeting thoughts of other, much crazier, possibilities such as an airplane crash or a full scale nuclear attack. I was confused and my head was unable to make sense of what was happening.

The truth of what had really occurred hadn't even crossed my mind. I watched in disbelief as a SWAT team poured into the house with gas masks, helmets, clubs, body armor, automatic weapons, tasers, shotguns, stun grenades and acres of attitude. Their high pitched repetitive screaming of 'FREEZE',

'POLICE' and 'DOWN ON THE FLOOR MOTHER-FUCKER' was designed to disconcert, confuse, befuddle and render helpless most normal citizens. It certainly frightened the hell out of Selma, Jennifer and Maddy. On the other hand Dan, Tiny, Rodger, Hakeem and I looked at the incoming wave of boys with their toys, shook our heads and resigned ourselves to the reality that the next few hours were going to be pure hell.

Just before this nightmare descended we had been relaxing in Dan's living room, having a somber discussion about our next step in unraveling why Brad had been killed. We had come directly from the airport. Hakeem convinced our bodyguards to remain with the plane so there was just the six of us.

Dan had been released from the hospital the day before. He still looked rough and was using crutches to get around but was clearly on the mend. Tiny had an uneventful several days guarding him until now.

Now Tiny was spread-eagled on the floor along with Rodger, Hakeem and myself while Dan tried futilely to get the testosterone pumped team, led by none other than 'he's a good kid' Bruce Kirkwood, to back down.

"God damn it, Bruce, what the fuck are you doing?" Dan screamed.

"Stay out of this, Dan," Bruce said. "If you hadn't been in the hospital until yesterday you'd be going to jail also. Even so the chief wonders if you aren't involved."

"Involved in what, Bruce?"

"Murder, kidnapping, perhaps white slavery as well," Bruce said.

Dan stared at Bruce for a moment and then glanced down at the three of us on the floor.

"I apologize," Dan said quietly.

"No need to apologize to me, Dan," Bruce said, "I'm just doing my…"

Dan's head snapped up so fast I thought he would injure his neck. The frozen look on his face was fearsome.

"I'm not apologizing to you, Bruce," Dan said coldly. "I'm apologizing to my three friends for not believing them when they tried to convince me how twisted up you were."

"Me?" Bruce said. "Your cowboy friends are the twisted ones and now they're going to get what they deserve."

Dan turned to face Bruce directly. The steel that came into his voice was enough to make Bruce take a step backward.

"I've known these guys all my life, Bruce," he said. "If I were you I'd let them up, apologize and work with them to find out what's going on."

"I know what's going on or at least parts of it," Bruce said. "We've got the body of a Sonic Ping employee who they killed because he must have been getting too close to finding out what they were up to."

"Where did you find the body?" Dan asked.

"I got a tip," Bruce said.

"Where?"

"In the dumpster behind the strip mall where Rodger has his business," Bruce said.

"Kind of convenient, wasn't it?" Dan asked.

"Guys like them are not usually very bright," Bruce said.

"I feel sorry for you, Bruce," Dan said shaking his head.

"Yeah? Well, I'm not the one who's going to jail," Bruce said.

⁂

Six hours later Rodger and I were sitting alone in a cell at the main police station. The midnight shift had just come on duty and things were quiet. We had been arraigned on an open murder charge and were waiting a bail hearing the following morning. Our longtime friend and lawyer shook his head at the weak charges that had been lodged against us, but even so, he hadn't expressed much hope that we'd be granted bail.

Bruce had been forced to release Tiny as dozens of hospital employees had seen him in Dan's presence for the past several days and barring charges against his partner as an accessory Tiny had an iron-clad alibi. Hakeem had merely pulled out his diplomatic passport when the screaming died down and they were forced to let him go. They weren't much interested in him anyway as the focus seemed to be putting myself and Rodger out of commission.

As I stretched out on the hard cot and put my head down on the pillow and tried to get comfortable for the night, I heard the security door at the end of the corridor open. It was way too late for visitors. In fact, as this was a fairly small town jail there should have been only one duty officer on guard in the office and he wouldn't have bothered to check on us. I sat up and listened. My heartbeat jumped fifty percent. I could see the tension in Rodger's shoulders as he got up and moved to the back of our cell. Four guards stopped at our door. Three were carrying semi-automatic shotguns. The fourth one was Bruce.

"Let's go," Bruce said.

"Go?" I asked. "Go where?"

"You're being moved," he said.

That didn't make sense. Our bail hearing was right next door at the courthouse tomorrow morning. Why would they move us? At midnight? Without cuffing us first? I glanced at Rodger and could tell by his frown that he had processed the same thoughts.

"Why?" he asked.

"Look, asshole," Bruce said, "we can do this the hard way or the easy way, I don't care."

"We're just tired and ready for sleep," Rodger said.

"Then the sooner you get a move on the sooner you'll get to bed," Bruce said, standing away from the door so we could pass.

Walking through that door was a certain one way trip to the morgue. Both Rodger and I knew that. If we went with this crew we would become just another example of desperate criminals who had tried to escape and were shot in the process. I rolled my eyes at Rodger. He scratched his right eyebrow and nodded. I lifted my chin to let him know I understood.

I stepped out of the cell first, moved to the other side of the corridor and turned the wrong way which drew Bruce's attention. He and one other guard stepped behind me.

"Hey, wrong way, asshole," he said.

I turned and smiled stupidly, spread my hands and shrugged.

"Sorry," I said.

Meanwhile Rodger had stepped out behind me, swiveled around and stepped back to the door of our cell.

"I forgot, uh," he said, pointing back into the cell, "I forgot my…"

The rest of his sentence came out as an unintelligible mumble that had the desired effect of causing the two guards watching him to glance into the cell to see what he was pointing at. With their attention distracted, Rodger went into faster-than-light mode. An eye blink later those two were unconscious with one of their weapons leveled at the two who were working on turning me around. They turned, saw the gun leveled at them and froze.

"Take their weapons, Daryl," Rodger said.

I took the shotgun from the one guard, lifted Bruce's 9mm and then patted him down. He had an ankle holster with a Glock 27 which I slipped into my waistband.

"You can't believe the trouble you guys are going to be in for this stunt," Bruce said.

"More trouble than being shot for trying to escape?" Rodger asked.

He opened his mouth to speak, then thought better and closed it. Rodger herded the four of them into the cell where I cuffed them to the bars and each other, made sure that I had all of the keys and anything else they might use to break out, then stepped out and locked the cell door. Bruce opened his mouth again.

"If you release us now I won't tell anyone about this stupidity," he said.

"Do they teach you those slick negotiating tools at the Academy or did you have special training?" Rodger asked.

"You're looking at aggravated assault on a police officer, asshole. That, along with the murder one charge, will get you life."

"Sounds better than what you had planned for us," Rodger said.

"Fuck you," Bruce said angrily. "Just wait until I catch up to you."

"I'm looking forward to a meeting on a level playing field," Rodger said.

Rodger turned and walked down the corridor with me trailing behind him. One of the keys we took from the group opened the door. The office was empty. We moved to the main entrance door, cracked it and peeked out. All of the duty cruisers were out and things seemed quiet. A black van was idling at the curb with a driver behind the wheel. He was smoking and glancing at the entrance. I closed the door.

"Looks like they were going to move us somewhere quieter to dispose of us," Rodger said.

"Yeah," I agreed.

"Let's go out the back and then you go around to the passenger side and get his attention and I'll get rid of him," Rodger said.

We slipped out the rear entrance, turned the corner of the building and walked to the back of the van. Rodger nodded and I slid around the right side, stepped to the passenger door and rapped on the window. The driver glanced up at me with a puzzled look at which point his door opened behind him and Rodger dragged him out. I moved quickly to the driver's side and helped Rodger carry his unconscious form to the back doors, then cuffed him to the prisoner seat in the rear. We were just shutting the doors when a police cruiser came screaming around the corner, lights flashing and pulled up behind us. Their headlights blinded us.

"Shit, Rog," I said, "we almost made it."

"Yeah, but at least we haven't killed anybody and now there are enough witnesses that they can't shoot us like they planned to," he said, laying his shotgun on the ground and raising his hands.

I followed suit and watched as both cruiser doors opened and someone stepped out of each side.

"I see you managed without us," Dan's voice said from the passenger side.

"I told you that there wasn't anything to worry about," Tiny's voice said from the other.

"Dan? Tiny?" I said, lowering my hands. "What are you guys doing here?"

"Just making sure that you didn't get killed 'trying to escape'," Dan said. "Tiny told me I was being a worrywart."

"Well…"

"You didn't kill any of my fellow cops or my partner, did you?" Dan asked.

"No."

"Where are they?"

"Resting in our cell," Rodger said.

"Sounds peaceful."

"Yes."

"Well, since you seem to have things under control I think I'll have Tiny take me home," Dan said.

"What about your partner?" I asked.

"I believe I'll make an anonymous call to the local TV station before the morning shift comes on so they can do a nice story about him," he said.

"It's not going to stop him, Dan," I said. "He was planning on killing us tonight."

"I know. I'm counting on you and Rodger to expose whatever is happening and put him away."

"We only have one lead. It's weak and it's out of the country, but that's where we're headed," I said.

"Out of the country? Where?"

"Do you really want to know?" I asked.

"Good point."

Chapter TWENTY-ONE

Three hours later we were sipping drinks at thirty-five thousand feet. The Wazir's jet had just crossed into international airspace over the Atlantic so the possibility of being forced down by U.S. Air Force fighters was over. Actually, we hadn't worried much about pursuit because it was still three or four hours before Bruce would be discovered and start the process of looking for us, and more like several days before he moved his mind out of the normal rut and thought about the possibility that we might have left the country. When he finally did he would still be on the wrong trail. Hakeem had the pilot file a flight plan for Barcelona, however somewhere over the coast of Europe we planned to drop down, cancel IFR, then disappear into the clutter of the thousands of airplanes that were in that airspace.

Our ultimate destination was Tripoli in Libya, but just to be certain that no one could track us, Hakeem arranged with the Wazir for us to first set down in Kampala, Uganda, where his father had important contacts. We would then refuel and file for Cairo, Egypt. Once we were on our way to Cairo we would again drop down and divert to Algeria where we could deplane and walk over to his father's Gulfstream II that was already on its way there. That plane would file a straightforward flight plan and move us to Tripoli while the Gulfstream 550 that we were using would return to Marrakesh. It was a convoluted way of getting to Tripoli but with a certainty that not even Interpol could find us before we had time to accomplish our mission.

As soon as we left the ground Rodger had his laptop open and was frantically pounding on the keys. When we leveled off I moved over and sat down next to him.

"Surfing for porn?" I joked, taking another sip on my drink.

"Some people might call it that," he said, his fingers flying over the keys.

"Did you find something more about the pay-per-click deal?" I asked.

"I did, but that's not what I'm working on right now," he said.

"Really? What then?"

"I'm working on setting up a way to extract Judy Green from her... situation."

"So what's the big deal?" I asked.

"We are going to need help."

"Poison?" I asked.

"That was my first thought," he said. "She's available. I'm hoping she can pull a team together fast."

"Why?"

"I want to be ready to go as soon as we hit the ground in Tripoli," Rodger said, "because we seriously screwed up Mustafa and Jabbar's operation. Their records were confiscated and if I were them, I would warn all of my previous clients that Interpol might come looking. In addition, if the buyer we took Maddy away from has told them that we were searching for her specifically, Judy's... owner might be expecting us also."

"Do we have a plan?" I asked.

"Other than locating her, snatching her and running?" he asked.

"Yes."

"Not really."

"What can I do?" I asked.

"Do some research on Tripoli and see if anything occurs to you," he suggested.

I pulled out my laptop, connected and spent some time reading the recent history of Libya and looking at the area where we would be on Google Earth. What I found was that Tripoli had been ruled by the Romans from just before the birth of Christ until it was conquered by the Arabs in 642 AD and, except for brief reigns by the Spanish in the 1550's and the Italians in the early 1900's, it has remained under Islamic rule. The present ruler, Muammar al-Gaddafi took over in a coup in 1969 and has ruled since.

I looked on Google Earth at Mitiga International airport where we would be landing and noted that there seemed to be decent highways leading both directions along the coast with the roads disintegrating the further inland one moved. The location of the compound where Judy was being held was about ten miles east of the airport on the coast road, but Google Earth didn't show enough detail to determine how heavily fortified it was. I assumed that Poison would have that information. It didn't seem like much, but I related what I'd found to Rodger. He asked a few questions and then looked at the satellite view of Mitaga airport and the sheik's compound for quite some time. When he was finished I turned off my computer, curled up and went to sleep.

ణ

We had a bit of trouble in Kampala because it was late in the day when we landed and the customs official who came out to meet the plane either hadn't been briefed or was taking advantage that our contact had gone home and was looking for an additional bribe. He insisted that we all deplane while his men searched the plane for contraband and verified all of our identities. Hakeem took him aside and after a few minutes returned grinning.

"We are all set," he said. "Our customs friend has had a change of heart."

"That's nice," Rodger said. "I hope it wasn't too costly."

"The man has limited ambitions," Hakeem explained, "plus I mentioned the name of our highly placed friend and suggested that we call him. He agreed that it wouldn't be necessary to disturb him after hours."

"So we're free to go?" I asked.

"Just as soon as we pay for the refueling," Hakeem said.

ॐ

At midnight we landed in Algiers. The Wazir had completely paved the way for us and as a result no one came out to meet the plane. We stepped off, walked the fifty feet that separated us from the Wazir's Gulfstream II and within thirty minutes of landing we were in the air again for Tripoli.

"It makes you wonder, doesn't it?" I remarked to Rodger as we leveled off at twenty-five thousand feet and the lovely attendant handed each of us a hot towel to freshen up.

"Wonder what?" Rodger said.

"When it's this easy for us to hop around to these different countries just to confuse our trail what really bad people are doing," I said.

"Money and power do seem to corrupt people," he agreed.

"How do you lose your moral rudder so badly that you think it's acceptable to buy and sell young women?" I asked.

"Don't know, bud. I just know we've got to get this one back so that we can unravel the mystery that Brad stumbled on."

"What's our next step?" I asked.

"We've got a meet scheduled with Poison and her crew at a nearby safe house she has as soon as we land," he said.

ॐ

Thirty minutes later we were on the ground at Mitiga International airport. Mitiga was formerly a U.S. Air Force base known as Wheelus before it was turned over to the Libyans in 1970. We pulled up close to the terminal and passed through customs and immigration along with a group of Germans off of a Lufthansa flight from Frankfurt and some Turkish families and businessmen who had just come in from Istanbul.

Outside the terminal was a uniformed limo driver holding a sign that said Seeker. The three of us piled in and sat back. Our driver turned left out of the airport on the main highway leading along the Mediterranean, eventually turning into the old center of the city where he spent the better part of an hour driving a circuitous route that eventually spit us out the other side. We again drove briefly along the water before we pulled into the Municipal beach parking lot with the Mediterranean directly in front of us. It was two in the morning and the lot was quiet. Our driver stopped three spaces away from the only other car in the lot, an older Mercedes, got out, lit a cigarette and strolled off toward the water.

We sat in silence for ten minutes watching the limo driver stand by the water's edge and chain smoke three cigarettes. He finally flicked the butt end of the third one into the water, walked back to the limo, opened the passenger door on the side where I was sitting and gestured for the three of us to step out.

It was a beautiful night, about seventy-five degrees Fahrenheit, with a crisp clear sky. The moon had not yet risen so we could see stars out over the sea. The soft breeze coming in off of the Mediterranean was humid but refreshing. Looking back toward the city the sky was bright, but directly in front of us it was dark enough that you couldn't see the line that divided sea and sky.

The driver motioned for us to follow him, then turned and walked back toward the beach. As we moved further away from the meager lighting of the parking lot we could see a sandy beach, completely deserted except for one small boat beached in front of us. The driver motioned to the boat, grunted something in Arabic, then turned and left us.

"I thought we were going to a safe house," I said.

"That's what Poison said in her email," Rodger said.

"What are we supposed to do with the boat?" I asked.

"Beats me, bud," Rodger said, "but Poison has never failed to deliver before."

Just then a shadowy figure peeked over the edge of the boat and said something in Arabic.

"He says come," Hakeem said.

We crossed the wet sand while the figure climbed out to meet us. He stood at the bow of the boat, made a gesture as if to push it back into the sea and spoke again.

"He says push and keep pushing until you are at least up to your knees," Hakeem said moving to one side of the boat.

Rodger and I moved to the other side. The boat slid backward into the small waves, the boatman clambered in, tilted the small outboard into the water and by the time the three of us had struggled over the side he had it started and was backing to deeper water.

For such a small boat with what appeared to be an undersized engine it was surprisingly fast. We headed straight out to sea until we were at least two miles offshore and then turned so that the coastline was to our left.

❧

Two hours later I was jolted out of a fitful sleep by the change of pitch in the engine. I poked my head up and saw that we were approaching a jetty. Silhouetted by the sky were two shadowy figures. The captain of our craft brought us expertly alongside, reversed and killed the engine so we could climb out.

"Sorry about the convoluted path here," Poison said from the jetty. "I just had to make sure you weren't followed."

"What's next?" I asked. "A helicopter?"

"No," she said. "Just a short walk to the house we are using."

"Lead the way," Rodger said, "and by the way thanks for the help in Marrakesh."

"You're welcome," Poison said. "Did you get your friend back without any trouble?"

"Without any trouble?" Rodger said. "Not exactly, but everything turned out well in the end."

"Is this one a personal job also?" Poison asked.

"We don't know her, but in some ways I guess I'd have to say yes," Rodger said.

"You Americans have a compulsion to save the world, don't you?" Poison asked.

Rodger squirmed but didn't answer.

"I'm not saying that's bad," Poison said, "it's just that this extraction is not going to be cheap."

"Don't worry," Rodger said, "we received a rather large donation from the men who sold her in the first place."

"That sounds like a story I would love to hear sometime," Poison said softly, dropping back and putting her arm through his.

"I… uh…"

I don't often see Rodger at a loss for words. I smiled to myself and enjoyed the walk.

ॐ

The safe house belonged to a Libyan professor and his wife. He was taking a year's sabbatical from Al Fateh University, the public university in Tripoli, to spend a year teaching in Abu Dhabi at the Kalifa University of Science, Technology and Research. He had put his house up for lease. It had been vacant for six months when Poison approached the management firm handling it and offered to lease it for one month at double the normal rate. Her cover story was that she and her husband wanted to spend their vacation in Tripoli researching the early Roman influence on the city.

This was plausible as the Romans had occupied Tripoli from the 2nd century AD until the 7th when the Muslims invaded. Few of their structures remain intact except for the arch of Marcus Aurelius from the 2nd century AD. Nevertheless, as there are still columns and capitals used in current buildings, it was a believable story and the management company had readily agreed.

It was a comfortable three bedroom, one and a half bath, two story home with a view of the Mediterranean located only a few kilometers from the center of the city. Poison had coffee, dates and tuna sandwiches for us to eat. We sat in the living room gazing out at the Mediterranean as dawn began to creep into the eastern sky. She handed us each a small packet.

"These pages contain what I've been able to find out so far," she said. "Not surprisingly there is good and bad. Which would you like first?"

I riffed through the pages quickly and glanced back up. I wasn't a speed reader like Rodger and preferred verbal explanations. He kept his head down.

"Start with the good," I said.

"We know where she is," Poison said, pausing.

"That's it?" I asked, disbelievingly.

"Pretty much," she said.

"Well, fuck. What's the bad part?" I asked.

"Just about everything else."

"Like?"

"The guy who has her is Shihab Aasaam al Shereef. He is a close personal friend of Muammar Gaddafi," she said, "which means that he has more resources than a normal citizen."

"Such as?"

"He has a military detachment on loan that guards his compound," she said.

"His compound?"

"As you know he has a villa on the Mediterranean about twenty kilometers east of the city. The bad news is, it's surrounded by a double razor wire fence, with motion sensors and guard dogs," she said.

"So how do we get in?" I asked.

"The best access point is for us to come in off of the Med. He has a long pier that sticks out where he keeps his boat, which is in France right now. I have rented a cigarette boat that can bring us right in to the jetty. It looks exactly like one that he owns so there shouldn't be any resistance until we climb out," she explained, "but even on the Mediterranean side he has two roving guards that we will have to neutralize."

"And?"

"Then we have to get into the house and find her," she said. "In the packet there is a schematic of the villa that shows the rooms where we think she's being held, and where our points of access and egress are. It also shows where we'll find the bedrooms, kitchen, bathrooms, living room, garage and any other miscellaneous space we'll need to secure."

"What are our chances?" I asked.

"I think we can safely sneak up to the shore, surprise the two roaming guards, neutralize the dogs and get into the house," Poison said. "After that it gets dicey."

"Dicey because?"

"Well for one thing we don't know for sure what room she is normally held in. Number two, we're not certain of the total number of people in the house, or how many of them are armed or dangerous. Number three would be the random factor."

"The random factor?"

"Yes, random, like the guy who should have been with the rest of the security detail in the kitchen, but who had to take a dump and comes out of the toilet behind us with a weapon."

"Can't we plan to eliminate the random factor?" I asked.

"Daryl," Rodger said, "the random factor always rears its ugly head just when you think you are home free. That's why you always need a plan B."

"So create one of your famous plan B's for us," I said.

"I'm thinking," he said.

"When are we mounting our raid?" I asked Poison.

"Tomorrow just before dawn," she said.

"Once we have her how do we get away?" I asked.

"We go out the same way we came in," she said. "The difference is that the cigarette boat will take us fifteen miles straight offshore where I've arranged for a two hundred foot motor yacht, with helicopter, that will ferry the three of you, plus the young lady, to Sicily."

"Sicily?" I blustered. "What do we do there?"

"Lay low until the heat dies down, then Hakeem can arrange for pickup and you can get back to the U.S.," she said.

We kicked the plan around for the next three hours, made some fine tune adjustments and placed all of the elements in motion. Then Rodger, Hakeem and I each found a place to stretch out and catch up on sleep.

ChapterTWENTY-TWO

At three the next morning we were idling about three hundred yards off of Shihab's compound sweeping the villa with our night vision binoculars. Things seemed quiet. The two rear guards had been standing together for the past five minutes in conversation. Both were smoking. We gave our captain the go ahead and he silently covered the distance to the beach and brought us alongside. The guards were still talking and hadn't noticed.

Rodger stepped out of the boat with Hakeem and walked slowly toward them. He was a mere fifty feet away before they noticed, swung their weapons up and shouted something in Arabic. Both Rodger and Hakeem raised their hands but continued closing the gap. One of the guards spoke sharply again. Rodger flicked both of his wrists and the throwing stars did their job. Seconds later both were on the ground clutching at their necks.

"Wow," 'Poison said softly, "how did he do that?"

"I'm not entirely sure and I've seen him do it before," I admitted.

We jumped out of the boat and joined them, trailed by four more armed men that Poison had for additional firepower.

"Nice," I said to Rodger as we reached them.

"Umm."

"We need to keep moving," Poison said, walking past us with her attention fixed on the house.

During our discussions we settled on a two pronged assault on the house. We didn't expect anyone to be awake at this hour, but nevertheless, by using two points of entry, if one encountered a confrontation the other would be able to flank the pocket of resistance.

Hakeem, myself and two of Poison's men went to the main patio sliders. Predictably they were locked, however whoever had locked up for the night had failed to engage the secondary blocking device. We were inside in less than sixty seconds.

Rodger, Poison and the other two didn't have any problem at the side kitchen entrance either. We met up in the living room. The house was silent.

"Any problems on your end, Daryl?" Rodger asked.

"No. The door was locked but…"

"But what?" he asked sharply.

"With all this security it almost seemed too easy," I said.

"I have to agree," he said. "But we're in the thick of it now."

"Did you ever develop a Plan B?" I asked.

He looked at me and smiled.

"I have one," he said. "It hinges on one thing I have to check yet."

"Which is?"

"Let's clear the house and I'll let you know," he said, turning to the wing he was responsible for clearing.

With one of Poison's guys to cover me I went down the corridor to the right to investigate the three bedrooms in that wing. The first two were empty. The third one contained a woman who I was pretty sure was Shihab's second wife along with two children. I put them in the closet and used plastic hand cuffs to secure the door so they couldn't escape.

Ten minutes later we were all back in the living room. Rodger had one guy in tow. No one had encountered Judy.

"Why'd you bring him?" I asked nodding at the thirtyish year old guy who was cuffed and gagged and clearly mad as hell.

"Did you find her?" he asked, answering my question with a question.

"No."

"Neither did we," he said. "We only encountered four guys who were playing cards. I… left the others, but this one looked like he had a brain. I thought he might be useful if we had a problem."

I looked at the man. It was obvious that he understood English, but looking at those cold eyes I doubted that we had enough time to convince him to tell us anything.

"Rodger," I said, "he's not going to tell us. We need to keep searching."

"I suppose you're right. Let's start with…"

"Just give me a minute," Poison said. "I think I can convince him to tell us."

"Really?" Rodger asked.

"Yes," she said, slipping her five inch stealth knife out of its sheath, grabbing a handful of the guy's hair and dragging him back down the hall.

The next five minutes were chilling. Even though I couldn't understand a word of what was being said the intent was clear. His bravado slipped to uncertainty and then further to outright pleading. Pleading is evident in any language. Especially the pitiful kind of pleading he was doing. I almost felt sorry for him, but I steeled myself by remembering the innocent girl we were trying to save, who no doubt put his pleading to shame. Poison walked back into the room about seven minutes after she pulled him down the hall with her. She was alone. Her left hand was covered in blood.

"She's in a secret room that is accessed under the stairs," she said. "Turn the third and fifth spindle from the bottom counterclockwise a quarter turn and pull up, then stand on the fifth step. It will open the passage to her room."

"How did you get him to tell?" both Rodger and I asked at the same time.

"Do you know what the most frightening thing you can do to an Arabic man?" Poison asked.

Both of us shook our heads. Hakeem looked as if he had swallowed the golden canary.

"You threaten to do something to his... um, manhood," she said.

"Threaten?" Rodger asked.

"You have to mean it," she said. "You have to be prepared to go through with your threat. He has to believe that you are serious."

"What kind of threat?" I asked.

"Do you have an understanding of what drives Arabic men?" Poison asked.

"Not really," I said.

"There is a lot about our culture that represses them, that causes them to be inhibited," she said. "They don't know how to please a woman and frankly they don't try. They are taught that sex is unclean. They are especially taught that if a woman enjoys sex it is dirty and very wrong. Thus, they justify the abuses they pile on us. They justify any and all behavior against women up to and including buying women as slaves because women are soiled, unclean and temptresses," she said. "On the other hand their own sexual organs are the center of their universe which, when you think about it, really isn't that much different any-where in the world, even in your country. I just threatened to remove them."

"What?" I said.

"I told him to tell me where she was or I would cut off something he valued dearly," she said.

"So he did?" I asked.

"Of course not," she said. "I'm just a woman. I had to show him I was serious."

"My god, Poison, what did you do?"

"What I had to."

Poison turned to Rodger and Hakeem and looked at them closely. Rodger was a bit jumpy, but Hakeem was very calm.

"You are quite a woman, Poison," Hakeem said. "I would like to get to know you better."

"Into a bit of hardcore, are you, Hakeem?" Poison asked.

"Actually, no," he said. "I'm just looking for a strong woman who believes that men and women should all be equal."

She took the few steps separating the two of them and looked hard into his eyes. She must have liked what she saw because she relaxed.

"I never thought an Arabic man would surprise me," she said, shaking her head.

"I have to say that I've always felt the same about Arabic women," he said.

"We are going to have to leave this courting dance until later, you two," Rodger interrupted. "We need to get Judy and get out of here before someone realizes we are here."

Poison turned immediately for the staircase, turned the third spindle, the fifth one and then climbed to the fifth step. A door popped open on the side of the staircase with a circular stairway leading downward. The four of us went down, leaving Poison's four armed men on watch above.

At the bottom of the stairway was a small foyer with one barred door. Through the bars we could see a very pretty pale skinned slim blond woman lying on a cot, looking at us with weary blue eyes. She was completely naked. Her body was badly marked as if she had been beaten frequently. The room contained pieces of equipment that were similar to devices I had seen in the basement of Teasers except they looked much more functional. One wall was completely covered with whips, floggers, canes and other implements.

The door was locked, but the keys were conveniently hanging on the wall just across from the cell, in plain sight but out of her reach. Rodger opened the door and the four of us stepped into the cell.

"Judy?" Rodger asked tentatively.

She looked at him but didn't respond.

"Judy Green?" he asked again.

"Is this your way of justifying beating me?" she asked.

"Huh?"

"Didn't Shithead tell you not to use my real name?" she said coldly. "He's going to be pissed. He has gone to great trouble to beat my response to my name out of me."

"Shithead?"

"I know his real name is Shihab, but I call him Shithead," she said. "When I'm feeling like I'm up to another beating, that is."

"Does he beat you often?" I asked.

"When he isn't busy trying to poke that three inch thing he likes to call 'the monster' into me," she said. "I keep telling him he'd be better off trading me for a young boy who wouldn't know the difference."

"I see you haven't lost your sense of humor," I said.

"I've lost a lot of other stuff, though," she said sadly.

"We're here to take you home," I said.

"Back to Mikhal?" she asked. "No thanks. He's the reason I'm here in the first place."

"Mikhal sent you here?" Rodger asked.

"Indirectly," she answered. "He had that asshole Victor take care of it."

"We put an end to Victor's operation," I said, "and the slave market in Marrakesh. Interpol will be trying to find all of the women that were abducted."

"You guys aren't from Interpol," she said matter-of-factly.

"No."

"So, why are you here?" she asked.

"It's a long story," I said. "A friend of ours was searching for you when Sonic Ping had him killed. Since then we've discovered a lot of things that don't make sense. We think you are the key to that puzzle so we came to get you personally."

"And we really want to hear what you know, but right now we need to get going," Rodger added. "Do you have clothing?"

"No."

"We'll find something upstairs," he said.

Poison and Hakeem led the way back up while Rodger and I helped Judy. Just as we got to the top of the stairs one of Poison's men came running in from the patio speaking excitedly in Arabic.

"He says that there are two navy gunboats with soldiers that just pulled up at the jetty," Poison translated. "Our ride out of here must have seen them coming and managed to outrun them, but we're stranded. It looks like they somehow found out about our plans."

"So, I'm not rescued after all?" Judy said.

Rodger snatched an afghan off of the couch.

"Put this on," he said, throwing the afghan at her and turning for the back of the house. "It's time for plan B."

"Plan B?" Judy asked. "What does that mean?"

"I haven't a clue," I told her, dragging her along with me, "but if anyone can get us out of this mess, he can."

Rodger pulled open a door and we all tumbled through. We could hear the sounds of serious gunfire coming from behind us. It sounded like Chinese New Year and the Fourth of July wrapped up in one package. Rodger flipped on the light.

Looking around we found ourselves in a six stall garage with every stall occupied by a vehicle. Rodger made a beeline for the fourth stall which contained a very large black SUV. He opened the doors and all eight of us tumbled in.

"I checked this out earlier when I did my sweep of the house," Rodger said. "This is a Hummer H2 that has been heavily armored, probably by 'The Armored Group, LLC' which has a sales office here in Tripoli. I doubt that any of the weapons out there can do much more than scratch us. Still it's going to be rough so, seat belts, please."

"But our boat has been taken," I said. "How is this going to get us to our helicopter?"

"It isn't. This is plan B. We are going to make a run to the airport, which is only about ten kilometers away and try to fly off in the Wazir's jet," he explained, starting the car. "Hakeem, call the plane, have them get the engines started and taxi it to the threshold of the active runway. We aren't going to get but one chance at this."

Rodger didn't bother hitting the garage door opener which would have drawn attention to us. He put the car in gear, revved the engine and popped the clutch. We blasted through the garage door like it was tissue.

Outside the garage the rear house guards had been alerted and were ready. In addition, some of the military force from the boats flanked the house to keep us trapped. A hail of automatic gunfire exploded in our faces. Bullets were coming from all sides. It was eerie and frightening to watch rounds coming directly at where you were seated, hit the windshield and bounce off. I couldn't help flinching. Rodger acted no differently than if it were a heavy rain. He ignored the possibility that we might die and concentrated on driving us out of there.

Our first problem was that the gate was closed and five men with AK47's were standing in front of it pouring fire at us. Rodger slowed for a moment looking right and left.

"The guys aren't a problem, but that gate is armored heavily enough that it might stop us," he said. "I think we'll have to go around."

Going around meant we had to bust through two heavy duty chain link fences topped with concertina razor wire. Rodger swung the wheel right, bounced over the curb, across the lawn, plowing into the fences just behind the guard shack. They barely slowed us down. The razor wire shredded all four tires. I heard the built in central tire inflation system trying vainly to keep them inflated.

"I hope you have a plan C again this time, buddy," I said to Rodger, "because I can't imagine being able to get ten kilometers on the rims."

"These Hummers all run on flat tires," he said, bumping back over the curb onto the driveway. "There is a ballistic roller ring around each inside that will allow us to keep going."

"Oh."

"The real problem is that about sixty miles per hour is all we can get out of them so if they have a vehicle that can chase us they are apt to catch us."

"Great," I said. "What's our plan then?"

"Worry about it when it happens," he said, making a screeching right turn onto the main road to the airport.

I looked back. No one was behind us yet. I glanced at Hakeem who had just flipped his phone shut.

"Did you get them?" I asked.

"Yes. Luckily they had already refueled the plane and all of the crew were in the lounge," Hakeem said. "They are going to tell the tower that they need to taxi over to the compass rose to recheck the magnetic compasses and then do some brief fast taxi's to check the brakes so nobody will be suspicious about them running around the airport. I will give them a heads up when we are a few minutes away."

"What runway is active right now?" Rodger asked.

"Two nine," Hakeem replied.

"Well, that's a bit of luck in our favor," Rodger said.

"Why's that?" I asked.

"Do you remember that Google earth view of the airport you showed me on the way here?" he asked.

"Yeah."

"If we turn off just before we reach the airport, the cross road runs right past the overrun of that runway," he explained. "We only need to crash through the fence and drive about seven hundred feet to where the runway starts."

I looked back again. There was still no pursuit. I started to feel optimistic.

"What about after we get in the air?" I asked.

"I don't think that Shihab will be able to convince Gaddafi quickly enough to scramble their fighters," Rodger said.

"They have fighters?" I asked.

"Yes."

"What happens if they do come after us?" I asked.

"Daryl, I think we should worry about the vehicle that's coming up behind us first," he said glancing in his side mirror.

I swiveled around to look. The roadway that had been clear moments before now contained a truck coming up on us fast. Standing up in the back, leaning over the cab, were four men with AK47's. When they got within three hundred feet they opened fire, hitting our rear window and making quite a display. It was impressive, but the rounds didn't penetrate.

"We have to get rid of them before the airport or else we won't be able to get on the plane," Rodger said.

"How?"

"Hakeem, have the guys in the back see if they can return enough fire to stop them," Rodger suggested.

Hakeem said something in Arabic, but before they could react Poison snatched an Uzi from the guy seated next to her, rolled down her window, stuck her head and half of her body out and sprayed a hail of bullets at the pursuer. Two of the men in back were hit immediately and fell out on the road while the other two hunkered down behind the cab. Hakeem yanked her back inside.

"Are you trying to get killed?" he shouted at her.

"I was closest to the window," she said calmly.

The vehicle must have been armored because the driver wasn't scratched. He kept coming, smashing into our bumper. Rodger fought the wheel as he hit us again and again, using his vehicle to beat out a tattoo on our rear bumper.

"Hold on," Rodger said. "I'm going to get rid of him."

Before I could ask how that was going to happen, Rodger swerved to the middle of the road and slammed on our brakes. The driver behind us wasn't ready. His truck impacted on the left quarter of our bumper which pushed our rear to the left. Rodger was prepared. He let off of the brakes and steered into the impending skid. The driver of the truck didn't have a clue as his vehicle began a slow turn to his left, which he failed to correct. As his vehicle turned broadside to its direction of travel it flipped over and started rolling, throwing the two men who had been riding in the truck bed into the street like rag dolls. The truck disappeared from our view as it continued to roll off of the road and into the desert scrub.

"See anyone else back there?" Rodger asked.

I looked and the road was clear.

"Nope."

"That's good because here comes the turnoff that leads us past the end of the airport. We don't have time to fight off another," he said. "Hakeem, where's our ride?"

"I'm talking to the plane now," Hakeem said from the back. "They'll be at the end of runway two nine waiting for us."

We went through a roundabout and took the exit that left the main road, paralleling it about two hundred yards away. One mile later a sharp left turn took us south. The scenery turned from scrub to residential. As we turned I looked back. I didn't like what I saw.

"How much farther," I asked.

"About two miles, why?" Rodger asked.

"There was a car that went through the roundabout and stayed on the main road paralleling us, but it just stopped and turned around," I explained. "I think they might be after us."

"Well, let's hope we are far enough in front of them," he said.

Two miles later we merged with the airport ring road. I could see the fence and a road on the inside paralleling the one we were on. Shortly after that the overrun tarmac to runway twenty-nine was visible and right where the runway started I could see our jet waiting with the door open and the front steps down. Rodger jerked the wheel to the right and we plowed through yet another security fence with barbed wire on top. We raced up the asphalt to within fifty feet of the plane. Rodger swung the car sideways to provide cover and stopped. We tumbled out.

"Rog, I think I see the car that was following us," I said, pointing back the way we'd come.

"Run, buddy," he said, scooping Judy into his arms and jogging for the plane.

I watched the car that had been chasing us bounce off the road and over the gap in the fence that we had just created. As it crossed the concertina wire I heard all four of its tires blow out.

It ground to a halt about five hundred feet away as its tires completely disintegrated. Two guys piled out and started running toward us. They were armed with pistols.

Poison's four muscle guys were at the steps of the plane facing toward us with their Uzis ready. Rodger had already climbed into the plane with Judy and I was just starting up the steps when the bad guys started shooting. Our guys with Uzis clearly wanted to return fire, but both Poison and Hakeem were between them and the targets. Given the extreme distance coupled with them trying to shoot while running, we should have been fine, but one of those one-in-a-million-chances reared up and slapped us. Hakeem took a round to the leg and fell to the tarmac. I climbed back down the steps and started back toward him. Poison looked over her shoulder to see why I was running the wrong way. She whirled and ran back to his side.

"Leave me and go," Hakeem said to her. "I have diplomatic immunity."

"Do you really think that's going to keep these guys from killing you?" Poison asked, trying to pull him up.

"Just save yourself, I'll be all right," he insisted.

"You fucking macho Arabs are all alike," she said in disgust. She let go of his arm, straightened up, pulled her nine millimeter Sig Sauer P226 Blackwater from her shoulder holster, took a shooter's stance and fired. The guy on the right dropped like a stone. She carefully shifted her aim, fired again and the other one was down.

"Now will you come?" she asked sweetly.

With her on one side of Hakeem and me on the other we helped him as he hobbled on one leg to the plane. The four guards climbed in behind us and one of the cute stewardesses pulled the door closed just as the captain turned the jet onto the runway and pushed the throttles to full stop.

I looked out the window as we lifted off and saw a convoy of three military vehicles racing down the parallel taxiway trying to intercept us. The one in the rear had a fifty caliber machine gun mounted on the back, which the gunner tried to bring to bear, but with the relative speeds and the bouncing of the truck our luck held and none of the rounds hit. The pilot kept the plane on full throttle longer than normal to climb us out of danger. We banked toward the Mediterranean and, as we crossed the coastline, the pilot pushed the nose over in order to increase our groundspeed and decrease the time before we entered international airspace. Five minutes later, when we were clearly out of Libyan airspace, the pilot turned toward Morocco and started a gradual climb. We all began to relax.

The bullet that brought Hakeem down had gone cleanly through his calf. Poison demonstrated another side of her character by using her stealth knife to slice Hakeem's pant leg off at the knee, getting out the first aid kit, applying disinfectant, antibiotic and expertly bandaging the wound. She sat back with a satisfied look.

"I told you to leave me," Hakeem said. "Why didn't you obey?"

"I'm not your wife, I don't have to," she snapped.

"And if you were?" Hakeem asked. "Would you have obeyed me then?"

"Probably not," she said. "I'm not good at taking orders from men when the course of action they are suggesting isn't the best."

"I have diplomatic immunity. They would not have harmed me," he said.

"You keep on believing that and it's going to get you killed," she said.

"They wouldn't dare to…"

"Did you see the machine gun firing at us as we left the ground?" Poison asked.

"Yes."

"Don't they know that this is your father's plane?" Poison asked.

"Of course."

"That's my point," she said. "In the heat of things people will ignore what is right. It is easier to ask for forgiveness."

Hakeem was silent for almost a minute digesting her remark. Finally his shoulders relaxed and he smiled and nodded.

"Well… I guess you have a point. Thank you… Poison," he said.

"My real name is Fatima," she said softly.

"Daughter of the Prophet," Hakeem said. "That is a very pretty name."

I could see the beginnings of a blush start up Fatima's neck and I opened my mouth to say something when I was interrupted by Rodger jumping from his seat and rushing forward.

"Hakeem," he said urgently. "Have the co-pilot get out of his seat."

Hakeem snapped a short sentence in Arabic to the co-pilot who quickly unbuckled, climbed out of his seat and stepped by us with a puzzled look on his face.

"What's going on, Rodger," Hakeem asked.

"I just had a premonition," Rodger said, pushing his way on to the flight deck and climbing in the co-pilots seat. "Buckle up."

"Premonition?" Hakeem asked.

"Daryl will explain. Buckle up!" Rodger shouted, buckling himself in and grabbing the controls.

Hakeem looked to me to explain. I opened my mouth and all hell broke loose. Rodger banked the plane sharply to the left, pulled the throttles back and pushed the nose down into a dive. Just as he did tracer rounds flew by above and to the right. They hit exactly the spot where we would have been if Rodger hadn't taken over. The cabin lights went out as Rodger cut power to all unnecessary electrical systems, killed the navigation lights and turned off the transponder. I watched a MIG 23 Flogger streak by, following the path of the bullets and still shooting. We spiraled down toward the water in a steep dive for five thousand feet before Rodger began easing us out of it, gradually increasing the throttles. We leveled off five hundred feet above the water.

Looking out my window I could still see the navigation lights of the MIG as it circled about ten thousand feet above us. Rodger flipped a switch and excited voices in Arabic came over the cabin speakers. It was plainly radio traffic between the MIG and ground control.

"What are they saying?" I asked Hakeem.

"The pilot of the MIG is telling his controllers that he intercepted the infidel and shot him down," Hakeem said. "He claims that he strafed us and we went out of control. He says he saw us spiral into the ocean."

"And they believe him?" I asked.

"He is up here alone and thanks to Rodger and his abrupt dive we went off of Libyan radar. What they see electronically jibes with what he is saying so yes, they believe him," Hakeem said.

"That's great," I said, "but why infidel?"

"That is a word used by Muslims to describe all non-Muslims," he explained.

"Don't they know that you are on board and who the plane belongs to?" I asked.

"Of course they do," he said, "but they also know that… infidels are a part of this and that…"

He trailed off at a loss for words then looked at Fatima and shook his head.

"I'm sorry," he said.

It took a moment for her to understand that the apology was directed at her. When she did she reacted.

"What?"

"I said I'm sorry," he said.

"Wow. An Arab man telling a mere woman he's sorry," she said sarcastically.

"Fatima, I see that you were right that they probably would have killed me and I apologize for being stupid," he said.

You could see the sarcastic reply bubble up. She bit it down.

"You're welcome," she said, then turned, walked to the rear of the plane and sat down in the last seat.

Hakeem followed her with his eyes and after she sat down he got up and limped down the aisle to sit next to her.

ChapterTWENTY-THREE

We landed in Marrakesh early in the morning and taxied directly to the Wazir's hanger where the doors closed behind us. The Wazir decided that the best course of action was to paint over the registration numbers on the plane with new ones and deny that either his plane or his son had ever been to Libya.

Evidently during the rest of the night Gaddafi had gone on television to speak about the 'serious attempt on his life by American imperialists.' He was very proud of how his 'brilliantly trained forces' had managed to thwart the 'sustained and brutal attack.'

The pilot who was credited with shooting us down was being hailed as a great hero. According to the CNN report he had 'engaged the infidel in a fierce dogfight from which, due to his superior training, preparation and flying skills, he had emerged triumphant'. CNN had a crew reporting from Tripoli with video showing the fences we had mown down, the truck that rolled behind us, and the car with the two dead bodies at the airport. According to the news, Gaddafi had been lucky to escape with his life. The talking heads went on about whether this had been a CIA operation or perhaps ordered by the President of the United States. I had to shake my head at how badly the reporters had been duped.

The Wazir was waiting in the entrance drive when we finally reached the palace. We all piled out except for Judy who had slept all the way from Libya, only rousing enough to stumble to the car and then fall back deep asleep. I was anxious to hear her story and put the last piece of the puzzle together, but a few more hours wasn't really going to matter.

"Quite an adventure, my friends," the Wazir said, greeting us warmly. "I thank you for returning my son still mostly in one piece."

"It was a freak accident, Achmed," I explained, embarrassed that we might have been to blame for getting his son badly injured.

"So I was told by my son," he said.

"They were at least two hundred and fifty feet away, shooting wildly," I said. "It was just one of those things."

"And yet this young lady managed to shoot both of them at almost the same distance," he said, gesturing at Fatima. "That sounds like some very impressive shooting."

Fatima was plainly uncomfortable with the Wazir's words. She nodded her acceptance of his praise but didn't speak.

"My son tells me that you did it to save his life," the Wazir pressed.

That got a reaction. She turned and looked at Hakeem.

"You told your father that I saved your life?" she asked.

"No, I told him that I was being a typical stupid macho male who thought everything would be okay and that you weren't willing to leave me to die," he said.

I don't know what she was planning to say, but that took the wind out of her sails. She closed her mouth and dropped her eyes. The Wazir stepped to where she was standing, took her chin and forced her to look up.

"I would like to thank you, young lady," he said. "My son means everything to me."

"Umm," she said neutrally.

"I'm sure you know who I am," he said, "but allow me to formally introduce myself. I am Wazir Achmed Baakam al Saadin."

"Poison," she said, "Assalam o alaykum."

"Poison?" the Wazir said, startled.

"Yes."

She smiled.

"Oh my," the Wazir said.

"Surprised?" Fatima asked coyly.

"That would be an understatement," Achmed said.

"You thought I was a man," Fatima said.

"And older," Achmed agreed.

"Can someone tell us what you two are talking about?" Hakeem asked.

"Do you remember that serious drug problem we were having about a year ago?" he asked Hakeem. "You were out of the country but I know I discussed it with you."

"Vaguely."

"Drug smugglers enlisted the help of the Tuareg to revitalize the old salt trade caravan route from Marrakesh to Timbuktu," Achmed explained. "They…"

"Wait, what are Tuareg?" I interrupted.

"The Tuareg are a nomadic Berber tribe that has lived in the Sahara for thousands of years," the Wazir said. "Because of their vast knowledge of the desert they were the guides of the Sahara. During the eighth to the sixteenth centuries they led the caravans that left Marrakesh carrying salt across the Saraha to Timbuktu in Mali, returning with gold."

"Timbuktu?" I asked.

"There really is such a place," the Wazir said. "It is known in your world as the end of the earth because of its location on the edge of the Sahara. It truly is the end of the earth in some respects, but at one point it was the center of the intellectual and spiritual propagation of Islam throughout Africa. The first university in the world is thought to have been founded there."

"Oh."

"Anyway, the smugglers revived the route. Instead of salt from Marrakesh the camels carried cash or gold, and instead of gold from Timbuktu the camels returned with drugs, mainly hashish or cannabis resin, from the interior of Africa," he explained.

"What does that have to do with you and Poison," Hakeem asked.

"I'm getting to that," Achmed said.

"Okay."

"We knew that the drugs were flowing in via some route from the south, but none of our normal police work was able to turn up anything. The King was getting more and more frustrated with the lack of progress. Every now and then we would manage to intercept a shipping container on its way to Europe, but that just made us aware of how much we were missing," Achmed said.

"Finally, the King formed a new task force and put me in charge," Achmed continued. "He told me he didn't care how I did it, but it had to stop and that's how I met Poison."

"Because of drugs?" Hakeem asked.

"Because I had to move our thinking outside of the box," his father said. "One of our tech guys got on the internet and found a firm that advertized that they specialized in providing 'special solutions to special needs.' The website claimed that they could trace missing loved ones, provide surveillance, help with 'identity problems', which I assumed was a euphemism for providing fake ID, supply bodyguards and armed escorts, do undercover investigative work and... well, the list went on and on. Anyway, we contacted them and asked if they might be able to assist us and that's where Poison came into the picture."

"So she had her firm investigate?" Hakeem asked.

"I hired them to do a preliminary look and tell us what they thought," Achmed said. "Poison got back to me and told me that they had discovered the caravan route, but the only way to really put them out of business was to infiltrate their organization and catch them coming into the country from Mali with the product."

"But how would you know?" I asked. "The Sahara is so vast and there are so many routes and…"

"We needed someone who was with the caravan to signal us," he said. "Poison volunteered."

I looked at the pretty, slight, thirty year old girl with increased respect. The trip each way in the desert had to be two weeks, plus another week at least in Timbuktu. To make that trip in itself was something, but to do it in a group of dangerous men, and not be discovered as either a spy or a woman, was extraordinary.

"Wow," I said.

"Yes, wow, Daryl," he agreed. "And especially now that I find out that…"

"I'm a mere woman?" Fatima said coldly.

"A woman you are, young lady, but I will never make the mistake of underestimating you again," the Wazir said. "Thank you for that service and again for saving my son."

Fatima dipped her head in acknowledgement.

"What about the gang?" I asked. "How did that go?"

"We caught every one of them except the main boss who wasn't on that trip," Achmed said. "The one leader we caught who knows the boss's identity refuses to roll over, so we don't know who he is and if he's still free."

"I've been meaning to contact your people about that," Fatima said. "I've done some more work on my own and I'm pretty sure I know who he is and that he is putting together another operation."

"Wonderful," Achmed said. "Now that you'll be a regular here at the palace we can talk about that and plan how to move against him."

"A regular at the palace?" Fatima asked.

"If the look on my son's face means anything," Achmed said.

Fatima blushed but didn't protest.

"Where… where are we?" a sleepy voice said.

I turned and Judy was climbing out of the SUV, wiping her eyes and trying to hold the afghan around her. The Wazir clapped his hands and two female servants appeared to assist her. I was dying to learn how he did that.

Chapter TWENTY-FOUR

"Do you want to talk about it?" I asked.

We were in the Wazir's living room, which was the size of a small home in the United States. The forty foot south facing wall was all glass and looked out on an exquisitely groomed garden with palm trees, flowers and a huge fountain.

Rodger and I were seated on the twelve foot long couch that faced the window with Achmed and Hakeem flanking us on two overstuffed chairs. On the opposing couch were Judy and Fatima. The staff had found her a very pretty Jilbab (a hooded floor length robe worn by Muslim women around the world). Even though she was now dressed and the windows were open to the balmy Marrakesh weather, Judy was shivering, rocking back and forth and keening softly. Her arms were wrapped around her body like she was freezing. Fatima was gently patting her shoulders and crooning in her ear. I waited but she hadn't seemed to have heard me.

"Judy? Are you okay?" I asked softly.

She stopped rocking and looked at me. The bleak look in her eyes was more than enough to send a shiver down my spine.

The fixer part of me wanted to make it right but I didn't have a clue how.

"I'm never going to be alright," she said.

I moved to where I could kneel in front of her.

"Of course you are," I reassured her.

"No, Daryl," she said. "I'm going to live and I'm going to go on with my life, but some part of me is never going to be right."

"I'm sorry," I said.

"It isn't your fault," she said. "It's…"

Her voice trailed off and she went off into her own private world. We waited in silence until she returned.

"At first I couldn't believe it," she said. "And then I…"

More silence.

"Thank you for rescuing me," she said, slowly looking into each of our eyes. "I know I seemed cavalier when you found me, but I had given up hope and it was my way of dealing with my personal hell."

"Oh, Judy," I said, reaching out and touching her knee.

I saw her body tense up with my touch and I immediately withdrew my hand. She looked at me with tears in her eyes.

"I'm sorry," she said, "but that's part of what I mean. I don't think I will ever bear to have a man touch me again."

I couldn't help the tears that started in my eyes.

"Judy," I said, "I know that it is going to be painful to remember, but we need your help. The reason that we came after you is because our friend Brad was killed and…"

"Brad's dead?" Judy asked.

"You knew Brad?"

"It's a long story," she said. "He's dead?"

"Yes. We think he was killed by someone from Sonic Ping because he discovered something…"

"Those fucking bastards," Judy said.

"He was looking for you just before he had his accident," I said.

"He had an accident?" Judy asked.

"That's what the cops think, but we have good reason to believe now that it wasn't," I said.

"He came looking for me?" she asked.

"Yes. At Teasers," I said.

"Did he get the key?" she asked.

"The key?"

"I gave a key to one of the other girls to give to him," she explained. "I told her he'd give her two hundred dollars for it."

That explained the ATM, except it looked as if when he tried to buy it the girl had held him up for another two hundred.

"I think so," I said. "What does it look like?"

"It's a special security key like the kind you see on pop machines," she said.

"Yes."

"So they caught the bastards?" she asked.

"No, Judy. As I was saying the reason that we came after you was that our friend Brad was killed and we believe that you are the answer to everything that has happened."

"So he didn't use the material?" she asked.

"Judy, I know you've been through a lot, but could you start at the beginning and fill us in?" I asked.

Her eyes got a faraway look for a minute and then she nodded.

"Do you know Mikahyl Dashkov?" she asked.

I nodded.

"He is… was my boyfriend," she said. "I have been with him for the past two years."

"Wow."

"I was in the adjoining room to his office one afternoon when Brad pushed his way past security," she said. "I could hear everything."

"Brad was in Mikahyl's office at Sonic Ping?" Rodger asked.

"Yes. Brad was going on about how he had proof that Sonic Ping's pay-per-click revenue was mostly a scam," she said. "He claimed that he had set up a site to demonstrate and he was trying to get Mikahyl to understand how it was being done."

"Did Mikahyl realize what Brad was driving at?" I asked.

"Oh, he got it alright," she said, "but he pretended like there was no way that such a scam could work."

"I wouldn't have believed it either," I said, "if I hadn't seen it working."

"Look," she said seriously. "Mikahyl Dashkov is one of the most brilliant computer geniuses in the world. He not only understood it was possible he knew it was being done because he was the one doing it."

"What?" both Rodger and I said simultaneously.

"Mikahyl is the one scamming his own company," she said, "but let me finish."

"Sure."

"Brad got mad when Mikahyl wouldn't listen to him so he stormed out. I snuck out the side door and followed him," she said. "I caught up to him in the parking lot, introduced myself and explained that I knew what he was trying to explain to Mikahyl and had proof that he was involved."

"What did Brad say?" I asked.

"He was flabbergasted," she said. "He couldn't believe that Mikahyl would be scamming his own company. He thought he was doing Sonic Ping a favor to let them know that they were being taken."

I couldn't believe it either so I asked, "Why was he doing it?"

"Because some is never enough for Mikahyl," she said. "He has some big investors in Sonic Ping who are mostly Russian Mafia so, even though the company is worth billions, only a small portion of that is really his. This was a way for him to skim billions off the top just for himself. Besides, the inflated revenue stream pumped up the value of Sonic Ping so it was a win win situation for him."

"I see."

"Of course as people got close to his secret he felt obligated to cross more and more lines to protect his good life, which finally included murdering people," she said.

"You know for a fact that he has been involved in arranging for people to be killed?" I asked.

"Yes.

"Wow."

"Yes, wow. So you can see that when Brad understood the whole picture he realized that he had placed himself in a very dangerous position by telling Mikahyl what he discovered. He had to get the authorities involved right away before Mikahyl did something rash," she said.

"Like having him killed?" I said.

"Exactly," she said, "so we arranged to meet at Teasers. I was going to give him the key to where I stashed the file I compiled, including passwords to all of Mikahyl's accounts."

"Why Teasers?" I asked.

"Because I was a regular there and I thought we would be safe," she said. "It was one of the few places where I was confident that Mikahyl didn't keep tabs on me."

"Why did you give the key to your friend?" Rodger asked.

"I was standing in the main room and saw the head of Sonic Ping security come into Teasers and…"

"You mean Victor?" Rodger asked.

"Yes. I just knew that something had gone terribly wrong, so before he saw me, I gave the key away," she explained. "It turns out I was right because a few minutes later Victor came over and told me that Selma wanted to see me downstairs in the office and…"

"You know Selma?" I interrupted.

"I'm a regular there," Judy said. "Of course I know Selma. She's one of the owners. Why do you ask?"

"You won't believe the string of coincidences that tie us together, but I'll fill you in later," I said. "First, just tell us what happened."

"I went down to the office and Jerry was there instead of Selma. Then two big guys came out of the back room and I was forced into a shipping crate," she said. "I woke up on some stage in the Middle East being sold to some drooling Arab."

"Africa," I corrected.

"Huh?"

"The auction was in Morocco in North Africa," I explained.

"Whatever."

"So Brad came to Teasers and couldn't find you, asked around, found your friend who sold him the key, and then before he could retrieve the material he was killed," I said.

"And, instead of having me killed, Mikahyl arranged to have me sold into the hell you guys rescued me from," Judy said.

"How good is your information?" Rodger asked, getting back to the subject.

"Iron clad," she said without hesitation.

"Who would be implicated?" Rodger asked.

"Besides Mikahyl and Victor and a few other Sonic Ping employees?"

"Yes."

"About half of the Pingree police force," she said.

"You're kidding," I said.

"No."

"For a pay-per-click scam?"

"No, the police force was involved either directly or indirectly by covering up all of the other things like murder, conspiracy, racketeering, white slavery, you name it."

"Wait a minute," I said. "If you knew that was going on why didn't you go to..."

"Look," she said. "Before I tell you the rest of my story, why don't you fill me in on what happened after Mikahyl took me out of the picture."

"Fair enough," I said.

I thought back on the phone call that had started everything. It had been less than two weeks ago.

"Just after our friend Brad was killed in what we thought was an accident," I started, "someone from Sonic Ping began calling his wife looking for money and some important papers."

"You originally thought his death was an accident?" she asked.

"Yes, but later on we found out his brake lines were severed," I said.

"I see," she said.

"When they didn't get what they wanted they kidnapped his wife's niece, Jennifer, which is where we got involved," I said.

"Do you have proof of the kidnapping?" Judy asked.

"Yes. Why?"

"Never mind right now just keep going," she said.

"Rodger traced where she was being held and managed to get her back," I said. "But the trail was cold because the guy was deported and…"

"The local cops didn't want to get involved."

"Right."

"So, then what happened?"

"We poked around and found Brad's laptop, notebook and the key," I said.

"So you figured out the scam from that," she said.

"Eventually," I said, "but not before they tried to kill me and killed my wife instead."

"How?"

"The same thing with the brakes," I said.

"Oh, I'm sorry."

"After they killed her they got really nasty and decided to 'send a message' by kidnapping Brad's wife and selling her into slavery," I said. "Rodger traced her cell phone to Teasers, and that's how I met Selma and found out about the back room where the girls were prepared for being shipped…"

I let my voice trail off as I realized I had to be bringing up bad memories for her.

"The type of situation you rescued me from," she said.

"Yes."

"Then?"

"Rodger had to kill a Sonic Ping guy who was just about to shoot me in the forehead and we ended up in jail for murder," I continued. "One of the detectives came to our cell to 'move' us in the middle of the night. We were forced to escape to save ourselves, and now we're fugitives."

"Bruce Kirkwood?" she asked.

"How the hell did you know that?" I asked.

"Just finish, please," she said.

"We were confident that you were the key to unraveling this mess so we flew over here to extract you," I said. "Luckily, the young lady sitting next to you is very good at what she does. We managed to get you out in one piece without losing anyone."

"Yes, you can't believe how grateful I am. I'd completely given up hope," she said.

"Judy," Rodger said. "Why didn't you go to somebody like the FBI when you discovered how twisted Mikahyl was? I know that you were in love with him, but covering up for murder makes you an accessory. We are going to have to report you."

I cringed. She had just gone through a horrible time, and while he was right, it seemed insensitive to bring up her short-comings and threaten her. Her head snapped up, and the fire in her eyes would have ignited a drenched campfire in monsoon season.

"*In love* with him?" she said. "I fucking hate the guy. He's an egotistical, overbearing asshole computer geek. I was just doing my job."

"Y-your job?" I stuttered.

"I'm a deep cover FBI agent," she said. "I've been after Mikahyl for four years. I worked at Sonic Ping as a secretary for two before I managed to seduce him and take over his former girlfriend's spot."

Of all the things I expected her to say that wasn't it. I looked over at Rodger and saw a little smirk on his face. He must have suspected her real identity and was just baiting her.

"You knew?" I accused Rodger.

"Not exactly who she worked for, but it was kind of obvious from her manner and the kind of questions she was asking that she was enforcement."

I thought about that. He was right. All of the clues had been there. I mean who gets rescued from the brutal life she was living and bothers to ask anything but *am I really safe?* and *when can I go home?*"

"What's our next step?" I asked.

My question had been directed at Rodger, but it was Judy who spoke.

"Do you still have the key?" she asked.

I looked at Rodger for guidance. He nodded.

"Yes," I said.

"If I told my office where the material was located they could easily break into the box that contains my evidence against Mikahyl, Victor and Sonic Ping without the key, but using it helps maintain our chain of evidence," she said. "How can I get it?"

"I can make a phone call and have it delivered," Rodger said. "Where?"

"Can you have them drop it off at the Boston FBI field office?" she asked.

"Who should they ask for?" Rodger asked.

"Special Agent Brandon Nichols," she said. "He's my controller and has been my only contact point with the Agency for the past four years."

"Judy, you've been missing for more than two months," I said. "Shouldn't he be going crazy worrying about you because you haven't reported in?"

"I only report in as necessary, to avoid someone blowing my cover," she said. "Even so, you have a point. When an agent's safety is a serious concern, we terminate an operation."

She thought for a minute.

"Actually, you're right, she said. "By now he should have raided Sonic Ping to find me, even if it meant that we compromised the entire operation and Mikahyl gets off without being charged."

"Why do you think he didn't?" Rodger asked.

"I don't know," she said. "He knows I'm resourceful so maybe he's giving me time."

She stopped again and I could see the wheels turn.

"The thing is, they have continuous loose surveillance on Mikahyl so they have to know I haven't been on his arm. They have to know I'm missing."

"Have you thought about the other possibility of why he hasn't blown the whistle?" Rodger asked.

"What other possibility?"

"That Mikahyl found out about the operation and turned your partner," Rodger suggested.

"I've known Brandon for ten years," she said, shaking her head. "He is a straight shooter. I can't imagine that happening."

"Which part?" Rodger asked. "That Mikahyl found out or that your partner got flipped?"

"Well, the first part is a definite possibility," she said. "For want of a better term, Mikahyl is 'hacker grade' when it comes to computers. He can and has hacked into every important computer system in the world just for fun and has never been caught doing it. For him to have hacked into the FBI computer system and discovered everything about the operation is a definite possibility."

"But you don't think your partner could have been corrupted?" Rodger asked.

"I guess at some level everyone can be corrupted, so considering that Mikahyl could have offered him more money than anyone could imagine possessing in ten lifetimes, yes it's possible," she said.

"So, what do we do?" I asked.

"Can I make a suggestion?" Rodger asked.

"Sure," Judy said.

"Let's call him and see how he reacts when you tell him that you've wrapped up the investigation and will be getting your package of proof to the federal prosecutor," Rodger said.

"How will that help us figure out if he's part of this?" Judy asked.

"If he's still on your side he'll want to help you and will be open to doing whatever you suggest," Rodger said.

"And if he's not?" she asked.

"He'll want to control you," Rodger said. "He'll probably want you to give him the information to keep it safe. For sure he will want to know where you are and if you've told anyone else and so on."

"But if I call him and he's in bed with Mikahyl he'll be able to trace where I am," she protested. "They'll send someone, won't they?"

"Don't worry," Rodger said. "We'll use an internet protocol similar to Skype so that he won't have any idea where you are."

ChapterTWENTY-FIVE

Thirty minutes later Rodger had an internet phone system set up that was totally untraceable. Anyone we called would see on caller ID a call coming from the Boston area, and if they tried to dig further that is all that would come up. After he had it set and tested he turned it over to Judy who dialed the emergency contact number she'd previously established with Brandon. He picked up on the second ring.

"Judy?" a surprised voice answered.

"You sound shocked to hear my voice, Brandon, who else did you expect to call?" Judy asked.

"No one but you has this number, but I..."

"What?"

"Where are you?" he asked.

"In a safe place," she said. "I've been putting the final details together on the case."

"But I thought..."

"Yes?"

"The final details?"

"Correct. I finally have everything we need," she said. "I have enough proof of various felonies to put Mikahyl and his people away for a very long time."

"You do?"

"More than enough," Judy said.

"We should meet," Brandon said.

"Why?"

"So you can fill me in and we can discuss strategy," he said.

"That's not necessary, Brandon," she said. "I've got everything handled. It would be foolish at this point to take a chance like that."

"I'll be the judge of that," he said.

"Pardon me?"

"I'm the leader of this team," he said, "and I think we need a face to face where I can put my hands on your evidence and make a judgment as to how to proceed."

"Brandon…"

"Look, Judy, you've been so close to this that you aren't aware of the big picture and how this case affects multiple things that the bureau is working on,' he said.

"Really? Like what?"

"I can't tell you over the phone," he said. "Just trust me, this is big and I need your findings to really break things wide open."

"My findings are going to break things wide open," she said. "That's what I'm trying to tell you."

"How many copies have you made?" he asked.

"Copies? What difference does that make?"

"How many?"

"I just have my original notes," she said.

"Who have you shared your findings with?" he asked.

"You."

"Just me?" he asked.

"Brandon, I'm in deep cover," she said in frustration. "Who the fuck else would I have shared that information with?"

"There is no need to get testy with me, Judy, we are both on the same side," he said. "I'm just thinking ahead."

"Are we?" she asked.

"Are we what?"

"On the same side?"

"Of course."

"Oh."

"Are you being sarcastic, Judy?"

"Not yet."

"Well, I need for you to meet me and give me everything you have," he said.

"You do?"

"Yes."

"And then what?"

"What do you mean?" he asked.

"Then what do I do?" she asked.

"Lay low until I put the case together and nail these guys," Brandon said.

"Why don't I just copy what I've got and send it to all of the major networks and the federal prosecutor so we can be sure that..."

"Are you brain dead?" Brandon said. "The news networks will twist this around, crucify us, and Mikahyl will get off."

"Brandon, I'm not ready to come in from the cold yet and, when I am, I'm perfectly capable of doing what is necessary to bring indictments against everyone involved."

"Judy, I'm ordering you as your boss to arrange to meet me. Bring me your files or else your career at the bureau is over."

"Really?"

"This is a matter of national security, Judy," he said.

"Wow, national security, wow."

"Are you being cute?" he asked.

"That's not cute, that's sarcastic," Judy said.

"Whatever it is, I don't like it."

"Well I don't like you ordering me about," she said.

"Look, I'm not going to argue with you," he said. "I need you to arrange to meet me."

"No."

"What?"

"I said, no, Brandon."

"Judy, this is not negotiable. I need you to…"

"Bye, Brandon," Judy interrupted, pushing the disconnect button.

She sat back from the computer with an angry look on her face. Rodger swiveled the computer and let his fingers go.

"Daryl, something's wrong," she said.

Before I could respond the computer screen came to life. It showed a fuzzy picture of a guy with a cell phone up to his ear. Judy looked at it and then turned to me.

"That's Brandon," she said. "What's going on?"

"Just listen," Rodger said.

"Mikahyl? Yeah, it's Brandon. I thought you said… No, I'm in my office. Mikahyl, I thought you said that Judy was taken care of."

Brandon stood up and moved out of our view, but we could still hear his side of the conversation. Rodger was busy on his own laptop.

"I just spoke with her," Brandon said.

Rodger sat back with a satisfied smile and said, "I should have guessed. That third Sonic Ping number is Mikahyl's cell phone."

"Well, she isn't in some fucking Arab's dungeon," Brandon said. "She's somewhere in the Boston area putting together a case against you and I tried to get her to come in and…"

Brandon stopped in mid sentence, moved back into our view and sat down, listening. I looked at Rodger and cocked my head. He smiled.

"That's a little program that can go into someone's laptop and turn on their web cam and microphone," he explained.

"So, as long as he sits here we can monitor what he plans to do?" I asked.

"Well… actually, I used his cell to trace where he called and that's what I meant about the other Sonic Ping number," he said. "We can listen in to all of their calls."

"Wow."

"Look, Mikahyl," Brandon said, "it's not my fault that your little scheme to punish her with a life of hell backfired. Why didn't you just have her killed like the rest of…"

Brandon stopped talking again. I looked questioningly at Rodger.

"I'm working on getting the other side of the conversation," he said, his fingers a blur on the keyboard.

Brandon hung up in a rage and slammed his notebook closed. Our audio and video disappeared. Judy looked shell shocked, head down and moving slowly from side to side. Without thinking I reached out and patted her shoulder. She didn't flinch.

ChapterTWENTY-SIX

"I can't believe it," Judy said, when she finally spoke.

"Which part?" Rodger asked. "The fact that Mikahyl found Brandon and corrupted him, or that your friend and partner of ten years – who has pledged an oath to preserve, protect and defend the constitution of the United States – thinks that Mikahyl should have killed you?"

That startled her out of her self-pity. I could see the flint return to her eyes and watched her back straighten.

"Get on with my life, huh?" she asked.

"Or let them beat you," he said.

"So, do you have another Plan B for us?" she asked.

"I do," Rodger said.

"I'm listening."

"Look," Rodger said, "over the years Daryl and I have made a lot of friends or at least trustworthy acquaintances in the Justice Department, the FBI, many state and local law enforcement departments, the TSA, the ATF and even the Secret Service. I think that we need to use them to…"

"Wait a minute," Judy said. "How is using one of your contacts going to be more secure than using my partner, which clearly would have been really dumb? It seems to me that one of your friends, even ones that owe you big time, are just as susceptible to being corrupted as my partner and then…"

"You're right."

"Huh?"

"They would be just as vulnerable," he said.

"So, what are you suggesting?"

"I think we should get a friend of ours that we know we can trust to retrieve your material, take it to Kinko's, make dozens of copies, and then distribute it to all enforcement people we know and trust. We'll also send copies to select U.S. Senators and congressmen and a few major media outlets," Rodger said. "Let's get the cat so far out of the bag that even Mikahyl with his billions can't put it back again."

"Let's start with the first part of that sentence," she said. "We are still going to depend on a friend that you know you can trust. Just why are you so sure that we can trust this friend of yours?"

"Well… in addition to the fact that he is a cop who has been friends with Daryl and me since childhood, Mikahyl sent someone who almost killed him, stole his girlfriend and had Victor ship her off to be sold," Rodger explained. "We rescued her last week, just before we came looking for you. I don't think Mikahyl would have a prayer of changing his mind."

"It's still a risk," Judy said.

"Why do you say that?" I asked.

"I've got a lot of stuff stashed," she said. "Proof of things that will put Mikahyl away forever, but it's one of a kind stuff, and if he intercepts your friend before they can get it copied and distributed, there is no case."

"I don't think that will be an issue," Rodger said. "Our friend comes with a tank."

"A tank?"

"Another friend," I said. "But your point is valid."

I turned to Rodger and nodded at the laptop, "Why don't we ask him how things are?"

Rodger tapped a few lines on the keyboard and within seconds the phone was answered by Tiny's gravelly voice.

"Cute, Rodger," he said, "but I doubt you are in Sri Lanka."

"True, but you knew it was me," Rodger said. "How's Dan?"

"He's moving around pretty well," Tiny said, "considering how agitated he is about being out of action and the problems he's having with his partner."

"Problems?"

"The guy was hounding us every few hours about something or another," Tiny explained. "It didn't make sense. It was as if he was checking up on us. I finally moved us into hiding."

"So he doesn't know where you are?" Rodger asked.

"I didn't say that," Tiny said. "He might know, but at least he's leaving us alone."

"Tiny, I need you to do something for me that is going to be dangerous if they follow you," Rodger said.

"And the fate of the free world depends on my success as usual?" Tiny asked.

"This time for real," Rodger answered.

"I'm listening."

"Can you move on this right away?"

"Yes. Why?"

"Because I have to assume that the other side is listening," Rodger said.

"Really?" Tiny said. "That is something for you to say, Rodger, because I didn't think there was anyone better than you."

"Tiny, there is always someone better."

"It still says a lot," Tiny said.

"Can you move or not?"

"Rodger," I interrupted, "I don't like the sound of this. We only get one shot at this and if they have Tiny covered and intercept him we are going to end up as fugitives from a trumped up murder charge that we have no hope of getting out from under. We can be there ourselves in eight hours. There's strength in numbers."

Rodger looked at Hakeem and lifted an eyebrow. Hakeem glanced at his father who nodded.

"We can leave within the hour," Hakeem said. "I will alert the pilot."

"Weapons?" Rodger asked.

"We came back from Algeria with quite a few," I said.

"And I can have whatever else you need delivered to the airport," Poison added.

"Tiny, can you and Dan pick up a couple of SUV's, get on the move, and make sure you don't have a tail?" Rodger asked.

"Not a problem," he said. "Call me on my backup cell."

"See you in about ten hours," Rodger said, disconnecting.

ChapterTWENTY-SEVEN

I woke up six hours into the flight. Rodger and Judy were awake and hunched over a laptop.

"What's going on, Rog?" I asked.

"In order to get us into the States without getting arrested I was planning on a maneuver similar to what we did going over to Europe where we drop down and get lost," he said, "but Judy says that they have special radar that will track us. If we try something like that they'll scramble fighters and we'll be forced to land where they want us to and be met with police and FBI."

"Sounds like we need another plan B," I said.

"Yes, and luckily Judy has a way for us to enter undetected."

"Really?"

Judy looked up from the keyboard and said, "Our government has identified several special corridors or flight paths where, if you fly an exact sequence of headings and altitudes, an incoming plane can evade detection."

"Why wouldn't the government plug loopholes like that?" I asked.

"They aren't something that a normal smuggler would stumble on by accident and they are very useful when... well, if you think about it I'm sure you can think of ways they could be used," she said.

"So you know one of these?" I asked.

"No, not from memory," she said, "but I remember the codes to access a server where they are stored."

"Won't that send up a red flag when you log in?" I asked.

"It would, but I'm using my old boss's login," she said.

"Old boss?"

"Before I went undercover."

"Wouldn't he have changed it?" I asked.

"Of course," she said, "but he's one of those old guys who hate to remember new passwords, so he only has two and bounces back and forth between them every time the IT people make him change."

"Oh."

She turned to the keyboard and typed a few more lines, then sat back in satisfaction.

"I'm in."

"And?"

"Give me a second," she said, punching some more keys.

She sat back, pulled the flash drive out of the USB port, handed it to Rodger and smiled, "Put this into the autopilot."

ରଛ

Two hours later the program she downloaded took over the autopilot, and for the next thirty minutes, it was as if we were on 'Mr. Toad's Wild Ride' at Disney World. First the program turned us north on a course that aimed us at the coast about midway up the shoreline of Maine. Next, it dropped us down to a scant three hundred feet off of the water, changed headings so many times that on a highway we would have been pulled over for drunk driving. Finally, we crossed into the United States at Spruce Head, Maine. A sharp right turn to the northeast brought us just east of the Knox County Regional Airport where the program made a left turn to line up with the heading of runway 31 and put us into a climb out as if we had just lifted off. The pilot switched the transponder to VHF when we got above 800 feet and turned us left. Beverly Municipal airport was less than ten minutes away.

"Impressive," I said to Judy. "I assume that no fighter intercept means that we got away with it."

"Yes."

I looked at Rodger, "Did you let Tiny know?"

"I sent him a text as soon as I had a signal," he said. "He'll be waiting at the FBO with Dan when we arrive."

"And then?"

"And then we go to wherever Judy has the stuff stashed and get it out there."

"What about the key?" I asked.

"I sent a text to the girls also. Jennifer, Maddy and Selma are bringing it to the flight center."

"Wow, Rodger," I said. "We've opened up an awful lot of ways they can track us."

"Can't be helped," he said.

∞

The fixed base operator at Beverly Municipal airport in Massachusetts is North Atlantic Air, located on the west side of the airport. We landed on runway 34, using most of the 5000 feet, turned left on the taxiway at the end of the runway and taxied back to parking. As the crew opened the door we tumbled out. Our five friends were waiting on the tarmac. Dan had his arm around Madeline. He looked great and so did she.

"Hey," I said, waving.

They waved back. I hurried to Selma, gathered her in and kissed her. Wow!

"Are you sure you guys weren't followed?" I asked when I was able to catch my breath.

"Pretty sure," she said, pulling me in for another.

Rodger looked at Tiny and Dan, "I'm sure that you guys are also clean, but based on some things that Judy has told us I think we can expect that won't last long."

"Who's Judy?" Dan asked.

Rodger gestured, "Judy is why we went to Tripoli. It turns out she is an undercover FBI agent who was pretending to be Mikahyl Dashkov's girlfriend. She is the key to everything that has been going on."

Rodger spread his arms to encompass Tiny and Dan.

"Judy," he said, "Tiny is a friend who's looking out for Dan. Dan is a detective in the Pingree police department."

She nodded and smiled.

"Judy," Dan asked, "why do you think we'll get found and by whom?"

"Now that Mikahyl knows I'm not locked up in some sheiks dungeon he'll be using every resource he has to find me. He knows that I can bring him down," she said. "He has unlimited amounts of money and he is one of the smartest people I have ever met. He will find us."

"But, what about the FBI?" Dan asked. "If you're an agent I would think that..."

"Have you been watching CNN today?" she interrupted.

"No."

"I have, during the last hour of the trip," Judy said. "Mikahyl and my FBI partner concocted a story about how I'm a rogue agent, armed and dangerous. My former boss, other agents who have worked with me and even people who I thought were close friends are speaking out about how they always knew that there was something wrong with me and so on. Essentially they are trying to get any law enforcement that catches sight of me to shoot first and ask questions later."

"But..."

"What? How do they trick a news organization into believing something like that without fact checking first?" she asked.

Dan looked sheepish, shook his head in disgust, "Yeah."

"I already found out that I can't trust my partner," she said. "Now I don't dare go to anyone else as Mikahyl might have gotten to them or they might believe the crap that's out there and…"

Dan turned to Rodger, "When you asked us to meet you here you clearly had an idea of how to go about getting us all out of this mess, so what's the plan?"

"Brute force," Rodger said. "Pile in the SUVs you brought and stick together while we pick up Judy's evidence, get it copied and sent out. Once the stuff is in enough other people's hands it will speak for itself. We only have to stay alive long enough for Mikahyl to realize that he's been beaten."

Dan looked at Maddy with alarm.

"Rodger," Dan said, "if you are so sure that they are out to kill us, shouldn't we put the women somewhere safe while we can and then expose ourselves?"

"That seems logical, Dan, but what would you do if Mikahyl got his hands on Maddy, and told you he would kill her unless you turned Judy's evidence over to him?"

The look on Dan's face said it all. He was smitten with Madeline and the thought that someone might harm her was not on any plate he wanted. He unconsciously moved closer, clutched her arm and nodded, "Good point."

"So, Judy, we're ready," Rodger said. "Where are we headed?"

Judy reacted to that question like a deer caught in the headlights. She looked like her world had been yanked from under her. I remembered how we found her, naked, alone and without hope. I couldn't help myself. I walked over and put my arms around her before I remembered how badly she had reacted to my touch in Morocco. I waited for her to freeze, but instead of rejecting me, she smiled up gratefully, her shoulders straightened and she looked at us with a bubble of amusement in her eyes.

"My apartment," she said.

"Your apartment?" I said. "Wouldn't Mikahyl have already searched it?"

"Of course. With a fine tooth comb, layer by layer, giving special attention to my panty drawer, but the stuff isn't actually in my apartment. I kept it within walking distance," she said.

"So the key is to a bank safety deposit box nearby?" I asked.

"No, Mikahyl would have discovered that," she said. "I had to find a place that I could monitor that was close but also a place that I could access twenty-four hours a day. A place that was secure but where nobody would ever think of looking. Someplace sheltered that wouldn't be stumbled over by accident."

"Not a PO box either then," I said.

"No, not that either. It's in a locked box that hundreds of people walk by each day and don't look at twice, which is why Mikahyl hasn't found it," she said. "Unfortunately it's located close enough to my apartment that we are likely to be spotted if he has my place under surveillance."

"I think we can count on him having someone watching," Rodger said, "especially now that he knows you are not in some private prison in Libya."

Judy shuddered at those words and nodded her head. I squeezed her again for reassurance. She looked at me in gratitude and it started a fire in my chest. I wanted her. Oh boy. I glanced at Selma guiltily, but she wasn't looking at me.

"Assuming that's the case, we have to get in and get out rapidly and begin converting your stuff to electronic form and sending it as we're driving away," Rodger said.

"So, where is it?" I asked.

"I made an arrangement with the cable guy," Judy said.

"The cable guy?"

"There is a cable junction box on the corner. I convinced him to change the lock to a special high security one and got him to arrange a cubby inside for me to use."

"The cable guy?" I said again.

"It was perfect," she explained. "It's partially hidden by a lilac bush so a normal watcher can't see me open it. I could stash stuff when I was out walking my dog with no one the wiser."

"And the cable guy left the stuff alone?"

"He and I had a flirtation going. Better yet, I told him it was stuff for my divorce that I didn't want my husband knowing about," she said.

"Clever," I said. "Let's hope the guy hasn't been fired and someone else is working his territory."

Judy looked stricken, "You don't really think…"

"No, I don't," I said reassuringly. "They wouldn't be so worked up if they had found your stuff."

"Right."

ChapterTWENTY-EIGHT

We stopped four blocks from Judy's old apartment and went over the plan. The SUV with Rodger, Jennifer, Dan, Maddy and Tiny would follow us to within two blocks of the junction box and then hang back in reserve. The one with me, Judy, Selma, Poison and Hakeem would approach the box from the opposite side of Judy's place and stop in front of it. Judy would scurry to the box, retrieve the material and, assuming we weren't interrupted, we would turn back and join the other SUV. After which we would head back to the airport.

Our idea was for Judy and Poison to start copying material right away and begin sending it while driving. The best case scenario was to return to the plane, get airborne and get lost in the clutter of eastern seaboard VHR traffic while we took our time getting the material disseminated. If that didn't work out we hoped to stay ahead of any pursuers long enough to send out enough documents to convince the world to take a hard look at Mikahyl.

The road was quiet as I approached the junction box, but there were red flags all over the place if one looked. Idling in the street were two cars that seemed out of place for the neighborhood. The house next to Judy's had a guy mowing the lawn even though it didn't need it and the woman pushing the baby carriage away from me screamed undercover like she was wearing a sign. Those were the first clues that we weren't in for an easy snatch and grab. I called Rodger on my throwaway cell.

"Rodger, we've got company," I said. "There are at least four that I can see. Two are in cars and two on foot. One of them is a female pushing a baby stroller, but I'm sure there is something a lot worse than a screaming brat inside."

"Have they made you?"

"Not yet," I said. "Their attention is focused on the house, but when we stop…"

"Go ahead with the plan," Rodger said, "we're on the way."

I pulled up to the corner as if I were stopping for the stop sign. Judy slipped out of the driver's side, using the van to shield her and ran to the box. I pretended to pull out a map and consult it, but eyes were already looking our way and wrists were being held to mouths. The lady with the baby carriage did an about face and started walking toward us, her hand reaching inside the carriage. I looked to the right. Judy had the box open and was stuffing material into her bag. I looked back at the baby carriage in time to watch it swerve into the street and tumble over as the woman's hand came out with an Uzi.

"Rodger?" I said into the phone.

I needn't have worried as he flew past our nose from the side street, did a skidding right turn and drove straight into her before she could fire. He hit her with a glancing blow that sent the Uzi flying and spun her into the gutter. I could see her moving, but she was clearly out of this fight.

Rodger swerved further right, sideswiping one of the parked cars, which effectively trapped the driver, rebounded, slammed into reverse and backed into the other one pinning that guy also. He reversed direction again, came back down the street and stopped opposite of where I was. I rolled my window down.

"Where's the fourth one?" he asked.

"He was pretending to mow the lawn at the house at the end of the block," I pointed, "but when you hit the nanny he disappeared behind the house."

"Did you recognize the guy in the Nova?" Rodger asked.

"Yeah. A Morton security guy, I forget his name," I said.

"Me too," he said, "but they don't come cheap and they're good."

"We've handled them before," I said.

"It makes you realize just how important someone thinks this is, doesn't it?"

"We've always managed to be smarter," I said.

He nodded and looked back at the two cars for signs of life. I heard the door close behind me and turned to see Judy.

"I've got everything," she said.

"Lead the way, Rog," I said, jamming the SUV into gear and fishtailing around the intersection to follow him.

As we reached the end of the block I glanced in the rear view and watched a green Camaro bounce out of the driveway where the fourth guy had been mowing, bump over the curb and straighten out about a block behind us. I flashed my lights at Rodger to alert him. My phone rang.

"Yes?"

"Is he alone?" Rodger asked.

"I think so."

"Our best bet is to get back to the plane and get lost in the low level VFR traffic here on the coast."

We turned out of Judy's subdivision and really pushed it. Our bubble burst when Hakeem spoke up.

"Daryl, the pilot says that two cars just entered the lot with four guys in suits. They ran into the office…"

"Tell them to get out of there," I interrupted.

"Won't they try to stop them?" Hakeem asked.

"They might, but they have no jurisdiction," I said. "Tell them to ignore anything but someone waving a gun in their faces and take off."

"To where?"

"Just have them get airborne, Hakeem," I said. "We'll figure out where later."

I got back on the phone with Rodger and filled him in.

"Not good," he said. "Somehow Mr. Clarence Morton or Mikahyl traced us to the Beverly airport."

"I agree," I said. "I told Hakeem to get the plane in the air."

"Great, but that means the plane option is out for us."

"Why? Can't we have the plane stop at a different airport and..."

"The guy behind us is already on the phone to backup. He'll have intercepts coming from every direction," Rodger said.

"Yeah. So, what do we do?"

"Plan B, buddy," he said.

"I thought we were already using Plan B," I said.

"Well, call it what you want, we have some tricky timing, so stay close."

"Right."

"And make sure those girls are sending out everything they can."

ChapterTWENTY-NINE

As we left Judy's subdivision we headed south. Just before the onramp to 128, Rodger pulled over to the edge of the road. I stopped behind him. I looked in the rear view mirror and watched the Morton Security guy following us pull over about five hundred feet behind, a cell phone plastered to his ear. Rodger and Jennifer jumped out and ran back to us with Jennifer climbing in the back. Selma got out of the front passenger's seat and moved to the back while I moved over to let Rodger drive. Rodger looked everyone over before throwing the van in drive and pulling back into traffic.

"Wait!" I said. "What about Dan, Tiny and Madeline?"

"They are going to keep their heads down until we're gone. Then Tiny will ditch their van," Rodger said. "The Morton organization will waste a ton of man hours looking for it. Meanwhile Dan and Tiny will work on lining up some law enforcement, that hasn't been corrupted, to review what we're sending out and keep us from going back to jail."

"Jail?"

"We are still fugitives from a murder charge," Rodger said. "Judges take a dim view of some of the things we've had to do."

"Judy's stuff will vindicate us," I said confidently.

We both glanced to the rear where Poison and Judy were working feverishly.

"How is the uploading going?" I asked.

"We're having trouble with the scanner," Judy said tersely. "We can't get it to work."

"Is there anything we can we do to help?" Rodger asked.

"How about giving us an hour at a Kinko's?" Judy said.

That got a nervous chuckle out of both of us, but at the same time brought home a reminder that if we didn't get Judy's proof out to the press and the authorities, anything we claimed in the future would just be the ravings of a bunch of crazies. Without concrete evidence no one would believe us. Our claims would become just another conspiracy theory put forth by a band of kooks.

After all, who would ever believe that a company as big as Sonic Ping could be based on a lie? And even if it was a lie who would want to believe it? If Sonic Ping's pay-per-click revenue stream of five billion dollars was mostly fake it meant that Sonic Ping would go under and take tens of thousands of related companies with it. No one would want to kill the golden goose and destroy their own meal ticket.

For the first time a shiver of real fear worked its way down my spine. I glanced over at Rodger to see the same tickle of terror mirrored in his eyes.

"Wow," I said.

"Wow, indeed, bud," he affirmed.

ᏇᎡ

Massachusetts route 128 parallels the coastline. If we had taken the west bound ramp we would have been headed back into Boston, into more traffic, more urban clutter and to my mind have become way more difficult to find. We turned eastbound instead, which caused me to look anxiously at Rodger. He swiveled his head and grinned.

"Just what Mr. Clarence Morton didn't expect either," he said. "I'll bet he has five cars lined up between here and Boston already waiting to intercept us and is cursing a blue streak right now."

"I'm sure that buys us some time, Rog," I said, "but aren't we boxing ourselves in?"

"It looks like it, doesn't it?"

"Well..."

"The road sort of ends at Gloucester and then there is nothing but ocean." he said.

"Uh..."

"Exactly what I want our friend Clarence thinking so he doesn't act precipitously," Rodger said. "Hopefully, by the time he realizes what we are up to it will be too late."

"How long do we need?" I asked.

"Judy estimated that it would take about two hours total to upload the stuff that will bury Mikahyl," Rodger said. "Of course she doesn't have the scanner going yet so that might be longer."

"Rodger," I said, "we can't possibly have more than a half an hour before we are captured if we keep going this direction. This is a complete dead end."

"Are you sure?"

"Rodger, there are no other roads out and no airport," I said calmly.

"Do you know what happened in June of last year?" Rodger asked.

"Are we playing twenty questions?" I snapped.

"So you don't?"

"No."

"Boston Harbor Cruises reinstated ferry service from Gloucester to Provincetown," he said.

"Oh my."

"Right."

"When does the next one leave?" I asked.

"If we hurry we will just barely make it," Rodger said.

CR

Barely was a good description. We got there with about three minutes to spare. Traffic had been light on 128, but when we turned on to 127 we slowed to a crawl. Rodger put up with the delay for a few minutes and then whipped into the left lane, barreling into oncoming traffic and forcing several cars to swerve to the curb with their horns blaring. He pulled into Rowe Square at the Rodgers-Main street split and drove right down to the wharf. We abandoned the van at the gangplank.

The seven of us piled out and lugged laptops, printers, the scanner, Judy's stash and a duffel bag of weapons on to the ferry just before they pulled the plank. As we moved into the channel I watched the Morton security guy screaming into his cell in frustration.

The main salon of the boat was spacious and about half full. In the fashion of people everywhere each group of seats had one or two people with their stuff spread out so as to keep others from intruding on their space. The very best spot for our purpose was right in the center of the boat, a large oval shaped table with eight chairs around it. Predictably it was occupied. There was one businessman on the bow end who was already frantically talking on his cell phone and an older couple at the stern end. The couple was sitting in two adjacent chairs and had staked out the two adjoining chairs with their backpacks. They were both reading Kindles. Rodger piled our stuff in the middle of the table and turned to the elderly couple.

"I'm sorry to ask you this," Rodger said politely, "I know it's an imposition, but I'm wondering if I could get you to give up your seats. My friends and I are smack in the middle of a serious project and…"

He let his sentence trail off, looking at them expectantly. The man's thin lip set made me think that we were in for an argument, but before he could speak his wife stood up.

"Why certainly, young man," she said graciously. "We'd be happy to."

She picked up her backpack and waited while her husband came up to speed and did the same. They moved to a table on the starboard side by the window. Rodger turned his smile on the businessman.

"Sir?" he said softly.

"There are eight seats and only seven of you," the man grumbled.

"I just thought you would be more comfortable," Rodger said soothingly, but the air of menace that emanated would have taken someone braver than that guy was to continue to sit there.

The guy grumbled under his breath a bit more and made a show of taking his time, but eventually he got up and moved. We spread our stuff out and restarted everything.

"What about the scanner, Judy?" I asked. "Is it still down?"

"It seems to be working now that we've rebooted it," she said.

"What's the plan?" I asked.

"I've divided what I have into three stacks," Judy said. "The first stack contains proof of how Mikahyl runs robot programs to generate key words that become the search strings, the real IP addresses he uses, the masking and IP spoof programs that make it appear as if real users are searching. Then, there's the shell corporations he set up as 'Ping Peers' that receive a portion of the click revenue, the money trail to multiple offshore Caribbean accounts, and the five accounts in which the money eventually appears."

"So where does the money end up?" I asked.

"He has one account in Bosnia, two in the Ukraine and two in the United States," Judy said.

"Isn't money that stays in the US easier for the authorities to trace?" I asked.

"Mikahyl is arrogant," she explained. "He doesn't think anyone is smart enough to catch him."

"What's the second pile?" Rodger asked.

"Backup material that verifies the first pile," she said. "It contains the URL's of every fake site he controls, links to the programs themselves, bank records, wire transfers and links to emails I saved on a secure site. It also has the bank routings so you can trace the money all the way through its convoluted paths, and most importantly the account numbers and passwords to every one of his bank accounts, including the five where the bulk of the twenty billion dollars that he has stolen resides."

"Twenty billion?" I said.

"He started small to begin with or it would be way more," she said.

"Wow."

"It also contains proof of all of the payoffs he's made to federal, state and local officials and includes verification of several serious illegal acts, including murder, by the Pingree police department."

"Names?"

"Yes, starting with the chief of police," she said.

"Does it include Detective Bruce Kirkwood?" I asked.

"Yes."

"And the third pile?" Rodger asked.

"That skinny pile is what I managed to dig up when I came across the white slavery ring," she said. "It isn't much, and I hadn't yet discovered that they were operating out of Teasers or I would never have continued to go there."

"We can probably help you in that area," Rodger said. "We downloaded the contents of the shipping computer in Teasers and another computer at the slave market in Marrakesh. Most of what we have has been turned over to Interpol, but it won't hurt to send it out again to the FBI and local law enforcement."

"And perhaps a television network or two," I said.

"Our first step is to start with pile number one and scan every page into the computer, then start sending them out," Judy said. "Then we do the same with pile two and, if we have time, pile three."

"We have less than three hours until we dock in Provincetown," Rodger said, "and unless we want a shootout with the Morton guys we're going to have to let the police know so they can arrest us. If we don't have enough of this information out there to bury Mikahyl and clear us of the murder charge Daryl and I are going to be spending the rest of our lives in jail."

I picked up the first sheet and laid it on the scanner.

chapterTHIRTY

It was like doing the dishes after a huge dinner party. If you look at the whole task in front of you it seems insurmountable, but if you ignore everything and just start with the first plate and then the next, eventually you have the last dish in your hand. Scanning sheets into the laptop was definitely the slowest part of the operation, but once we established a rhythm we began eating away at the pile, and by halfway into the trip we had enough hard information sent out on the web that it was like a snowball rolling downhill.

Judy had pre-compiled lists of organizations that she wanted to alert, a broad cross section that included news organizations, business, regulatory groups, local, state, national and international enforcement agencies. We traded off the boring job of standing at the scanner to keep the pace up. The rest of us were either on a laptop emailing, uploading documents, twittering, posting to Facebook or MySpace, or on a cell phone texting or talking to someone.

It wasn't long before the whole world became aware of what we were doing, as did the other passengers on the ferry.

Some of them because of the television in the lounge and some of them because friends or family had called concerned that their relatives were on the ferry where the latest story was taking place. People looked our way, some with curiosity, some with fear and some with anger. The older Kindle couple came over and got my attention.

"Yes?" I asked frantically scanning sheets.

"Are you guys really murderers and white slavers?" the older gentleman asked.

I thought about how brave or stupid he had to be to ask me a question like that.

"Do we look like it?" I asked.

"The news says…"

"Keep listening," I said. "They often get it wrong to begin with."

"Is there going to be a shoot out?" the wife asked.

"You mean when we dock?" I asked.

"Yes."

"Only if someone does something really stupid," I said.

That seemed to satisfy them, but they didn't go back to reading.

ଔ

When our time was almost up we weren't completely finished, but it didn't matter. The odds and ends left were just more nails in a coffin that already had the cover screwed on tightly. The proverbial cat was so far out of the bag that getting it back in again was a feat that even Mikahyl with his billions couldn't accomplish. He was finished.

All of the major networks and cable news organizations already had 'breaking news' banners running on the bottom of their screens. Judy was scheduled for interviews on most of the morning shows, and both Fox and CNN were vying for hour-long exposés.

The stock price of Sonic Ping went into free fall, declining fifty percent before the SEC stepped in and suspended trading.

There were calls for a full scale investigation. Several major law firms had already announced their intentions to file class action suits. Mikahyl had disappeared.

As the ferry pulled around the end of Cape Cod and headed into the Provincetown harbor I could hear several helicopters in the air and realized we were in for one hell of a reception when we docked. I picked up the bag of weapons.

"I'm going to go dump these overboard before we get any closer to shore," I said. "I think we will beat all of the other charges and I don't want to give some overzealous District Attorney an excuse to continue harassing us."

Rodger looked at the bag glumly.

"I suppose you're right," he said. "It seems like a horrible waste but…"

"Give them to me," Hakeem said.

"So they can arrest you instead?" I asked.

"I have a diplomatic passport," he said, "and, while in Libya they might shoot first and ask questions later, I don't think that will happen here."

I handed him the bag.

CR

Five minutes later we docked. I could see three helicopters circling overhead, two were TV news and one had FBI in big letters, but I could hear more. The quay was crowded with so many police cruisers with flashing lights that it seemed as if Providence had started their Christmas display early. There were also enough troopers in swat gear waiting to board to invade a medium sized country.

Except for the gawkers with their attention focused on us, the majority of passengers were queued up to exit the boat. It created a huge buffer zone between the enforcement officers and us. It should have slowed them down, but they pushed through the crowd as if ESPN had offered free sports programming for life to the first ten officers who brought us to heel. They boarded without letting anyone off, pushing everyone back into the lounge area of the ship. We stayed seated and waited while testosterone filled the lounge.

"Everybody on the floor!!!"

"Hands where we can see them!!"

"Down, Down, Down!"

"Move and you'll die, motherfuckers!"

The screaming went on and on. Both Rodger and I had been through it before and knew what to do. So did Judy who lay down under the table with her arms and legs spread. Jennifer was a bit unsure, but Rodger pulled her down next to him and kept her calm. I did the same with Selma. Hakeem kept standing with his passport in the air, holding tightly to Poison screaming, "Diplomatic Immunity!" She looked amused.

The first swat team members tried to get Hakeem and Poison to lie down, but he kept waving his passport and refusing. Eventually, someone with half a brain realized that it might be prudent to treat him differently. They pulled the team back and pushed the two of them into an alcove where one guard could watch them. At no time did anyone look into the bag of weapons that he had slung over his shoulder.

We were patted down and cuffed and then allowed to sit while the team mopped up. Judy hadn't been treated any differently by the initial invaders, but when the suits showed up they crossed to her and uncuffed her.

"Sorry about that, Ms. Green," the lead suit said. "We had to secure the boat first and there wasn't time to…"

"I understand," she interrupted, "you were just doing your job."

"Thank you."

"These people are all with me and are not a threat," she said, waving her hand in our direction.

"I'm sorry, ma'am," he said. "I can release the women, but those two are wanted for murder among other charges."

"Those are trumped up charges by some of the very people we have exposed," she said.

"That may be, Ms. Green, but we have orders to bring them in until this gets sorted out."

Judy didn't like it but she knew better than to argue. She looked at me and shook her head.

"I'm sorry," she said.

"Don't worry about it," I said. "We talked to Dan on the trip over. He took a chopper over to the Provincetown airport and will be taking jurisdiction of us shortly."

As if on cue Dan walked through the door waving his badge and a fistful of paperwork.

"I need you to release these two into my custody," he said. "The town of Pingree has jurisdiction and I have the proper paperwork here."

The lead FBI agent didn't like it much, probably because he wanted to be the one to march us out past the waiting TV cameras, but after a few minutes of grousing he agreed.

"Did you bring cuffs?" he finally asked.

"No need," Dan said. "I'm sure they'll promise to behave."

That really pissed the agent off, but he took our cuffs off mumbling something about hick police departments. Dan escorted Rodger and me, the two girls, Hakeem and Poison out to a waiting police van. Because we weren't cuffed we waltzed right by the media who were craning their necks trying to get a look at the bad guys.

"I'm the new acting chief of police of Pingree," Dan said when we were safely under way. "The chief has been arrested."

"What happened to Bruce?" Rodger asked.

"He disappeared. We're not sure. He may have left with Mikahyl."

"To where?" I asked.

"No one has a clue," he said. "Mikahyl took off in his jet when the story started to break. He didn't file a flight plan."

"What's next?" I asked.

"Tons of paperwork, but I'm fairly certain that the DA will be dropping the charges against you two," he said.

"So it's over?" I asked.

ChapterTHIRTY-ONE

Things settled down over the next two weeks. The DA dropped the murder charges against Rodger and me. He also made it clear that he wouldn't be bringing any others. Judy became an instant celebrity as the woman who brought down Sonic Ping and was busy making the talk show rounds. Her ex-partner, Brandon, was languishing in a federal prison awaiting trial. Hakeem and Poison returned to Morocco with promises to hook up with us very soon. Victor Underwood was arrested trying to leave the country via El Paso and Selma's partner Jerry was taken down at his home and was now awaiting trial for kidnapping, white slavery, money laundering and racketeering.

Rodger spent most of his time glued to his laptop working on something that he didn't share with me, but I got a whiff when all of the news stations had a field day of breaking news about Mikahyl Dashkov being found dead in a luxury apartment in the Recoleta area of Buenos Aires. I bit my tongue as long as I could and then broached the subject.

"I see someone found Mikahyl," I said.

"Umm."

"You have any hand in what happened?"

"I didn't kill him," he responded.

"I guess I could have figured that out since you've been glued to your computer and Argentina is at least nine or ten hours away," I said. "So you didn't, huh?"

"You know what the trouble with smart guys like Mikahyl is?" he asked.

"Not really."

"They get to thinking they are so smart that no one else can possibly match them. They think they can disappear and no one can find them."

I didn't respond, because now that I had him started I knew he was going to tell me, and prodding him wasn't necessary.

"He was smart enough to switch cell phones," he said, "but when you've got all your really important stuff on a laptop it's hard to stop using it."

I nodded.

"He was pretty good at not using his computer for almost two weeks, but then he must have needed something that was only available on it. It wasn't on for more than two minutes before he changed the IP," he said. "If I hadn't had a permanent trace on the old IP address…"

He looked up at me and smiled. I smiled back.

"I sent an anonymous email to his investor group, which happens to be some seriously bent and pissed off Russians."

"And they killed him?" I asked.

"Things worked out for the best."

"Did you find Bruce also?" I asked.

"Not yet."

"He wasn't with Mikahyl?"

"Not that I could tell," he said, "and no traces anywhere else either."

❧

The phone rang a half hour later. We were still at Rodger's shop making plans to use the millions of dollars from Brad's account and the slave market proceeds to set up trust funds for the women who had been abducted. All but two of them had been recovered, but we had assurances from Interpol that they had leads on those two and it was only a matter of time. We could see from caller ID that it was Judy calling. Rodger pushed the speaker-phone button.

"Hey, how goes the talk show circuit?"

"Hi, Rodger," she said.

"Hi. Everything okay?"

"Just tired," she said.

"You've been through a lot," Rodger said soothingly.

"Can you do me a favor?" she asked.

"Sure. What?"

"Can you come over right now and help me sort something out?" she asked.

"I think so," he said. "Daryl and I were just winding up the preliminaries on those trusts I told you about."

"Daryl's with you?"

"I'm right here," I chimed in.

"Can you come along?" she asked.

"Don't see why not," I said. "We'll be there in about thirty minutes."

"Rodger?"

"Yeah?"

"Can you bring your computer?" she asked. "I need you to sort something out for me and you know how bad I am with computers."

"Oh, uh, sure."

"Thanks," she said. "The door will be unlocked, just come right in."

Rodger pushed the speaker-phone button again to cut her off and looked at me.

"What?" I asked.

"Have you seen her on a computer?"

"Oh."

"Yes."

He opened his desk drawer and handed me a Glock 26 and an ankle holster.

"Put this on," he said.

"What are you thinking?" I asked.

"Our missing man."

"Bruce?"

"I think so," he said, pulling another one out for his ankle.

Ë

We walked into Judy's apartment twenty-five minutes later and sure enough Bruce was there. Judy was trussed up in a kitchen chair while he stood behind her with a gun to her head. She looked a little shaken up and scared, but otherwise he hadn't appeared to have harmed her. She looked beautiful and vulnerable.

"That's close enough," Bruce said.

As I stopped I stepped to the left instinctively and Rodger went right. It wasn't much but it divided his attention.

"You fucking hotshots sure screwed things up for all of us," he said.

"You mean by exposing the corrupt and downright illegal things that were going on?" Rodger asked.

"Did you bring your computer?" Bruce asked, ignoring Rodger's jibe.

Rodger lifted the laptop in his right hand and placed it on the table. Bruce looked at it greedily. Thinking about it I realized that computer contained paths to the thirty million we had recovered plus all of the links to the billions that Mikahyl had stolen. It was quite a valuable commodity.

"Guns," Bruce barked.

Neither one of us moved.

"Listen you assholes," he snarled. "I know both of you are probably carrying so if I don't see them right now I'm going to shoot her."

"And lose your only bargaining chip?" Rodger asked.

"In the leg," he said, moving the gun from her head to her left thigh.

It was a stupid move. Rodger could have taken him before he could kill her, but it meant she would be shot in the leg. That was too much for me. I shot Rodger a look to insure he wouldn't move.

"Okay," I said.

"Slowly, Daryl."

I crouched down carefully, pulled the Glock from my ankle holster, laid it on the ground and stood up.

"Kick it away," he demanded, his eyes flicking back and forth between Rodger and myself.

I kicked it. It slithered across the floor toward him but not near enough for him to reach without exposing himself. I watched the wheels turn in his head but decide against it. He focused on Rodger.

"Now you."

Rodger stooped down, removed his gun and stood back up with the weapon dangling from two fingers of his right hand.

"Toss it on the table so that it lands over here close to me," Bruce said.

Rodger's toss was a bit long. The gun hit the table in front of where Judy was tied up, bounced once and slid off of the table into her lap. Bruce's eyes followed it down. As they came off of Rodger he reached behind his neck, came out with three throwing spikes and flicked his wrist. Bruce looked up but he was too late.

The spikes hit Bruce square in the face. One penetrated each eye socket and the third imbedded itself in his forehead just to the right of his nose. He dropped like he had been poleaxed, dead before he hit the ground. Rodger walked to him, looked down and grunted.

"What?" I asked.

"The one in his forehead is a half an inch to the right of where I aimed," he said.

"Half of an inch?"

"Yes."

"You're way too hard on yourself," I said.

"Maybe so."

I crossed to Judy, bent down and touched her face.

"You okay?"

She looked up and smiled, "Uh huh."

She was so beautiful and vulnerable in that instant I would have loved to lean in and kiss her. Considering her situation and everything she had been through it would have been totally unfair. I busied myself setting her loose instead. As the final ropes fell away she stood up, grabbed my shirt and pulled me in. Our lips almost touched. The electricity between us could have lighted up New York City. She moved her face back before I could crush her lips on mine. My mind flashed back to our first meeting and the memory caused me to shiver. She noticed.

"You are quite a nice guy, aren't you?" she asked.

I nodded.

"Are you still seeing Selma?" she asked.

I nodded again.

"Serious?"

"She sees other people," I said.

"Daryl, I know I said that I would never be able to let a man touch me again but…"

"But?"

"Would you like to… call me sometime?"

My whole body was telling me yes. I managed to nod.

Acknowledgments

Like many of you I've had fantasies all of my life of writing a novel. I think I even started a few times but I don't recall putting more than a sentence or two on paper before I was completely out of ideas as to what to say next. The dream languished and I finally decided that it was never going to happen.

Then I read a book by Sarah Bird titled: <u>The Yokota Officer's Club</u>. It struck something deep inside of me because, like her, I had been an Air Force brat who had lived in Japan during the same time she had. I had stories that I wanted to share, so I sat down and started my book. Of course with absolutely no experience in writing anything I hadn't a clue as to how to make those stories that bubbled inside of me come alive for a reader.

Then I met Cheryl Howe, the wife of a hang glider buddy, who has three published Romance Novels (<u>After the Ashes</u>, <u>The Pirate and the Puritan</u> and <u>Stealing Jewel</u>). She gave me the best advice I've ever gotten about writing. She told me to write and keep writing. She was right because like any exercise the more you do the stronger it gets. My writing got better. It improved enough that I scrapped everything I'd written and started over. I picked up a story that I'd started many years before, and over a three week period I turned it into a short novel. I sent it in.

This is how I met Paula Hatton, the author of nearly 150 novels and non-fiction works. She was the editor to whom I sent my first effort. She took pity on me and took time to edit the first ten pages I sent her. I was appalled at how badly written they were, but it changed me for the better. I revised that book twice more and am still working on the third revision.

I couldn't stop by this point so I turned to short stories. I was obsessed, turning out two to three stories a week, sending them out for free on the internet, which is how I met Deborah Dormitzer. She loved my stuff and somehow could pick me out no matter what pen name I used. Flattery drove me to keep writing. Then there is my writer's group (AnchorInnCastaways, a Yahoo group) whose advice and encouragement to each of the other writers in the group and whose sheer output of great writing continued to inspire me to sit down and finish.

The list wouldn't be complete without mentioning a great author I met along the way who has continually encouraged me, Lori Gordon, (look for her coming book State of Panic) and my long suffering wife, Cid, who has put up with each of my obsessions including this one.

Finally, I would like to express special thanks to the Program Director of a Masters of Fine Arts program in writing who had the final say in rejecting me for admission into their program starting January of 2010. He told me that they just didn't feel that I was ready. I hung up the phone and within the next two hours wrote the first twelve hundred words of what (with tons of revisions) became "Sonic Ping." He was probably correct in not admitting me but the sting of rejection was a powerful incentive.

Orlando Stephenson
Grand Rapids, Michigan

Orlando can be reached at: orlandoworth@yahoo.com